Changes

Seven Short Stories

John Guthrie

My thanks to Robert Harrison of Seneca Author Services for his formatting, cover design and invaluable assistance with everything even slightly technical.

Cover image: "Evasive" by Wassily Kandinsky, 1929. Public Domain Image Library.

Paperback ISBN: 978-1-0684612-1-7

CONTENTS

CHANGES

Why did you marry that person? Because she or he is so different from you, or because she or he has certain qualities that exactly match yours? And do you want that person to be changed, to be more like you?

My Mother always wanted me to join a tennis club and meet a nice girl. We had nothing to do with tennis clubs, and we even had a bad case of inverted snobbery about them. But long ago, she had gone to a tennis club with some local boys, and it had lodged in her mind as the place where nice young men went to meet nice young girls.

Well, I didn't. For one thing, I was always useless at tennis. Weak wrists, poor eyesight, and an inability to do a serve without hitting the ball into the net or into the next county. And there's only so much socialising you can do without actually playing the game.

Plenty of people wanted to socialise with me since I inherited a lot of money. I soon saw through the superficiality of that. But in the end, I did find what I wanted, and needed; with the help of patience, all my other good qualities, and the little matter of scientific breakthrough.

Saying 'little matter' is just one of my euphemisms. An

immense scientific breakthrough would be more accurate. But being available only for those with the money to pay for it, well, we with that sort of money don't shout about it. In fact, we've been told pretty sternly, confidentiality documents and all that, to say nothing. So, it looks as though for a while, this will be restricted to the wealthy few. But who knows? The wealthy few used to be the ones to visit exotic places; now, all and sundry are dragging their noise and bad taste all over the world.

But, being realistic, it would be a bad thing if this particular benefit became available to everyone. It is too big, with too many implications, and too much opportunity for misuse. It needs to be reserved for those who can use it properly.

Such as I.

So, here we go. I am talking about the fast and easy reversible sex change. As many times as you like, provided that you have the money and are willing to spend it.

I have, and I am.

And I think it's a good thing to share my experiences with people who might be considering it, perhaps feeling a little nervous. I hope that this will be helpful. But one thing with which I can't help is the old problem of ethics. Morals, if you prefer. I can't advise on that. And don't even think about throwing religion at me. That's your problem, your affair. My help is restricted to the practicalities of the thing.

So, thoroughly preambled out, I'll make a start.

Having no job, and no real friends, no-one missed me for the short duration of my first change. The Adjustment Centre, as they liked to be known, issued instructions in the traditional way, reminding me to bring a change of clothes, cosmetics if desired, and all the other minor, and major, things that went with being a woman.

"There's a lot more to it than people think," I was told. "A lot of changes, physical and mental, are involved. Putting a man into a woman's body is only the first step. Only *you* can complete the change."

There were lectures, written guidance, legal documents. There was essential training. Most sex-changers have been drifting towards that other sex all their lives, or at least for years. Many have virtually become that other sex in the way that they behave. I was going straight in. There was a big difference.

The teaching and advice weren't just for my benefit. Too many women clumping about with no attempt to behave as women would eventually draw attention to the Adjustment Centre, and that was precisely what they didn't want. They wanted the custom, they wanted the money, they didn't want the publicity.

Of course, I didn't mention that my intention was always for this to be temporary. Changing back was available, but not part of the deal. The Government didn't want people popping back and forth between the sexes. The implications were massive.

As soon as the operation was done, they came at me again with their instructions, warnings and advice. They probably detected within my polite responses the implied 'Yeah, yeah' of the know-all. I was impatient. I wanted to go out into the world as a woman. It would be like starting again. All the mistakes of my life would be written off, by me, as man-mistakes. I was already looking back disparagingly, thinking, '*Well, what do you expect from a man?*'

I was very pleased with the result. It was very strange to see a woman's face in the mirror, my face, looking at me as though assessing me. I wasn't exactly pretty. They couldn't change basic physical defects, such as large ears, and a large head, but I had a vague sort of elusive goodlookingness. I don't want to be too flatteringly descriptive of myself. Let's just say I was pleased with my new appearance, which is what mattered.

As a sort of souvenir, they took my photograph. The tourist thing. I tried to pose as a woman, then as a man, then I relaxed and just posed as myself, regardless of sex. It worked very well. I liked that photograph, and still do. I keep it on the little table beside my bed.

Of course, as with any big change, like passing your driving test, you want to go out and try the thing in as many places and ways as you can. Yes, I had a lot of trepidation, but again, that's like your first time driving on your own. On my first time out, driving I mean, someone blew his horn at me and I nearly drove off the road.

In telling you about my first time going about as a woman, I must, with a lot of reluctance, do a confession. My initial desire to have a sex change was not prompted by my desire to be a woman. I thought that being a woman would be the perfect disguise for going into those places which men were forbidden to enter You see, I thought that I could be a man in a woman's body, soak up the details in as many women's changing rooms as I could visit, and enjoy the recollections when I returned to being a man.

At first, it worked well. As Sarah, my chosen name, I enjoyed going through those sternly closed doors into the forbidden places. But you know how it is when something which you particularly desire is no longer unattainable: the novelty soon wears off. Besides, even though I was safely clad in a woman's body, I was rather conspicuous because I used to stand staring at the other women. Some of them used to stare back at me, looking annoyed, and I used to panic and quickly touch myself in various places to make sure that I wasn't changing back as I stood there.

Another thing was that after the initial novelty, I realised that being in a women's changing room felt right to me. Not just because I was, after all, now a woman; even as a man, which to some extent, I still was, it felt right. Partly because of the reduction in changing room jokes, but mainly because as a man, and as a woman, I detested being amongst naked men. Now, in addition to the natural aversion of anyone to the sight, I began to see men as the enemies of women; their physical difference and ugliness being a manifestation of that threat.

Gradually, I managed to stop staring, at least ostentatiously. I did a combination of peeping at those nearest to me as I dried and dressed, and I did occasional casual panning round while doing a vigorous bit of rubbing with the towel. And it was while I was doing this panoramic viewing one day that I made a friend. I had pivoted round, almost in a circle, when our eyes met and I stopped turning.

Her eyes seemed really to see me, and seemed to say, "I know that you're a man under that superficial covering." But she seemed not be bothered about it. She smiled, then came over and introduced herself.

"Alison Foster," she said. "You like it here?"

"Yes," I said, too low. I tried again, too high, coughed and settled for a nodding grin, like one of those dog things that people used to have in their cars. I felt painfully aware that I was still in the transitional stage and was currently treading water in mid-channel.

We finished dressing, and then she came back. We chatted about trivial matters for a while, but I was becoming aware that those eyes were now transmitting a lot of passion. I could feel an intense force pulling us together.

Suddenly, she said, "It's okay. I know your secret. And that's fine with me."

"Secret?" I laughed nervously.

"I know the signs." She smiled pleasantly. "You might have the body of a woman, but you're a man really. Inside, I mean."

I managed to say, "Er, well, yes."

So she'd seen through my disguise. I felt horribly exposed, naked, which I had been very recently. But I felt man-naked, now.

But at least she was still smiling in that warm, friendly way.

"It's all right," she said. "So am I."

"Ah," I said.

I didn't know what to say. I hadn't expected to find someone else who'd had the operation. How many of us were walking about? Were we all heading straight for the women's changing rooms?

She said, "When did you first become aware of it?"

She was making me even more confused. "Er, well, it all happened very quickly. I mean, it seemed as though one moment I was one thing, and the next moment, I was the other."

"Ah," she said wistfully. "That's the best way, even though it might be the most traumatic. Mine took much longer."

"Oh. I thought they all took roughly the same time."

"Oh, no," she said earnestly. "Mine took years."

"Years?"

"Oh, yes." She laughed. "I suppose I just kept resisting the truth about myself. All the signs were there, but I kept turning my head from the direction in which they were all pointing, and pretending not to see."

Ah. Right. Now, very slowly I admit, I understood. Not an operated one. She was a woman who wanted to have a relationship with a woman. And I was a . . . well, what was I? I was physically a woman, gradually becoming a woman, but I was only a visitor, as it were, and I intended to be a man again before any lasting damage was done. But Alison liked me, was attracted to me, apparently, which wouldn't have happened, and wouldn't happen, when I was a man.

And I liked Alison, and was attracted to her.

What choice did I have?

I became a lesbian.

It was difficult at first because I was still thinking as a man, and I had always been bad at the sharing sexual needs thing. For me, a woman was the supreme masturbation kit. If she could enjoy it, too, that was an additional source of pleasure. But the main thing was *my* pleasure. Doing things which the woman liked me to do was distracting. It interrupted my rhythm. It made me aware of my defects, especially when all this need for sharing suggested all the people who had gone before. I didn't want to be part of a long procession of sexual artists: I wanted to go in, so to speak, and have my pleasure, and move on.

But now, unless we were going to do butch and docile role-playing, which we definitely weren't, then I was going to have to change my ways and learn how to do things.

As a woman.

I had to learn to do things slowly, delicately, at least for a while. Alison really liked the slow building up. That was the most difficult part. It was a struggle to keep my concentration on *anything* for that long. It was a bit like those big occasion meals, where everyone else seems to be enjoying the long, slow event, but I want them to hurry up with the food. And even when they bring the food, they do it a little bit at a time. All the other people are happy being sociable, but I just want to enjoy my personal pleasure.

But with the obvious aid of my new body, I adapted to the new methods, and to the new form in which the pleasure came. And, as with most things, I found that going slowly helped me to work out the best ways of doing things. Often, I did things slightly later than Alison, following her movements, her techniques. I made myself familiar with my own body.

But as our relationship developed, I forced myself to accept my original plan. I had wanted to dabble, not make a permanent change. I was in danger of becoming a woman to such an extent that it would soon become almost impossible for me to return.

I might start being attracted to men.

And another thing. Although Alison and I were well-bonded, I couldn't see her as someone with whom I'd be happy in a permanent relationship. We had so many differences. She liked this music, I liked that music; she liked this food, I liked that food; she wanted to go to this place, I wanted to go to that place. Apart from our feelings for each other, we didn't have anything in common. So many people have come adrift, thinking that feelings are all that matter, or thinking that the other person will adapt, will improve.

How do you devote your life to someone who enjoys different things, wants to do different things? If you keep your own personalities, your own tastes, your own interests, you're going to be living separate lives. Some people think that's the recipe for a happy marriage. But what's the point of it? If you have jobs, you meet in the evening and do your different things. Again, what's the point?

———

So I came back. I told Alison that I had to go away on business for a little while, and took my very sad leave of her, while trying to hide the depth of my sadness. She looked very vulnerable. There was nothing tough about her. She didn't conform to any stereotype. She was a beautiful person.

And I was leaving her. I was going to be a man again. And so, soon after, I was. I adapted very quickly, apart from some alarming mannerisms which I'd acquired, and which still seemed natural to me. Before leaving, so to speak, the first time, I had made the permitted arrangement with my bank to have a dual account. So far as anyone knew, I was two different people, two different official identities.

After the strain of trying to be a woman, being a man was so much easier. If I slouched, or lurched as I walked, no-one cared, or even noticed. No-one looked twice when I went to a pub on my own. Peeing in a hedge was easy. No-one leered at me. They hadn't when I was a woman, but the point is still valid. And although female attire is better for movement, those movements have to be done just right, or heads turn and eyes stare. Legs apart, elbows on knees, just doesn't go down well with critical men, and women.

I was still fond of Alison, and knew that I'd always be so. I took to going to, or near, places where I knew she would be, and looking at her. But that made me sad. She looked lonely, and I wanted to help. With that desire, the sadness became grief for my loss, for her loss. I expected to see her with another woman, or even a man. But she was always alone, always with that sad look.

One day, very upset, I went back to my apartment and lay on my bed, brooding. I turned my head and looked at the photograph of me, just after the first change. At that moment, a massive truth struck me: I was looking at my perfect woman. A female me was my perfect woman. That was what I wanted. That was what I could never have.

That was what I must never have. Because what I wanted was my own selfish, egotistical self, duplicated to my satisfaction.

Isn't that what we all want? Ourselves in the other sex? In many divorce cases, the reason provided is 'irreconcilable differences'. Of course they are, because even after years of determined efforts and adaptations, it all becomes too much hard work, and some parts of the other person refuse to become exactly *you*. Those are the irreconcilable differences: those parts of the other person which stubbornly refuse to change to what you want them to be, which is *you*.

From the moment that you are born, you see and feel everything through a filter, reducing everything to what it provides for *you*. When you cry for milk, you're not interested in bonding: you want to be fed. But it isn't just a matter of egotistical impulses: everything is arranged to make you focus on yourself. Even when you give to charity, you do it for you, for your conscience, for your good feeling about yourself.

And that is why we are never truly happy.

I remembered a line from The Waste Land: 'the awful daring of a moment's surrender'.

Love, real love, is the love of someone else, and real love always puts that other person first. Spouse, partner, child: all must come first. Discard all that stuff about losing your personality. That will survive, or change into something better. Most of your personality is formed by responses to other people, most of it is formed by the need to protect oneself. Let it go. That isn't what you are. What you aren't is what you are. Whatever happens will be for the best because love requires surrender. Even surrender of your personality. Love doesn't just give love: it gives everything.

Let it all go.

So, there it was, and there I was. Staring at my irreconcilable sameness. At *me*, the centre of the Universe, in whom, of whom, for whom, all thoughts and desires were created.

And in the centre of the Universe, there was nothing but futile loneliness. Not because I had to have someone, but because I needed to surrender, to let go of *me* in order to become me, instead of a mere collection of egotistical and selfish thoughts and impulses, constantly spinning in a pointless orbit around myself.

———

At the Adjustment Centre, they weren't pleased to see me again. I assured them that it would be the last time, and, as I said, money is very persuasive.

I caught up with Alison as she was leaving the office.

"Sarah!" she said excitedly. "You're back."

There was such joy in her eyes.

I nodded and smiled. "And I'm here to stay."

# # #

CLASS

We've all read the books and watched the films about the people who will fly space ships and settle on distant planets. The scientists. But those scientists will need to be looked after. Supplies, catering, cleaning, laundry, sanitation. So, like it or not, some of those early space travellers will be clerical staff and manual workers.

CHAPTER 1

Someone that you don't want round a ship on take-off day is someone with no sense of time. With ship take-offs, that sort of thing is rather important.

And that's where it all went wrong.

The pilots and passengers, the guys in the control room, all the support technicians, were all fully focused on all matters pertaining to time.

Except for one man.

As humanity reached once more for the stars and the infinity of space, one man stood alone and apart from it all.

Wendell Drake was that man.

As everyone else looked up, he looked down, at the instruction which had slowly come to him through an administration system which had defied all the advances of the human race.

The instruction was three weeks late.

Down in the admin level, where time was relevant only to starting and finishing work and meeting deadlines, where the only mechanical sounds were the hums and sighs of thousands of computers linked to the vast admin system, Wendell Drake saw an instruction.

On the level below his, in non-tech engineering support, Barton Wood received his order. He was to take his brush, go into the engine sub-system area and sweep all the poffle out of the C-Tubes.

As a non-tech, Barton had limited knowledge. You would have called him a simple man, with no insult intended. It wasn't so much that he was simple, more that he tried to keep everything simple, in a very complicated world. And he had a very simple, realistic view of his own abilities. He aspired to be good at whatever he did, which meant staying within his realistic attainment levels. He didn't see anything wrong with that. Better to stay at that level than go to a higher level where his deficiencies might be exposed, and might cause problems. He believed very strongly that the man, or woman, who cleaned the poffle was just as important as the man or woman who flew the space ship. Different parts of the same process.

All that wasn't to say that Barton felt fulfilled in his mundane work, but who was? By not letting dissatisfaction creep in, he was at ease with himself. He had no wife and children to draw attention to his inadequacies, so why worry about them? He knew just enough to do his various jobs. He knew that poffle was the fluffy stuff that accumulated in the C-Tubes because of the magnetic interference with the testles, which were the . . . well, that was it. He was non-tech for a reason. When he was told to go and sweep out the poffle, that's what he did. He just followed instructions, and that was that.

Or so he thought.

Anyway, there you have the basic background. It just remains to be said that when Wendell Drake sent him to perform his little task, he gave no thought to the imminent departure of the ship. Ships came and went, and he didn't hear them or see them. He was in the depths of the admin area, doing his job.

And Barton? Well, he just assumed.

And we all know what *that* does.

Barton followed all the standard safety procedures of closing and locking doors, to keep the in things in and the out things out. He checked his equipment: one brush for the removal of the poffle from the tube, and one receptacle for the removal of the poffle from the ship. One hygiene mask, to prevent the inhalation of poffle fibres. One 'space suit' because the rules stated that everyone in any part of a ship must wear one. And he set about his simple but important task.

He actually had his whole arm inside a C-Tube, reaching for a last bit of poffle which was stubbornly resisting the attentions of his brush, when it happened.

Earthquake!

Volcano!

Tornado!

Don't be silly, he told himself. They're just doing a run-through, making sure that everything is working okay. Of course they test the engines before they go.

But there was a lot of vibration, and a sort of pulling and pushing, somehow outside and in. He didn't like it one bit. Well, even a non-techie has a bit of brain function. He decided that this testing was a bit too vigorous for just standing there and that it would be sensible to fasten himself down.

But how, what and where?

Once more in this sudden crisis, the old brain sparked again. He removed the fat fire extinguisher from its moorings and replaced it with his thin body. A bit tight but it wasn't going to be for more than a few seconds.

A few seconds later, he was beginning to think that this had gone on long enough. The vibrations were increasing. So was the noise. And the pulling and pushing. Well, obviously, if you're going to test the engines, it's no good just having them in bottom gear; you have to give them the full wumpf. But he didn't like being so close to it all. He was a non-tech person with non-tech ways. He had a brush. And a cloth. And buckets and cans and packets. Basically, he cleaned and polished things. And he did it all when everything was motionless and silent.

He tried talking sternly to himself, to tell himself to stop being such a softy, that this was just normal testing, but he couldn't hear what he was saying to himself. He tried thinking the words, but he still couldn't hear them. And he couldn't see them because they were jumping about all over the place, then falling into their separate letters.

Any moment now, he managed to think, in a rattley sort of way, it will descend into a hum and a whine and stop.

Rooooooaaaaaaaarrrrr.

Damn. He just managed to think that as he felt the pulling and pushing extend into compressing and stretching and his brain vibrated inside his head, banging about, hitting the sides.

Pointlessly, he whispered, "Help."

It even felt as though the ship was starting to move.

Suddenly, that point was clarified.

The ship shot.

The fire extinguisher hurtled across the room and conked him on the head. His helmet banged against the wall behind him. And with all these other things going on in and around him, he sank into welcome blackness.

As they say in the stories, he knew no more.

CHAPTER 2

Although time has no measurable relevance in space, it was two days before someone found him, still strapped, still terrified, still confused.

It had taken two days for the highly technical people to check all their systems thoroughly before deciding that the tapping sounds might be loose somethings in the C-Tubes area. When one of the crew floated down to examine, he found one detached fire extinguisher, one rather lonely brush, and one dejected member of the very low orders, with not one idea of what to do next.

For people who are supposed to be clever, technical guys can be pretty impenetrative at times. Barton had told the one who found him, very simply, what had happened, but the technical guy seemed to find it difficult to understand, like an obscure and complex technical problem. He sorted him out with a spare suit, for space rather than for poffle-brushing, and showed him how to perform the very necessary washing of his body in a very small and unstable area, and then took him to meet the gang.

The flight crew just did some disgusted shrugging and head-shaking and weren't bothered. Flying a ship was what interested them, not cargo, which people were. Just some items to be delivered. That attitude didn't please this little party of scientists.

"Glorified bus drivers," the technical guy muttered as he lad Barton away from the flight area to meet the items to be delivered.

After a rather surly round of introductions, Barton was pressed for an explanation of the catastrophe, as they immediately viewed it.

"Say that again," said Hanson Sloan when Barton had explained.

He said it again.

Sloan winced, frowned and shook his head. "But I still don't understand why you went in to clean the C-Tubes when the ship was about to take off."

Barton explained again.

"What do you mean, you didn't know it was about to take off?"

Barton sighed. This was very hard work. Of course, a large part of the problem was that these guys lived lives that were remote from all the vital work that people such as he did. They didn't know that he was told only what he needed to know for any task.

He said, "You need to understand that those people who are directly involved in take-off know all about take-off. I have no involvement in take-off, and my boss has no involvement in take-off; therefore, we know nothing about take-off."

What? Not even that it's about to happen?"

"It's not a part of our function. Our tasks and responsibilities are laid out very clearly. My boss was told to ensure that the C-Tubes were cleaned. He wasn't told when to do the job. He wasn't told when the ship would be leaving. That isn't part of his job. His job was to arrange for the cleaning of the tubes. He told me to do it and I did it. Well, I was doing it when this happened."

They just could not let it go. Those in their seats kept leaning forward and leaning back, those who were standing, well, floating, kept trying to pace about while weightless, making them look as though they were learning how to do the doggy paddle. All the time, they all had these screwed-up faces, looking as though they had smelt something horrible, then eaten it. And the head-shaking was almost continuous.

"But surely. . . ."

"But if you didn't know. . . ."

"But doesn't anyone check. . . ."

He kept shaking his head. Eventually, a little irritated, he said, "Well, don't you do something to warn people? Perhaps shout, 'All ashore that's going ashore'? Perhaps ring a bell or a buzzer?"

He was fighting back with some very pertinent questions, delivered calmly and clearly, so different from their enraged and bewildered splutterings.

"Besides," he added, very sensibly, "how I came to be here has rather lost its relevance and even importance, compared with the simple fact of my being here. Is there a plan, or shall we make a plan, for an additional crew member?"

"Well, hardly crew," snorted a guy called Harcourt Ringer. There was some background snorting, more pig than intellectual.

"It doesn't matter what we call me. I am an additional human being in your little society. I have already taken one of the spare suits and used some of your soap. I shall also need some of your food."

That was throwing a live one amongst them. They had been so busy babbling and being pompous that they hadn't considered that nasty bit of reality to be faced.

"Our rations," Ringer said slowly and solemnly, "are calculated precisely for the number of the crew and the length of time. We don't have additional allowances in case we pick up someone on the way." He warmed to his subject. "I mean, we don't look out of the windows for people who might be wandering about in space or whose ship might have broken down. Our job is to go as quickly as we can to our destination, do what we have to do there, then return, as quickly as we can. There are no extras built into our job descriptions."

"Rather like my situation," Barton said.

"Nothing like it," Ringer said indignantly.

"Yes, it is. You do as you are instructed, with no deviations, and without objections or enquiries."

"Until we have a stowaway," said Lang Pollitt. "Then we have to improvise."

"Go on, then," Barton countered. "So far you haven't made any constructive suggestions."

Pollitt accepted the invitation. "The sensible course, for the good of the official crew and the mission, would be to jettison you."

"You mean murder me?"

"Not doing it could mean the death of one or more crew members."

"Better a non-techie die than a skilled technician."

"Well, yes. That's it."

"Here's my suggestion. You eat less and we'll all survive."

"Our rations assume certain levels of activity."

"What activity?"

"We have to survey and maintain station equipment and liaise with existing station staff."

"For how long?"

"One month. But it will be six weeks before we arrive, and there is the return journey of the same duration."

She tried to keep the pleased look off her face. Barton smiled at her and said, "I saw the sleeping capsules on the way here. I have read about space travel even if I haven't been involved in it. You will shortly be enjoying extended sleep, in sleep pods, and not of the long distance frozen variety."

"A pod for each of us," she said, the pleased look now spreading into a smirk of triumph.

"We'll nap. In turns. I'll wake one of you after a week."

Barton could see them trying to think of ways round this, still contemplating his removal. He said, "My work record shows where I was working when the ship took off. So, obviously I must be on the ship, so jettisoning me …"

"Yes, okay," Sloan said irritably. "Don't go on about it. We're stuck with you."

Barton smiled. Actually, the people back on Earth would have very little interest in what happened to him. But some bluffing was going to be essential.

"So," he concluded, "with periods of sleep, and work which is not physically demanding, I think that you will manage with slightly smaller rations. I shall manage on the minimum. A month will soon pass."

Sloan said, "This will all be fully reported when we return."

Suddenly, Barton lost his temper. "Are you supposedly very clever people with strong, spacey, characters, going to spend this entire trip moaning and threatening? The small crew unexpectedly increased by one. A space problem requiring careful thought and adaptation. Be resourceful. Show strength of character. Let's have some teamwork. Okay?"

Grumble, mumble. Interpreting, he understood that they would do it, but they damn well weren't going to be cheerful and pleasant about it. He tried to lighten the mood by saying, "Right. What's for lunch?" They weren't having any of that. Levity, that is. Reluctantly, they agreed that it was time for lunch. Like old misers, scowling and glaring, they each broke off a tiny bit of nutribar and passed it to him. Not equal shares, then. But he hadn't expected it. He was hungry and not looking forward to any part of this trip with these grumpy people, but it was a new and exciting experience, and he was going to make the most of it.

CHAPTER 3

Those guys had been pretty crabby before the sleep, but that was nothing to Sloan's mood when he was woken. After he had growled and snapped for a while, he did the sensible thing of explaining that space travel sleeps aren't like normal night sleeps: the pod is designed to maintain a very light sleep, spreading it it out over the timed period. When Barton woke him, he hadn't had a week of sleep: he'd had the equivalent of about four hours sleep. Hence, the increased crabbiness.

"Ah," Barton said, sympathising. After all, he might not be in the sunniest of moods when it was his turn to wake.

After a cup of coffee, Sloan was courteous enough to show him how the pod controls worked. Barton lay down, and after pressing the switches and setting the dial, and turning on the gentle electronic hum music, off he went. None of his usual restless wriggling and twisting as he worried about all sorts of things. The worry things were all back there on Earth. There was nothing that he could do about them. He was sure they would wait for him. Probably, like children, they would have grown a bit, but that was several months away. Just before he went into a pleasant sleep, he had the pleasant thought that regardless of what these people said, he was now an astronaut. He was travelling through far space, eating through it, and now about to sleep through it. Definitely an astronaut.

Perhaps he should ask for increased pay for the duration.

———

I shan't bore you with an account of the wakings and sleepings of the journey. There was general irritation, and even

Barton wasn't at his best after a week of very light sleep. And surviving on bits of nutribar like a bird was much more of a struggle and an annoyance than he pretended. But he was determined not to show any signs of suffering. They'd have been all over him with 'I told you so' and 'That's why only the top technical people are sent on these missions.' They call them 'missions' to impress. Most of the time, they're deliveries, collections, or system reviews, as this one was. Being a long way from Earth doesn't change a job. The travel is really just a long commute.

Condor 8 is one of those inhospitable lumps that scientists decide have potential for the establishment of mining and research stations. The big attraction, for everyone, of asteroids and small planets is that no-one is living on them, and no-one wants to. So, no competition, no potential for territorial disputes, as wars are euphemistically called.

At that time, there were nine domes of varying size and design, linked by passageway tubes, the whole thing called a village. As you would expect, the settlement was populated by scientific people with the social skills of a lamppost. Like large white ants, they hurried and scurried and worried, rarely even glancing at what was outside the domes (which, to be fair, wasn't much). The planet was merely a source of statistical information to be collected, measured and assessed.

Finding suitable accommodation for him was clearly not going to considered by anyone but Barton. Modestly, understanding how things stood, he chose a small cubby hole of a storeroom, in which the storage of six space suits on hooks and some drawers of simple tools left just enough room for him to sit and lie down. When Barton threatened to use several of the space suits, Sloan found some layers of foam for a bed. After some further persuasion, he provided a chair and a pocket computer, on which Barton could see incoming mail, but not send any messages, and on which Barton could keep a diary, and write notes to himself.

As cubby holes go, it wasn't a bad choice, having a thick door which could be thoroughly locked.

Barton and everyone in the vicinity would have preferred his room to be somewhere else, rather than on the edge of a large working area. When he opened his front door, the view that greeted him, so to speak, was about eighty scientists tapping and staring and scurrying with an intensity of concentration that kept their brains on full power for their work, and didn't admit the presence of the undesirable one.

It was obvious from the beginning that the attitude of Barton's fellow crew members was shared by everyone in the settlement. He soon understood clearly that it was only the scientists' ignorance of his dispensability that prevented them from opening a door and shoving him outside. With a mid-day temperature of -60 centigrade, some very nasty poisons in the air, and with no food, water or protective clothing, his life expectancy would have been very short. And no murder ever stood a better chance of not being detected. He had already disappeared back on Earth; it was easy for him to disappear again on Condor 8.

They had a sort of roaming committee, and the pushing outside was pointedly discussed loudly and frequently in his vicinity, to be rejected by correspondingly loud and frequent insistences that their high moral level would not permit what their scientific logic recommended as the most practical course.

Of course, scientific logic and being practical can be very selective. Barton's suggestion that everyone participate in the sharing of food for the extra mouth increased the general resentment in number and intensity.

But what *really* vexed these people was his mere presence. He was spoiling the party. This was Great Boffinland, settled not by poor immigrants, but by the cream of humanity. This was not going to be another . . . well, you choose. . . . Oh, no, not at all. This was going to be the beginning of an elite planetary annex; a new development of the human race, as significant as the split of the Neanderthals and the Cro-Magnons.

And there *he* was, a non-technical labourer, walking amongst them, trying to have conversations with them, cheerily greeting them with such low level colloquialisms as 'How Do?' and 'How's it going?'

It seemed to him that what these people needed was some teaching in how to be practical, preferably without moaning, and with good manners. For a start, he took the food sharing from the theoretical to the actual, by obtaining a list of all the residents and making a rota, which he put on the communal notice board in the recreation area. He felt like an ancient king or sheriff, demanding his share of their alimentary wealth, but these things must be done. He appointed himself as the collector of these little bits of nutrition and suggested that they might prefer to place their contributions in a convenient receptacle in the recreation area rather than have him wandering all over, interfering with their work or rest. They did prefer, and he found a box.

He had to do the same sort of thing with water and clothing. They seemed to be surprised that he might have liquid and clothing needs, too. He placed an empty bottle beside the box for their water contribution. Clothes were to be placed in a pile. The village folk did not like all this. Their faces became longer, their frowns became darker, and in their eyes the glint of scientific enthusiasm was replaced by the glint of resentment. But Barton knew that he had to be firm from the start.

Firm, but friendly.

"How's it going?" he asked Sloan one day when he returned from duty in one of the research domes.

He gave Barton a weary look of contempt. Clearly, he wanted to tell his troubles to someone, but he didn't want that someone to be this someone.

"You wouldn't understand," he replied.

"Well, if you explained as you complained, I might. It isn't my fault that from age eleven my career path went off sideways then down the steep cliff. My parents were poor. Being a non-techie doesn't mean that I'm thick, although I probably am."

Sloan shrugged. "The osterior crosspostulators keep flagellating."

Perhaps he saw the several suppressed responses in Barton's eyes. He said, "They have very fine hairs, for want of a better word, which spin at, well, very quickly, to create a delicate membrane of energy which is held in place by the magnetic equalisers. In spite of the momentum, which is supposed to keep them erect, most of them are bending and, in effect, beating their own cogs."

"Have you tried increased speed?"

"Yes," Sloan said with ostentatious patience. "Yes, we tried increasing the speed. That was the first thing we tried. We have tried many other things."

"Have you examined the crosspostulators for defects?"

"You mean a piece of equipment which has been manufactured by WorldCo Spacestream, to our exact specifications, and tested and accepted by three independent quality controllers."

"Yes."

"No."

It was Barton's turn to shrug. "You've done all the scientific testing. My scientific approach would now be a non-scientific one. It's all a matter of saying, 'What if?' and 'Just suppose that…' Identify all those possibles and check them. And do bear in mind that if money could control my career path from age eleven, it can certainly play a significant role in the quality of equipment which is to be sent to obscure places where even the most angry complaint would take a couple of weeks to arrive."

Sloan sniffed, shrugged in a looping sort of way, sighed and said, "I'll put it to the others."

"Or just do it."

Barton gave him a little nod, and received a stiff little nod back.

He was trying to humanise Sloan.

Three days later, Barton asked Sloan had the problem been solved.

"Oh, yes," Sloan responded dismissively. "Yes, we sorted it."

"Was it the crosspostulators?"

"No, no. They were fine."

"So what was it?"

"You wouldn't understand."

"Oh, I think I do," Barton said, with a smile. Sloan scowled, then tried to pretend that it was a look of concentration.

CHAPTER 4

By the time that Sloan delivered his bit of information, Barton had risen from a parasitical state that was annoying even him, and had gone all over the station, looking for jobs that he could do. An easy one to spot was what you might call household management, but extended into this domed village. In short, the boffins were a lot of slobs. They displayed the sort of attitude that sets all this emigration and colonising off on the wrong foot. In spite of knowing that there was a very limited population, of very superior people, on Condor 8, they could not adapt to being away from the simple luxuries of life back on Earth. Back there, lots of menials looked after them. That wasn't exaggerating, now that he was seeing it clearly. An example will help the explanation.

Back in their various scientific establishments at home, litter bins were emptied every night. And the area around the bins was cleared. The great brains might be dependent on computers and all the associated electronic gadgetry, but they still liked to print documents and show how clever and intense they were by excitedly working things out with pencil and notepad. Rejects were flung petulantly into, or in the vicinity of, the litter bins. As were drink cartons and plastic food containers. But no matter how much mess they made, in the morning the bins were empty and stood on clear and clean patches of floor.

The designer of the village had included a very efficient single-blast incinerator in the plans, but the drawback was that none of the scientists considered that they all had a collective responsibility to take relevant items to the incinerator and put them into it. Their attitude was that other people did that. The complete absence of the other people didn't have any effect on this attitude. The result was a lot of screwed-up paper, drink cartons, boxes and instant meal trays, in every room, on every floor. Occasionally in bins.

Sloan had the decency to look rueful. "Some of it was put there by the previous lots," he admitted. "Each new team inherits mess left by the previous team. We found mess when we arrived and just learned to work around it. We're pretty adaptable."

"*Adaptable?*" In his excitement, Barton forgot all about proper forms of conversation. "No-one here has adapted to being without the people who clear up all these messes back on Earth. They aren't here! But you've all just carried on accumulating mess as though there were non-techies all over the place to do it for you. They aren't here!"

"*You're* here," Sloan said brightly.

"I have already decided to start sorting out the mess. I don't want to be given the job as a non-techie. I have chosen to do it because I am available and have identified the problem, and because I want to be useful."

"Well, that's good," Sloan said happily. "I'm glad you've found a way to be useful. Let me know if anything else occurs to you."

That was the start.

Soon, Barton was a familiar sight around the village, lugging large black sacks, hauling bins and pushing trolleys. He also instigated a recycling scheme, stopping all that drink once and throw away idiocy. He washed the cups and put them back in the dispenser. Again, like it or lump it.

All the time that he was doing this, he was also investigating and assessing, until at a weekly meeting, he insisted on addressing them and dropped a few bombs on them. First, he announced a rule that nothing, *nothing*, was to be thrown at bins. A rule? By a non-techie? Was this too much for them?

"All right," he said. "Compromise. You may throw items *into* the bin, but when you miss, you must go over and pick them up and put them in the bin. That is just being civilised and considerate."

"What if we don't?" asked one truculent and heavily scowling guy at the front.

"Then you announce that you *aren't* civilised and considerate, and unless you can see the importance of those qualities, then you aren't as clever as you think you are."

Barton wasn't sure whether he had contracted haughtiness from them, or whether it was a suppressed feature of his own character. Anyway, out it came. He spread the haughty look around, avoiding the black looks and said, "Look. We are many light years from home. We are a very small community on a small space station. It is important, no, vital, that we operate as a team. Scientific brilliance isn't enough, especially when combined with snobbery. I know my place in this organisation. I am the non-techie. I shall do non-techie things for the good of the village, and for my own satisfaction, and I shall do them well. That in turn will make your lives more pleasant. But I am still a member of the team, and I am entitled to request, even to insist on, your cooperation in helping me to do my work well."

Had anyone ever talked to them like this before? Born to be boffins, raised as boffins, taught as boffins, and turned loose in the vast research and development organisations within vast commercial organisations, they had barely if ever taken so much as a peek over the walls. Even after travelling many light years from Earth, they were still in the same channel of statistical information and calculations, always looking down and never caring what was up.

"Are we clear on that?" he asked.

"It hasn't been accepted yet," said another grump.

He'd had quite enough of this absurd opposition. He said, very smoothly, "I shall be doing the rounds regularly. Anyone who misses the bin and doesn't put the item in the bin will subsequently find it somewhere amongst his documents. And it won't have been cleaned first. Try following the simple rule, guys."

At least they were now in a sulky sullenness. The revolt had been quelled. So, what better than to go on to the next difficult topic? They expected him to sit down in his low-level triumph. He almost smiled at their disappointment.

"Sewage," he said. "You have marvellous toilets, with the most powerful sanitary chemicals, but even so, sewage accumulates and must be cleared. The receptacles are almost overflowing and it looks as though previous occupants have let them overflow. What is the point of pure air systems when you are producing foul air and germs?"

"What? You want us to empty and clean toilets now?"

"No. I'll do it. It's a non-techie job. But I want you to know that I am doing it, and I want you to take some responsibility for cleanliness and for occasionally checking the sewage levels. This is Condor 8, not Sterile 8 or Antiseptic 8. Sewage must be controlled and disposed."

After a moment for that to sink in, he asked, "*Is* there a disposal system?"

Blank looks all round.

Ridiculous. Had *anyone* thought of these things? At that point, he'd had enough. He asked Sloan for access on a spare computer to the relevant documents and sat down.

Three days later, after looking in every bit of every available (not confidential) documents, he had failed to find anything about sewage disposal. When Sloan, checking on progress, made a wry face, Barton said,"What is the gravity on this planet?"

"Similar to Earth's."

"Do we have access to outside?"

"There is access, for those scientists whose work takes them outside, which doesn't apply to the present team. We are internal researchers. The people who were here before us went outside, and no doubt the people who will come after us will go outside. We have neither need nor intention. It isn't nice. There's nothing out there, except extreme cold, and air so acidic that it would burn your lungs to shreds in a few seconds."

"But we could put something outside, couldn't we? An early bit of terraforming?"

Another bold idea to cause perturbation, even agitation. But Sloan soon subsided into a reasonable, "Well, I suppose. But you couldn't just keep dumping it out of the door."

"Not on our own doorstep, you mean. Okay, then. Would those suits in my room provide adequate protection against cold and poison?"

"I understand that they are fitted with a short term air supply. I don't know how long that is. I advise you to keep checking your dials."

"But what about the early explorers. Did they just go out for a few minutes at a time?"

"No. There are some air cylinders somewhere for long visits, but we aren't interested in those. If anyone *had* to go out, it would be very short term, for which the fitted air supply would be adequate."

"Right then. I'll be your muck-spreader."

"You mean go outside?"

"Yes. That's why I have been asking those questions. If other people can do it, I'm sure that I can. I don't intend to go far. Just far enough to keep the muck from the door."

So, that was general cleaning and tidying duties and sewage disposal, combined with some unofficial basic terraforming, which to Barton's simple mind seemed the best sort that anyone could do. Let those tough little bacteria go to work. They'd colonise the planet long before humans did.

Next was laundry. There was a powerful steam and disinfectant contraption, with a drying frame attached, but no-one had thought of using it. Partly because they were too important and busy to be concerned about such matters as personal hygiene; and partly because great scientists have trouble with such operations as off and on. Barton told them to put out their clothing every three days, with a name on a piece of paper and he'd put it in the machine, to be washed and dried, and then he'd return it. Most of the time, they forgot the piece of paper, and he just made a big pile for them to come and claim their clothes. They soon settled in this additional routine.

Cleaning and tidying, sewage disposal and laundry.

He decided that for all their sakes, they should stop the melodramatic eating while working. It was no good for health or temper, and no good for his cleaning. Even though generally they put bad shot items in the bin, they were never going to stoop so low, really, as to clean greasy messes off the floor. He made a separate section in the recreation area to be a restaurant. He told them to have short breaks, to be decided when practical in advance, and to send a message to him and he'd heat whatever their chosen meal was and put it on a table in the restaurant. Although at the beginning, there was the inevitable ordering, then missing, of meals, and lots of variations on ways to hinder the success of a system, gradually he had them trained, to order, slip away and have a gobble at the table. Soon, the gobbling was accompanied by lunchtime chats with one another, and soon again, little cliques were having regular lunches at regular times.

Cleaning and tidying, sewage disposal, laundry and catering.

They were reporting things to Barton, asking questions, requesting assistance with finding lost items, and, of course, they were being civilised and organised.

He was effectively in charge of Condor 8.

CHAPTER 5

But what mattered most to Barton was that he was being useful and doing his work well.

To use an old phrase, he was earning his keep.

But he had to admit that even he put off sewage disposal for as long as he reasonably could. There were two unappealing elements to the job: sewage and outside. Being a typical non-techie, he was still in awe of, and a bit afraid of, the system that kept their little home planet spinning away in the vastness of space. He didn't even like going up ladders, even with the safety harnesses and fall-breakers. But he had his duty. The sewage must go and, very briefly, he must go with it. After all, he had created this task, then volunteered to do it.

The sewage drums were in a utility area, opposite what was, in effect, the back door. There were the drums, with two spare empty ones, spare air cylinders, boxes of tools, and the control panels for the entire heating, cooling and air purification systems. After some nervous moments, Barton managed to seal and detach the drums, and dragged them out to the exit.

"You don't have to do this," Sloan said, rubbing temptation into his weak spots.

Barton smiled. "Yes, I do."

"Okay." Barton gave the helmet a final twist until there was a reassuring click. He checked all the bits which screwed or bolted into place, and, less reassuringly, the flaps which merely stuck to one another.

"Remember," Sloan said, "that the gravitational pressure is close to Earth's. 'Close to' can be a significant distance out there. Press down hard into your boots. You won't float away, but you might float about. That isn't recommended for your version of sewage disposal. We don't want the stuff to float about and follow you back in here. And don't lose your card for opening the outer door."

At least he was providing important information. The rest were like a lot of eloi. Not the slightest concern or even interest. Apparently. Although the suit was light and flexible, walking around inside the dome in it was difficult, but they seemed not to notice his clumping about. Oh, well. In a way, he was glad. Attention from that lot was usually of the disapproving sort. Better to be ignored and left to go on with his job.

He prepared by putting all the sewage drums in a line. They would have to be carried out one at a time. He picked up the first one by its two handles and lugged it to the inner door. He tapped in the code and pressed the button. The door hissed open in the traditional manner and he dragged the drum through and closed the inner door. There were more buttons and levers for the outer door and it didn't hiss; it slid slowly, as though doomily giving him a last chance to decide not to do this.

He was not to be deterred by a dismal door. He rolled the drums out, then out he went, rather enjoying being outside on another planet. A big step for a poffle-sweeper. He'd have preferred to be taking minute dust samples or photographs instead of dumping the contents of sewage drums, but he wasn't going to spoil the moment by being fussy.

He immediately understood what Sloan meant about pushing down into his shoes. He didn't like the constant feeling that if he relaxed, he'd float away. A bit like reverse drowning, except that in this case there was no faint prospect of touching the bottom and bobbing up again. If he went up, that would be it. He couldn't swim back down. He'd just keep going into the infinity of space and whatever death that would produce for him.

And his last view of the safety of the domes would probably be those annoying people, not caring, or not even knowing, that he was departing into the great void. And some of those who did know would probably not try to conceal their smug relief.

Imagine that as your last view of the human race: a smirking scientist.

They wouldn't want to give him the importance of a celebration. Someone would just give the slightest glance and murmur, "There he goes."

Barton enjoyed having the ballast of the full sewage drums.

He rolled each drum a reasonable distance from the dome. Not as far as he'd have liked, but the walk back each time with an empty drum was making him nervous and he just emptied them at the first spot that he had selected as possible. It was still a long, slow job. He was glad when the task was finished and he stood at the outer door with his empties. He showed his card and tapped out the codes and waited for the door to open.

It didn't.

He tried again, and again, and again. He tried variations of the code, and after three attempts, it denied him entry for two hours. He thought of knocking on the door and the wall of the dome, and yelling, but in space, no-one can hear you knock or yell. But he stood at the window wall of the dome and waved his arms and shouted. The people inside looked everywhere but at him. Even those walking in his direction somehow avoided looking at him. It was as though he was already dead. He threw empty drums at the thin but hideously strong plastic. Still, there was no response. He looked at his air and temperature dials. He didn't have much time. The supplies were set for a very short visit. No-one expected anyone to be outside for long.

No-one?

Anyone?

Everyone?

Had they, with the utmost irony, managed to work together as a co-ordinated team?

He set off round to one of the smaller domes, taking a drum with him. He banged and shouted and leapt about, briefly levitating. No: still they didn't hear and didn't see.

He was a couple of minutes away from death.

He started to move away, then turned sharply back. Just for a moment, he saw the eyes of one of the techies being turned away. He'd caught her. She'd peeped and Barton had caught her. He stood before her, waving his arms. She stared at the computer screen. Barton moved into what would be her line of vision if she'd only look up.

Of course, she didn't.

The couple of minutes had almost gone.

He went to the door of this minor dome.

At this moment, on the brink of a horrible death, he was *annoyed*.

But, remembering something obvious, he was looking forward to disappointing them.

People who had no intention of going outside had been very careless with their cards for opening the outside doors. Barton had an ingrained habit of picking up anything that might be useful. He took out the card which belonged to Sloan and presented it to the main entrance. The outer door slid open. As soon as there was a big enough gap, he darted through. He closed the outer door, opened the inner door and stepped back into safety.

Safe, that is, apart from being in the company of one hundred and forty two attempted murderers.

It was amusing to watch those people trying to hide their amazement, disappointment and perhaps a little fear, while trying to pretend that they hadn't noticed his return any more than they had noticed his crisis outside.

But of course when the notorious drudge had just returned from a dramatic first venture out of the dome, you *would* notice. Even if you didn't like him or approve of him, you would notice.

He went straight to Sloan and said, "That was close." After a brief hesitation, Sloan said, "Why? What happened?"

"My card wouldn't work."

"Oh? That's odd. Er, so how did you . . . open the door?"

"By always thinking ahead, and preparing for possible problems."

Sloan sat nodding. "Did you do the sewage disposal?"

"Yes," Barton said, very pleasantly. "Another satisfactory task performed for the good of the community. But next time, if there *is* a next time, I shall insist that someone comes out with me. As insurance against any more problems."

Sloan tried to look indignant, with a dash of astonishment for good measure. "I hope you aren't suggesting that a member of this research team tried to kill you. After I stood there, giving you careful instructions and advice."

"Yes, you did," Barton replied. "I'm not accusing anyone. I'm saying that there were some very odd aspects of the occurrence."

"Such as?"

"Why was my access blocked?"

"One of those freak things that occasionally happen even with the best electronic systems."

"A rather important part of the system, access to the dome from outside. One would expect lots of vigilance and support. When my access failed, a reserve system should have stepped in. That didn't happen. Why was no-one supervising my exit and return? Simple safety control. And why did no-one, *no-one*, at any time, glance in my direction or detect my waving, drum-flinging, body in his or her peripheral vision. Put all those things together and you have a lot of bad luck, a lot of coincidences, a lot of procedures ignored."

Sloan tried being haughty and offended. "What a terrible thing to say, to *think*. Doubly, no, trebly, offensive. To accuse your fellow residents, scientists of the highest repute, and, putting it quite bluntly, your superiors in all respects, of such a callous act, is appalling. I think that an apology to the whole settlement is in order."

"I was left outside, with a small amount of oxygen and heat source, with not one of my supposed superiors doing anything in the way of watching, timing or checking in any way. I'd like to look at the procedure manual. There must be one. And there must be a procedure for when a team member goes outside."

"I haven't time to go searching through manuals. I've wasted enough time talking to you."

"One last thing. Scientists, on a distant small planet, in a space station? I'd have thought that procedure manuals would be essential reading."

He started to walk away. But he saw resentful looks, and he heard murmuring, done just loudly enough for him to hear.

"To think," Pollitt said with disgust, "that we could have just jettisoned him into space on the way here."

Murmur, murmur.

Barton murmured back, "According to procedure?"

There is nothing like the truth for making people indignant. They had failed and been caught out. They had dropped the great superior façade, and resorted to lowest level skulduggery. And made a mess of it. They had been out-thought by the dogsbody. It all combined to make them even more dangerous.

He showed them his palms in a concluding, let's move on, gesture and said, "Look. Let's just forget it. Let's pretend that whatever it was never happened, and go on with our lives. Okay? I'll carry on being your general assistant and you carry on with your research. Let's try to be on good terms with one another, and cooperate with one another, and in a few weeks, you can be rid of me forever."

"A few weeks?" muttered Mr Truculent. What he meant, implied, was, 'Do we have to wait that long?'

As a way of moving on, Barton turned back to Sloan and said, "Someone will have to bring in those drums or come out with me while I do it."

"I'll find someone to help you," he replied.

"Preferably, not the second least popular person in the village, or I might still worry."

A haughty look was the response. Barton added, "And please arrange for my access to be restored."

"I'll look into the problem."

"Which is exactly what would have happened in the case of a genuine malfunction. You aren't even covering your tracks well. The obvious and immediate response should have been: Someone's access card didn't work! How did that happen? We must investigate. So sorry about that, Wood. We'll take all the necessary steps to ensure that it won't happen again."

Sloan ignored him.

———

When a guy called Mellor approached Barton, he said, "Ah, Wood, I notice that our sewage drums are still outside. That won't do. We need them inside and functioning. Organise it, will you?"

He didn't wait for a response and prevented any potential conversation by walking quickly past. This wasn't the first time this had happened during the last few days. Barton couldn't decide whether they were feebly trying to reassert their imagined superiority or whether they were trying to confirm and reinforce his imagined inferiority in order to make themselves feel better in the event of another 'accident' involving only him. Perhaps both. But he had no doubt that another attempt would be made to slip him neatly and without fuss into the cold and silent void.

Not the least annoying thing about all this was that he had made their dome lives so much better. The village was relatively clean, meals were prepared and served, documents, in whatever form, were carefully stored, spares for defective equipment were quickly provided. Of course, having ignored all these things before, they hardly noticed what was being done now. And they even resented some of the systems, such as meal breaks by rota. Damn it: he'd been civilising these slobs.

He was also beginning to suffer from the loneliness of being ignored in a large crowd. Monosyllabic responses to questions, with a carefully raised eyebrow and a blank look were worse than outright insults.

He refused to bring in the sewage drums unless someone went out with him. Eventually, Sloan volunteered someone who very grudgingly stepped outside, and stood impatiently while Barton dragged the drums into the chamber. He didn't help at all, but Barton didn't expect him to offer. All that mattered, for a little while, was that the the drums and he were safely back in the dome.

Nodding towards the door, he asked his recent companion, "Your first time?"

"Of course not." It was said with *the look*.

It was like this all the time. Anger, irritation and grumpiness he could have tolerated, just about, but this cold aloofness and contempt was very upsetting. He wanted to go home, in every sense. And because of that, he felt horribly trapped.

He also felt *watched*.

Sometimes, often, it seemed not so much that they were trying to make him miserable as that they were inadvertently releasing their menacing, malevolent intentions. He'd observed that they were bad actors. Too much egotism. They couldn't imagine being anyone else.

As for their being 'top brains', Barton would have said that history contains many examples of people who were clever, but did wicked, and very stupid, things. Cleverness isn't an indication of intelligence. You could have a conversation with a parrot or a mynah bird, but try asking it for its views on the current political situation.

His further response would have been: based on what you have read so far, what do *you* think? Your further response would probably be that it was his imagination, that he was resentful in the presence of his superiors, jealous, bitter, para-noic, a typical non-technician response, and on and on. That business with the access? Just a glitch in the system.

And the incident with the freezer? Same thing.

Which incident with the freezer?

This incident with the freezer.

Barton had taken it upon himself to be the head of cater-ing. That didn't involve hours of slaving over a hot stove: just some boring minutes in front of the large microwave cooker. Things had moved on considerably from the days when space travel fare consisted of powders and pastes. Now, the typical traveller takes a supply of frozen meals, real meals, sort of. It works pretty well. Delivery around the Galaxy is big business for FoodCo. Easy profit, too. In most places, there's no problem of leaving the items when the recipient is out or hasn't arrived yet. So long as the temperature is minus what-ever, they can just dump the food and go on to the next planet.

Yes, Condor 8 is chilly. You wouldn't last for long in tee shirt and shorts. But it isn't a frozen waste by any means. It even has a summer, in the middle of which you might just be able to venture out in all your gear, for about three seconds. Not that you'd want to; I'm just saying that you could if you wanted.

The point of all this is to explain, in a rather rambling way, that the food on Condor 8 was kept in a very large freezer.

And I expect that you saw about ten minutes ago where all this is going.

Now, Barton would have admitted that the large door of the freezer room had a strong tendency to adopt a default position of firmly closed. After opening it, as wide as you could, it was advisable to place something heavy in the doorway or keep glancing over your shoulder because it liked to swing back on a powerful hinge. Not just swing back. It was one of those doors that like to pretend they're closing forever. In certain circumstances, that is what it would be doing in effect. The obvious thing was to visit in pairs, with one to hold the door. Barton's problem with that was in forming a pair.

That was entirely the scientists' fault. He didn't trust them.

Before he even entered the freezer room, he placed a stool where it would prevent premature closure.

Thinking about it later, he was stupid about it because he didn't anticipate the removal of the stool. There was a small and persistent thought which kept saying that a bunch of top level scientists would not be cold-blooded killers.

Yes, the same top level scientists who tried to kill him a few days earlier.

Even the method, and effect, were similar.

In spite of the cold, he felt a chill when he heard the clunk and deep click of the closing door.

But he wasn't *that* stupid. He merely walked over and pressed the emergency door release button.

Nothing happened.

He spoke into the voice box.

Nothing.

He tried his personal communicator.

Nothing.

They were being thorough this time.

But not thorough enough.

They had forgotten one important thing. The freezer was no more than a storage facility for frozen meals, assembled out here from a kit. It was powerful and reasonably well-constructed, but only so far as its single purpose went. That purpose was to keep frozen food frozen, not to withstand an internal attack by a desperate man. It was a plastic kit, which meant that everything fitted into slots. Barton knew that when everything fits perfectly into everything else, there is a lot of strength in a simple construction. There was probably only one relatively weak area.

He didn't have much time because the cold would soon make him numb and weak. He hauled frozen meals off the shelves and made a large, roughly square pile at the far end of the room. He stacked as well as he could because he needed it to be firm. When it was what he hoped would be the right height, he clambered up some shelves and stepped very carefully onto his pile. There was only room to crouch, which was what he intended. He paused, took some big breaths, then simultaneously pushed down with his feet and up with his shoulders, in one quick, powerful movement.

He felt the roof move. Great. He felt the frozen meals move. Very bad. But he'd had encouragement from the movement. He repeated, with a snarl and a whoop and an uuuurrrggghh.

Bang. Sudden and dramatic cooperation. Up went the lid, up and up, as he enjoyed his triumph by leaping onto the rim still dropping the section of roof back into place. He leapt onto the firm part of the roof and looked triumphantly, contemptuously, down from his high platform.

There was no-one there. This was the kitchen area.

What a waste of a moment of triumph.

It might be his only one.

On his way back, he made a detour, and filled his pockets with the most important items in the medical box. He was starting to prepare. Two attempts. There would soon be a third.

Of course, when he walked through into the main areas, everyone tried very hard not to notice him. But he looked closely at them and could see that slight suppressed double-take, with perhaps just a dash of discomfiture.

He walked straight through them to his room and closed the door. He had built a supply of various nutribars and sealed cakes, and drinks, for just such a crisis as this. Apart from bathroom visits and an occasional stroll, he decided to stay in his room until it was time for the return to Earth. From now on, these people could heat their own food, eat it cold or do without. They could live in their own filth and clutter. They could go about in dirty clothes. He didn't care. He had tried to help them, they hadn't appreciated his efforts, and now he was withdrawing his services.

After all, they wouldn't have had his services if they had killed him.

CHAPTER 6

He didn't have to bother about visits from begging scientists or curious scientists. That was all well beneath them. His isolation was the next best thing to his being dead. It was regrettable that he was there, but at least they didn't have to see him, share their air with him, be infected by him.

He had to admit that it seemed to work better for everyone. They avoided or ignored him and he did the same. They were happy in their dirty chaos and even they could manage to walk to the freezer, grab a meal and heat it.

Being top-level scientists, even with the defects which have been mentioned, you would have expected them to notice that the frozen meals soon weren't. The roof panel needed to be put firmly back in place, not dropped, as Barton had done.

It was an important point. Those meals had to be frozen hard, then taken out and blasted by the old waves, then eaten. There was no variation on this, no half-way stage. I mean, not in the healthy eating plan. In any stage between frozen and instantly cooked, the food became extremely bad for the health. It was all to do with methods of freezing for long journeys. Slight defrosting did something spectacular in the germ-producing line.

Over a few days, Barton noticed in a distant, peripheral sort of way a large increase in the number of people hurrying to the lavatory area. That could be interesting in view of the removal of his sewage assistance. Then, it was groans and people curling up on the floor, gasping out vomit. A horrible job for him if he had still been doing that sort of thing.

He expected a request soon.

What was he thinking? Those people didn't do requests. Not of a social and professional inferior.

All that information about the effects of partially defrosted food had just, belatedly, occurred to him when Sloan staggered over to Barton's room and hovered and twisted and coiled in the doorway, as though he had a couple of angry things having a fight in his trousers. "It's all your fault," he gasped, with a touch of snarl. "You clean it up. All of it."

"What's all my fault?"

"The food. It's all defrosted."

"Why is it all my fault?"

"You left the panel loose in the freezer."

"And why did that happen?"

"I don't know. Probably because you're trying to kill us."

"It's an interesting and attractive thought. I admit that it was careless of me to leave the panel loose. However, there would have been no need to loosen the panel if I hadn't been locked in the freezer."

"Well, that was your fault. Oooh. Everyone knows that the door swings back and you have to be careful."

"Which I was. I placed a stool where it would prevent the door from closing. It was moved."

"Well, no-one here ..."

"*Anyone* here. You're a crowd of callous ingrates, and this was the second attempt to kill me."

"Do you, oooh, really think that the people here would be capable of such an act? Just thinking that is a clear display of your inferiority."

"All right, then, superior people, clean up your own mess."

"No! That's your job."

"It's my job because I volunteered."

"You...ooooh ... volunteered because we politely waited for you to do so. Obviously cleaning up the rubbish and disposing of it was your role."

Barton walked over to him, put his hand on his chest and lightly pushed him off the threshold and out of his room. "Go away," he said. "I have to use those toilets, too, which puts it in my interest to do it. But I'll do it when I'm ready to do it. In the meantime, and for the rest of this trip, all you superior people keep right out of my way."

He didn't notice the man just outside and to his left until he said, "That might not be quite that simple."

Dover Hemingway was a thin, bald man with a large head; the old idea of a boffin type. So far, he seemed to have adopted a policy of strict neutrality, not speaking aloud against Barton or for him. He just watched. Now, in one of those curious, indefinable moments of certainty, Barton knew that he was the controlling malevolence in all this.

"What do you mean?" he asked.

"The food is inedible. Very soon, this village will consist of a lot of very hungry, and very valuable, scientists. Staying alive will be a matter of duty to them."

Turning to Sloan, he said, "I've called a meeting. In the circumstances, I think that we need one."

"Yes, yes, of course," Sloan said following him away from Barton's room.

With a loud sigh, Barton said, "And I'll start cleaning your mess."

Barton watched that bald head moving away, looking like a twentieth century mountain observatory that had come loose and was rolling away. Was the man saying what he seemed to be saying?

Why not? With no moral restrictions, no danger of detection, their cold, analytical minds would immediately look for and find an obvious source of sustenance.

All that they needed was an inferior being. A lower, less important species. The cow, the pig, the sheep, the non-technical guy.

Physically, he'd be outnumbered. Mentally, he'd be outeverythinged.

The plan had come to him in an instant.

His survival plan.

———

The meeting was a big one. It looked as though everyone had gone to attend. Gone in a hurry, too, because most of them hadn't even bothered to log out of their computers.

He sat down and sent a message back to Earth, giving them his name. It was a brief message, but at least it would be on record in the event that something horrible did happen to him. When he had sent the message, he deleted it at this end.

Weapons!

What weapons were there? The planet was known, or at least believed, to have no inhabitants, and scientists were expected to stay in the safety of their domes.

Think! He needed to do this quickly. A meeting about killing him was not likely to be a long one.

He took down all the space suits, and managed to shuffle quickly round to the control area. He put the space suits, the tool box, except for one screwdriver, the medicine box, and the spare air cylinders into one of the spare drums. He dragged the sewage drums into a line by the rear exit door, with the spare drum beside them. Next, the freezer room, where he used the screwdriver to slash open most of the remaining food cartons.

When the meeting ended and the mob, the contents of all nine domes, came out, Barton was busy mopping and disinfecting.

Dover Hemingway came to the front of the mob. He didn't push and Barton didn't notice anyone moving out of his way. He seemed just to appear at the front. He said, lips barely moving, "The meeting was about our chronic food problems. The snack machines are almost empty. Obviously, we technicians must do what we can to stay alive. The matter has now become severe."

"And what did you decide?"

He tried to do a little smile. "That we scientists must do what we can to stay alive."

He turned and walked away, the crowd somehow melting away from him, then following him and returning to their desks.

Well, that was clear.

In order to survive, the superior species was going to dine on the inferior species.

Isn't that always the way?

CHAPTER 7

Barton had done his planning and his preparation. He was very glad because he didn't know how much time he had. He doubted that they were going to wait until they were starving. They might do it as soon as there was a general peckishness.

Would they go for straight slaughter, or would they wait for an opportunity such as his going out with the sewage drums?

It would have been very helpful to know, but his planning assumed either. His plan provided for survival in a variety of circumstances, possibly all of them. The door of his tiny room was thick, but probably wasn't strong enough to keep out a demented mob.

As soon as he opened his door, they all watched him, all pretending that they were thinking of other things.

They were no longer wondering where their next meal was coming from.

He walked through the desks, trying to look casual, to where the sewage drums were stored.

He tried to look merely busy in his usual way, emptying litter bins in the vicinity, and generally fiddling about. He moved slowly, carelessly, showing no indication of stress or urgency, or nervousness. He was increasingly glad that people were ignoring him.

The drums weren't full, but the recent illnesses had been productive. When he saw people looking furtively at him, he shrugged and said, "You dream and plot all you like. I'll carry on doing my work at this end of the social scale."

They stared at their computers, a collective version of a sub-shrug for someone who was too far down the social scale to be acknowledged. Talking to them had been a dangerous bit of improvisation, but he was glad that he had done it. It displayed a scepticism about what they were intending, and showed his stupid and menial person's determination to go on with his duties.

As he pretended to work, he saw slight movement in his peripheral vision, a slight flickering of shadows.

"What's your plan?" Dover Hemingway somehow called, whispered, insinuated, verbally crept.

"To keep working," he replied. Hemingway was standing only a few steps away, having advanced like one of those monsters who come from the far end of the corridor to right beside you in the moment of darkness when the light is switched off. His bald head and blandly intense scientist's face didn't reduce the horror that Barton now felt. He was too close, too knowing.

"No," he said. "I mean your *big* plan. The one on which you are now working, thinking that you can out-think your superiors. Because that's what you've been doing, isn't it? Thinking. *Big* thinking."

"What? One thick menial against all you?"

"I've been watching you. I'm watching you now. You're so easy to read. You're trying to think, to plot."

"Why should I need to plot anything?"

"Because you know what is going to happen; what must happen. The gulf in intelligence between us is as great as the one between you and a pig."

"So, I'm the animal here, am I? Or is that the person who eats an animal?"

"Having ruined all the food which was provided by even lower forms, yes, you are. You are all that is left. What would you have? All these great scientists die because of your idiocy?"

"You caused it."

"That is your view, but we have established that your view is the equivalent of a snuffling grunt in the mud. Besides, it is irrelevant. Your status is quite clear. Our duty is quite clear."

Barton looked down, defeated, afraid, sad, weak. "Call everyone together," he said. "I need to speak to you all."

"You're still plotting."

"I hate to say it, but you're overestimating me. I've just been keeping busy to keep the small flame of hope burning. That's how we lower orders think. Always be busy to keep away harm, to keep away sin. Call everyone. A gathering in five minutes. I want to explain. Go on. It's the least you can do."

"It won't work!" Hemingway called.

Barton shouted, "Do it, or just clear off!" He had wanted to have more time, to do it slowly and steadily, letting it all take place smoothly, without their knowledge until the last moment.

Damn Dover Hemingway!

But at least he had gone to round up the scientists.

By the control panel, just out of sight, Barton put on his space suit. Then, he switched off the air purifier, and turned up the heating.

"Now!" Dover Hemingway's voice, suddenly harsh, slashed across the room.

Barton dashed back to the drums. The entire population of the nine domes was rushing at him. One hundred and forty-two homicidal maniacs. Trying to be calm, Barton tipped the first drum, sending a slime of sewage sliding across the floor. The people at the front, stopped, and tried to step back, as those behind continued to advance. Two people fell into the mess, and bellowed.

Over went the next drum, and the next, until they were all empty.

Pulling his supplies drum, Barton slammed his hand against the button to open the chamber, and again to close it. The mob was screaming at him, horrified by the splashing of sewage on their legs, enraged by his escape, and bewildered.

Just before Barton clicked his helmet shut and locked, he was delighted to see the face of Dover Hemingway as he began to understand the plan. Contempt was replaced by horror, and fear. Barton raised a slow arm, and gave him a thumbs up.

He opened the outer door, rolled the drum out and closed the door.

And that was that.

He was outside, with the suits, each with its air supply, and with the cylinders.

They were inside, with no suits, and with a lot of food and sewage germs which were quickly going to spread in the clean, warm air. And those clean scientists, protected all their lives from nasty things, were soon going to become very ill. That's why the defrosted meals had affected them so badly. Tummy aches were to be expected, but they all had the result of defunct immune systems.

And he had all the useful medicines.

Waiting outside was going to be tedious and not at all pleasant, but he had his bars to nibble, his air to breathe slowly, and, of course, his show to watch through the brightly lit screen of the dome window.

CHAPTER 8

The next three days were slow and dreary. The suit air supplies were soon gone, and he had a few moments in which to regret an important omission in his planning: he didn't know how to use the air cylinders. Stuck on them were some incomprehensible pictures, and some stern warnings about what he must NOT do. He didn't understand any of it, and the only people that he could ask were some very angry, homicidal, and dying, scientists. But all that he needed was some incentive. Painful suffocation, in full view of the enemy, was a pretty strong incentive. He did what he always did when faced with such difficult challenges: he ignored all the instructions and did what seemed to be the obvious thing. He removed his air nozzle, punched the cap on a small orifice on a cylinder and shoved the end of the nozzle over it. It worked. There was a small wheel with which to control the flow. He turned it to minimum. This had to last. Shallow breathing from now on.

He was going to be okay for a while. Would it be long enough? Probably not, but it looked as though he was going to live for longer than the suffering people in the domes.

Feelings of triumph and revenge soon faded, and he stopped watching the rapid, dismal decline and deaths of the scientists. He just glanced occasionally to check on how things were going. Long-lost immunity combined with clean, warm air and some eagerly opportunist germs were a devastating combination. After two days, he could have moved back in because everyone inside lacked the strength and the desire to do anything to him. But his departing mess, the subsequent mess and the dying people made him very reluctant. The only cleaning equipment consisted of disposable cloths and an electric mop. It needed a lot more than that.

He soon regretted not adding some of the full-scale junk food to his relatively sensible collection of nutribars and little cakes. He needed more food and he needed variety. He was bored and lonely. For a while, he even looked keenly through the window, hoping to see someone who was resisting the infections. He'd have gone in and tried to help, just to have some company.

But he was going to have to dispose of one hundred and forty two bodies. At that point, he wondered whether he really intended to kill them all. No, he told himself; he had done what was necessary to prevent them from killing *him*. They had tried twice, and they had told him that they were going to kill him, and eat him. He couldn't overpower all those determined and hungry people, other than by doing what he had done. Their deaths were inevitable, but the intention was to prevent, not kill. A neat bit of justification to ease his conscience.

He couldn't wait for absolute completion. He needed to start clearing and cleaning. He needed to destroy the evidence.

He stopped and pondered.

He checked his pocket computer. The dying scientists had sent desperate messages, and the cops were on their way from Aztec-9, and would arrive in six days.

He sat back and thought about it.

He considered his responses, from the comical *They went out* to the incredible *They were going to eat me*. Then, he knew what he must do.

The evidence must stay where it was.

CHAPTER 9

The cops strode about spraying cleaning fluids and swear words. The dead bodies had to go, but they had to go in some sort of order, their names, titles and ranks being recorded, photographs taken. As each one was recorded, out it went, to float away into the darkness. They hadn't died with any consideration for the task, and were all over the place, in nine domes. It took two days to dispose of them all.

The cops were not pleased. Disposing of dead bodies and disinfecting a space station was not cops' work; but they had to do something. They couldn't just walk away leaving one hundred and forty two dead bodies in a space station.

"What's that?" Two cops turned abruptly, as they heard erratic thudding against the door of the cubby hole. Pointing their guns, the cops approached. One put a linkaphone against the door and spoke into it. "Who's in there?"

A quavering voice replied, "Barton Wood. Is it over? Is it safe to come out?"

"That depends on what you mean by 'safe'. You see, some very strange messages were received saying that Barton Wood was killing everyone."

"I know. They went mad. They were all being sick, and blaming it on me. Because I took charge of things like the food, and the refrigeration room leaked, and the food went off. I told them not to eat it, but they said in that case, they'd eat me. I ran in here, and locked myself in. It was horrible. They kept trying to break the door. I've been in here over a week, with no food or drink, except a couple of things that I grabbed when I saw them going peculiar. Oh, what a nightmare. Please help me."

"Well, you can start by unlocking the door."

Barton did, then staggered out, and collapsed at their feet. He began to sob, looking around anxiously. "Have they . . . did you …?"

"They had to be removed," said the cop. "But we've made records and taken photographs, so we have all the evidence we need."

Another cop stepped forward and said. "It's says here that a few days before they sent their messages, you sent a message, saying they were going to kill you."

"Yes. For a few weeks, they were unpleasantly resentful and ungrateful. But then it turned sinister. They kept making comments about needing more food because of the extra person."

"Which extra person?"

Barton said patiently, "Right. Let's start at the beginning."

He soon had them thoroughly bored, which is the best thing for interrogators to be. For the person being interrogated.

"Okay," said the main cop. "I have the idea. Skip the details."

That was good. One, he wanted to skip the details; two, if challenged later over omissions, Barton could explain that he was told to omit the details.

"Well, when they insisted on eating food which should have been cooked from frozen, but was now thoroughly defrosted, there were some internal disturbances, and then threats. I panicked and locked myself into my little room. I was expecting them to break through eventually, but the pounding on the door became weaker, presumably as they did. Then a lot of groaning. Then silence. It might have been a trap, so I stayed in here, and waited for something to happen."

"What about all those overturned sewage drums, and sewage?"

Barton shrugged. "I've no idea what they were doing. They were mad."

"I'm not sure I believe it," said the cop.

Barton looked at him, raised an eyebrow, and tilted his head for a moment. "Well, yes, I suppose that one hundred and forty two diseased dead scientists, and one nearly starved and terrified man who has been locked in his room for a week might look suspicious to you. I shall be submitting a detailed report of this entire horrible business, and my report will include the complete lack of sympathy, and the failure to provide nourishment and medication for the sole survivor of this catastrophe."

Take that! Barton put into his voice a nice blend of self-pity and aggression. He had learned quickly, having been fully exposed to a lot of pompous and nasty superior people. A small collection of cops was no problem.

"Okay. Calm down," the cop said. "Miller, dig something out of the rescue box."

Barton exhaled, and said, "Thank you. This has been a very difficult time. I am not at my best. Excuse me. I need to sit down."

The cops were startled out of their customary slowness, when a strange little outside wind put on a very impressive show, by returning the dead bodies, as though deeply offended, at a high velocity to whump against the transparent side of the dome. Nerves of steel were nowhere to be found. The constant thuds, and the staring faces of the dead bodies quickly convinced the cops that a rapid departure was the right course to take.

"We'll take you to Aztec-9," the cop said as they hurried

away, and you can go back to Earth on the next cargo ship that unloads, which shouldn't be long."

"Very kind of you," Barton replied. "And when I'm back there, that's where I'll stay. No more space stations for me. I know my place. I know where I belong."

But as the cop ship roared up into the darkness, he looked out and thought, "Or do I?"

# # #

NEWTOWN

Have you ever stood in the crowded centre of a newtown, and had a panic attack? I did. And as I came out of it, I wondered, 'What if?'

Newtown. Already shabby, but always a newtown by design. Adapted, assimilated, the people of Newtown scurried, dawdled, stamped and shouted through the harsh, sharp shapes of the shops and offices. A dizzying, suffocating scramble of bodies.

"Shopping centre," Jenny said.

Tom raised an eyebrow or two. "Do you mean centre as in heart and mind, the throbbing hub of the town, the essence, the culmination of all the aspirations of the people who designed this horror?"

"Yes. Exactly. This really is the centre. All the big stores, the silvery abstract town centre symbolic sculpture, the rectangular pond containing empty cans and fast food wrappers, the fountain which isn't working. This . . . is it."

"This isn't doing street view, or looking from a train window, and wondering about all the far away people with their own lives …"

"No. We're going to be part of it. Very soon."

The grim truth. Tom's very simple choice, which was no choice: be made redundant or move to another division. The division which was here.

Redundancy was tempting. But frightening. Especially with the move to this place being dressed up as a promotion. Besides, he wasn't the sort to walk out of employment. Too old-fashioned; too independent to take risks. Ignore the reputations; people who took risks always had someone or something to provide a safety net. Or they had no qualms about living off the state and charity.

And looming over, and lurking under, all these considerations was the biggest, darkest one: at his age, and with his limited capability, the only job for him would be a trolley-pusher. Staying in one company, and behaving reasonably well, could lead you gently up to a salary level at which no other company would employ you.

"Let's eat."

"Okay. But it won't make the problem go away."

"It'll be a few minutes away from all these people rushing about. It's like being in another country, but without the interesting people, buildings and language. The centre of a town of a million identical houses. The people are identical, too, apart from their shape variations."

She almost dragged him to the inevitable town centre fast food place. Never mind the quality, just have some instant flavouring to calm the nerves. She made him go and find a seat. She didn't want to stand in a queue while he tactlessly insulted everyone around him.

When she arrived at the table, he was already fidgeting and scowling. The food didn't improve things. "I give them full marks for consistency," he said. "The quality here is as bad as it is in every other one that I've had the misfortune to visit."

"Well, isn't that a little bit reassuring?"

"Not really." He smiled. "But I know what you mean."

"We'll find the good things about the area, and settle in. We'll adapt. "

"Yes." He hesitated. "I was talking to a chap who worked at the other division, at Polstock. The one they closed. He'd heard that even the divisions which survive the chop will have some big reductions."

"Well, we know they keep reducing. That's why we're having to come here. They wouldn't bring you all the way out here, relocation costs, and all that, and shortly after, make you redundant."

"Yes, they would. Look at Dunning. One year, they took it over from Nessa, two months ago, they recruited, one month ago, they announced it was closing. There's no great plan, no long-term strategy; the accountants produce some sheets of figures, and then make recommendations. For the company, it's the same as you and I turning down the heat to reduce expenses. They chop a site, move anything and anyone worthwhile to one of the other sites, and cast the majority of the people loose to fend for themselves. There: a nice little cost-saving."

"But that was a small site on the south coast. This is the main division, where the big cheeses are."

"It's the main division now that Dunford has been closed. Four thousand people, old site with a lot of history, whump, gone, just like that."

"When the lions catch a zebra, the other zebras are safe."

"Until the lions are hungry again."

"Well, everyone is reducing, everywhere. We know that. But you've been promoted. You're a medium cheese now."

"That was a small bribe. I'm replacing people who are being retired. Dead wood out, rotting wood in. I don't think we're looking at 'if': it's 'when'."

Jenny shrugged. "Well, we'll deal with it when it comes."

Her cheerful stoicism wasn't making it easier for Tom. He decided to head straight for what he needed to say.

"Mike, that's the chap who was made redundant, warned me. He and his wife moved this way as we're going to do, He said that now he has no job, he can't move back. He has no job, short service, so not much severance pay, so there's no point in even trying to buy a house. They're stuck, and his wife is blaming him for moving and for losing his job. I don't want us to be stuck as they are."

"So we need to look at something small, with a small mortgage?"

"That's one possibility. But with my short service, we'd still be stuck. What I'm thinking is that we keep our home, you stay there, I stay in one of the company transfer apartments during the week, and come home at weekends."

It didn't go down well. He could see that clearly. The stoicism had evaporated. But he could see the mixed feelings in her face. Weekly separation against keeping their base where they wanted to be, away from this newtown horror.

He pressed on. "Including travelling to and from work, we're out each day for about ten hours. So, it's really just our evenings together that we'll lose. And I can do all the calling-up, we can see each other as we talk. And we can enjoy a Friday night reunion every week."

She smiled as she acknowledged that. "You're doing a

good job of selling it. If the worst comes to the worst, you could work as a salesman."

He shook his head. "No. That's lying; this is telling the truth. If we sold our house and moved here, which is horrible anyway, eventually, I'd be kicked out, and we'd have Mike's problem. This way, we keep our base, I put in some more service, hopefully increasing my severance pay and pension, and when the time comes, I'll pay off a bit of mortgage and stack shelves or push trolleys. Or both."

She nodded. "Okay. We'll do that. Let's have a walk. I'm sick of this place."

"Well, say goodbye to it. You won't have to see it again."

Outside, she said, "But you'll have to. If not this one, others like it."

I'll just think of you and the weekend. The five working days. I'll go to work early on Monday morning, and come home on Friday evening. It'll be …"

"What's up?" she asked anxiously. He was pale but sweating. He took some deep breaths.

"It's this damn place," he said. "All these people rushing at us, veering away at the last moment, as though they can't see us until they almost collide, as though we're invisible, until they're right next to use. We're not fully in this world. We're like partly materialised spirits."

It came again, stronger this time. The ground seemed to throb and ripple beneath his feet. The movement was throwing him off balance. He was sweating heavily, so afraid of losing his balance that he became more unsteady. He staggered, and Jenny reached out to hold him.

"Hold me," he said. "No. I mean both arms. Hold me tight."

He needed the comforting reassurance, but something

else. He was convinced that if she didn't hold him down, he would lose all substance and float away. Not so much into the air, as away from this life, this dimension, away into something unknown and terrifying.

He muttered, "Don't let go," because Jenny was the only thing that could keep him from disappearing into that other place, whatever, wherever it was.

"Deep breathing," Jenny said.

Gradually, that worked. Still hot and cold, shivering and sweating, he calmed down. As Jenny stepped back cautiously and came into focus again, he saw the deep concern in her eyes. Not the concern of an anxious partner, but the infinitely loving concern of someone who had become a part of him.

He exhaled and managed a thin smile. "Thanks, love," he said. "I just came over all peculiar."

She shrugged. "Just a panic attack. It's this place. We've seen enough and made our decision. Let's go home. I'll drive."

"Yes. Perfect. Not all the way. Just the first half, then I'll take over. As soon as we're away from here and on the way home, I'll feel much better.

"Right. Damn. I should have gone in there. Will you be all right if I pop to the toilet? There's a sign pointing to one across the square."

"Yes. I'll be fine. If I have another turn, I'll sit down. Or lie down."

As he watched her walk away, he felt very lonely and vulnerable. He realised now that he'd become dependent on her, in so many subtle ways. Through several big decisions in the last few hours, she'd agreed, always seeing the good points, putting her own fears and doubts aside.

He felt a strong surge of love, knowing that he could

never love her enough. He could never give her the quantity, the intensity of love that she deserved.

Oh, Jenny.

It started again. He needed her back, urgently, desperately. It was worse this time because she wasn't there. He closed his eyes, but that merely increased the sensations of rising and falling. He was floating and stumbling, light as gossamer, heavy as iron, leaving the ground, being pressed into it.

The people began to stampede, squealing and bellowing, the big shops began to spin round him, the ground tilted one way, then another. The buildings leaned towards him until they were almost touching. He could hardly breathe. He tried to clench his fists, but he was too weak. He knew that he was about to drown and suffocate in this spinning, shrieking tumult.

"So, there you are," said a voice right in front of him. "Why can't you stay where I leave you. Ten minutes. That's all it was. But you had to go wandering. I suppose you went into the pub, as you usually do."

He blinked and stared at the large and lumpy woman who was talking to him. A complete stranger, jabbering at him.

"Just a couple of pints," he said. "It's been a hard week."

What was he talking about? He didn't know this . . . Mary . . .was her name.

"Dad's a dirty boozer," shrilled a scruffy girl, standing next to a loutish boy with a fixed sneer. Where had he gone wrong with them? Lissy and Pad were obnoxious brats.

What?

"Well, you can come and wait outside the shop this time.. I'll only be a couple of minutes. But remember that sometimes, *I* need a break from the kids. You're not the only one, you know."

"All right," he said. "Don't go on."

He shook his head. Jenny. I'm married to Jenny. Who are these horrible people?

These horrible, *familiar*, people.

"Well, are you coming?"

"Yes. Right." He followed her and the two children across the square to a clothes shop.

"Wait here," Mary said. "And I mean here, not the pub."

Pad said, "You're always upsetting her. I'll sort you out when I'm a bit older."

"You tell him," Lissy added.

Then he saw her, making her way through the surging crowds. Jenny. Darling Jenny. Oh, the relief. He tried to walk towards her, but his legs wouldn't move.

He didn't want any more trouble.

No, that wasn't it. Was it?

It must be easy. All he had to do was just walk over to her.

Look! The poor thing is starting to worry, looking around. She was worrying about him, but soon she would also worry about herself.

Poor, dear Jenny. Don't be frightened, love. I'm on my way. I'll be there in a moment.

His love and his grief grew as one until they became an unbearable power.

"I asked you a question," said the harsh voice of his wife. "But you'd rather stare at that woman over there."

"Sorry," he said. "For a moment, she looked familiar."

# # #

THE SEA GIRL

Eleanor's parents might not appreciate her qualities, but the sea does. And if her parents don't want her, the sea does.

CHAPTER 1

"I must go down to the sea again, to the lonely sea and the sky,

And all I ask is a tall ship and a star to steer her by…"

"Is that what you are learning at school, Eleanor?" asked her father, breaking his long silence as they walked along the sea front.

"We learned it last term, Father, but being here reminded me of it."

"A poem for a boy, I suppose, but still a good one for learning. Good poems have the correct structure for learning."

It was a hot day. Eleanor's straw boater with a ribbon didn't provide much protection from the sun. Her long frock and smock did, but the result was a tiring clamminess. How much worse, she thought, for the older people. Father was in a woollen suit, with a tweed waistcoat, above which his firmly fastened wing collar suggested that to look down at his daughter could cause a serious injury to his throat. Mother was in a long taffeta dress of pale cream. This, too, had a high collar, and on her head she wore a hat which looked like a miniature garden, discouraging head movements in any direction, and requiring a day of no sea breeze.

To their right was the long beach, the tide slowly coming in. Some children were playing with buckets and spades, the boys in sailor suits, the girls in frocks, with larger straw hats, better suited to protect from the heat. Most of them had further protection from long, curling hair, unlike Eleanor's neat bob cut, which left her thin neck exposed.

Nearer to the sea were some individual baskets to protect from any wind, and some bathing machines, from which an occasional woman appeared and slid into the water like a seal.

The water! The beautiful turquoise sea. It whispered to her, "Eleanor, Eleanor." She longed to be a part of it. Not a paddler, not a dipper, but a sea girl, swirling in its embrace.

"I am the sea,

And the sea is me."

"What was that, Eleanor?" asker her mother.

"Just something which came into my head."

"Don't let things come into your head, unless they are put there by a respectable person. Your father and I put things into your head. So do your teachers. So does the vicar. But other things are like litter blown by the wind. Do not be a receptacle for them. Let them go on their way."

Like a doomed ship, blown to its fate on the rocks, Eleanor said, "I was thinking how lovely it would be to go in the sea."

"Fish go in the sea, Eleanor, not people."

"Some people," said her father slowly, "seem to have formed the idea that the presence of an expanse of salt water entitles them to discard all constraints of propriety. We do not consider ourselves to be amongst them. Fishermen sail on the sea from necessity, agricultural labourers work on the land from necessity. People of refinement look at and admire God's great work. They do not wallow in its pleasures. This is your celestial art gallery."

Even across the expanse of sand, shrieks and laughter came from beyond the bathing machines. Women wearing bathing caps were splashing one another.

"That is the sort of low woman that goes in the sea," pronounced Mr Greystalk, Accountant, Father and Husband.

"Is that," asked Mrs Greystalk, Wife and Mother, "what you *really* want to indulge in, Eleanor?"

"We-ll, not that, as such," Eleanor replied, carefully treading the very thin line of diplomacy between complete honesty and complete denial. "I meant that it would be lovely to swim on my own, in a deep part of the sea, near the rocks and caves, well away from frivolity and gaiety and staring eyes."

"And what would happen in such a place if you encountered difficulties? Who would rescue you? Who would even hear you?" Mr Greystalk shook his head in gloomy contemplation of his daughter's death by drowning.

"Such a silly notion," added Mrs Greystalk. "And do not think that because you are away from human prying eyes, you are out of sight of the one who sees all."

Eleanor thought that her mother made God seem like a snooping old man, loitering out of sight, waiting for girls to come swimming, then rushing out to chastise them. Immediately, she thought of the park keeper, who liked to jump out into the midst of boisterous children, waving his stick. He was small and bald, with a large nose and large ears, giving him the appearance of an overgrown pixie.

"What are you smiling at, Eleanor?" It wasn't merely a

question from her mother: it was a suspicious probe, an interrogation.

"Nothing," Eleanor replied.

"Smiling at nothing? That is what idiots do, the sort that
are put in Badstock Hall."

"I have stopped smiling," Eleanor said with heavy politeness. "The moment has gone."

"One should remember," Mr Greystalk said oratorially,
"that the trains have enabled all sorts to visit the seaside, and
as for the lower classes, they express their release from the toils
of work with a regrettable, but I suppose understandable,
degree of ebullience. They are like children having their first
play, excitable and silly. One must be tolerant. However, the
danger of permitting access to the same areas in which their
superiors go presents the problem of assimilation and
mimicry. Do not be tempted, Eleanor, to lower yourself to
their level. Shouting and laughing are what they do, but we,
never!"

The sea continued to whisper to her.

CHAPTER 2

"Are you enjoying the gardens, Eleanor?"

Eleanor longed to say that the gardens were much better than the dark and gloomy museum. Instead, she said, "Yes, Father. There is such a good view of the sea from here."

He drew in a sharp breath. "We brought you up here to enjoy the flowers."

"I *am* enjoying the flowers. I am enjoying being amongst them, and looking out from here is an additional enjoyment."

"Hm," he said, and looked again at the catalogue. It contained a plan of the gardens, and he and his wife were carefully using it to go round the flower beds. The garden was terraced, with three levels, joined by stone steps. Each level contained different sorts of flowers and shrubs. As expected, Eleanor had ignored the guide, and every attempt by her parents to persuade her to approach the walk in an orderly manner. She hadn't actually disobeyed her parents, but she had a propensity for drifting sideways, falling behind or dashing ahead.

"Well, try to stay where we can see you," he said. "And don't touch the flowers."

"Yes, Father. No, Father," she said with patient submissiveness. That wasn't perfect for Mr Greystalk: he wanted enthusiastic submissiveness. Why couldn't the girl be happy?

All the way up here to these world famous gardens, and she liked the view of the sea. He tutted and went back to his wife.

Eleanor did enjoy the flowers. She said to herself, "The flowers smile, the sea whispers."

Her favourite flowers were the large lilies, but she liked them all. What she liked best was their living happily together, tiny flowers, medium ones, big ones; familiar ones, exotic ones; dazzlingly colourful ones, and plain ones. Each one stayed in its allotted space and minded its own business. The effect was harmony. Beautiful harmony.

Was the sea calling more loudly now, its whispering more urgent and insistent?

Was it jealous, or impatient?

She whispered back, "I can't come. I'm not allowed."

Even if she were allowed, what could she do? Raise her dress to, well, nearly to her knees, and paddle. She had no desire to paddle. That would be like trying to quench your thirst with one tiny sip of water.

Her mother's voice hissed angrily in her ear, "You are a stupid and ungrateful girl, standing daydreaming when you should be looking at the flowers. Now, behave as though you are happy to be here."

"I *am* happy," she snapped back. "This isn't just a place for looking. It's a place for contemplation."

"Well, you little . . . don't you tell me the purpose of a garden, child. Now, look at the flowers and enjoy them. I'll test you later."

Eleanor looked listlessly at the flowers. They seemed to have had their colour drained out of them as she started the slow business of memorising their names. There was no chance of enjoying them now.

She hadn't made much progress when her parents told her that they were ready to go. Mr Greystalk sniffed and said, "At least *look* as though you enjoyed it, Eleanor."

"I did enjoy it. However, as a respectable middle-class lady, I restrained my feelings, and exhibited my pleasure inwardly."

"You were staring at the sea, and, according to you, contemplating."

"Yes, Mother. In the first case, I was inspired by the flowers to look out beyond the garden, at the surrounding trees. While doing that, I noticed the sea. And the beauty of the flowers made me aware of their, and my, place in the great order of things. That was the form of my contemplation."

Mrs Greystalk looked at her husband. He sniffed again and said, "Well, all right, Eleanor. That seems to be reasonable."

He took his watch from his waistcoat pocket, snapped it open, pondered, then said, "I think a brisk walk back to Mrs Fuller's will leave us with time to wash before the evening meal."

The path from the garden wound round several times. On each side, there were tall shrubs and bushes, some with spikes all along their thick stems, some with immense leaves, looking like gigantic rhubarbs. There were trees, too, with furry trunks. What games could be played in there! If . . . if rather a lot of things.

In one sense, it would have been better if her parents had been cruel tyrants, starving and beating their daughter. Then there would have been justification for a determination to escape from them one day. But her parents weren't cruel, at least not in a physical sense. They believed that in all things they knew what was best for Eleanor. Not from experience or study of the matter; they had no doubt of their infallibility in the development of a child into a respectable adult.

Their great ally in this was the Reverend Shoebury, who could easily, and with the utmost willingness, find an admonitory Bible quotation to suit every occasion. In view of the mandatorily increased donations, it could be said that he ran a Bible quotations business, opposing or justifying everything, according to what was wanted. Of course he wasn't directly asked for a quotation: he was presented with a problem, and, like a senior civil servant who ensures that whatever he does is in accordance with a book of rules, the Reverend Shoebury would always ensure that the advice which he gave to his worried parishioner was entirely in accordance with his own book of rules, which was the Bible. Hence, the quotations to provide unimpeachable corroboration of what he said. More even than that, because the Bible said it first. The Reverend was merely the messenger.

From the few vague remarks of her two grandmothers, Eleanor had formed the impression that her parents had not become so dour and upright with the passing of the years; they had always been that way, even as children.

But this was a new age, with the passing of the Queen, and the coronation so recently of the ebullient Edward. Even while the Queen was alive, there had been developments, with women being permitted to do long-forbidden things, and working class men rising to prominence.

The return to the sea front took them along the grassy area in which families had their picnics and strolled. Then, down the steps, they walked past the entrance to the pier. Her parents' synchronised sniff at the frivolity didn't matter much to Eleanor because she had her own objection to the pier. It was a monstrous iron intrusion into the sea. It was one of those things which was done somewhere, and soon imitated everywhere else. *They* had one, so *we* should have one. That was the version of moving with the times that appealed to certain influential men. Never mind developments in education and society, build a vast iron edifice into the sea. That demonstrated progress!

The tide was now in, pressing against the long, curved wall. The weather was calm, and so was the sea; but in one moment, a wave hit the wall with a loud smack. Eleanor flinched, and was unsteady.

Mrs Greystalk commented, "Now, do you understand the dangers of the sea?"

"It wasn't dangerous. Just for a moment, I thought the wave had washed over me."

"Huh," said Mr Greystalk. "That provides further proof of your unsuitability for fooling about in the water. Look how calm it is."

Eleanor didn't argue. Arguing was called insolence; and she could never win against her parents' combined obduracy.

But there was something else. She *had* felt the wave wash over her, and it seemed, in that tiny, timeless moment, to be trying to pull her into the sea.

CHAPTER 3

Eleanor supposed that most guest houses called 'Seaview' were like this one. A portion of the sea was visible from the main bedroom, views of various parts of the neighbourhood from the others. Her parents' room provided a view of the town park, and, provided that one stood on the window sill, the barest glimpse of the sea. But, of course, respectable young ladies do not stand on window sills, and she was appropriately admonished.

Her own room was at the back of the house, up another flight of stairs, and her view was of a rather ugly town. Beyond the row of rooftops and chimney pots, she could see a gasometer and several factory chimneys.

So, she thought, with one thing and another, her holiday wasn't having much to do with the sea. On the way back from the gardens, she had suggested in an airy fashion a boat trip. Oh, no was the response. The cost, the danger, the fumes, the seasickness, the proximity of other people. She didn't protest. Her parents' objections to pleasure were like parcels being sent to faraway places: thoroughly and tightly wrapped, sealed and stuck down. With the sender and recipients name and address.

From Mrs and Mrs Greystalk. Message of disapproval. Deliver to: Miss Greystalk.

The food which Mrs Fuller provided was reasonable in quality, unreasonable in quantity. It looked as though it had been carefully measured, a culinary equivalent of the comments by which Eleanor was surrounded. For, in fairness to her parents, she admitted that they were not alone in this house in their constant displays of sober caution.

Mr and Mrs Drewett peered at life as though examining

its fine details. Mr Drewett liked to clip a pair of round spectacles to his nose, then look over the top of them. His wife brandished a pair of lorgnettes with which to verify the merits of anyone who addressed her.

Mr Peabody directed the same sort of visual scrutiny at his food. Thinking that perhaps he shared her opinion about the inadequacy of the portions, Eleanor smiled at him. His look was an icicle thrust into the heart of her warm gesture, and the poor thing fluttered fatally wounded to the floor.

Miss Dilkin had come 'to take the air'. She did not say what she intended to do with it after taking it, but Eleanor thought it was probably to somewhere dark and dismal.

Why did these people come to the seaside? Why didn't they just walk in their nearest park? If they didn't like the sea and the sand, the boats and the rock pools, the hills and the trees, why come here, where there were plenty of all those things?

In spite of what was beyond her window, she opened it, and breathed deeply. No, not a trace of the salty sea air, no smell of seaweed and crustacean. Even the occasional gull cry was a dispirited rendering, a token call for old time's sake.

The evening was warm, so she left the window open and made herself as comfortable as she could in the lumpy bed. After a little wriggling, she settled and soon fell asleep.

It was dark when she woke. The night had become sultry, but there seemed to be a cooling draught from the open window. And something else.

She could smell the sea!

A powerful and pungent smell of salty sea and seaweed.

She could even *feel* the sea, throbbing and surging within her.

And she could hear it, whispering her name.

She could even *see* it, coming through her window, as soft as smoke, rolling and flowing down to the floor, then rising again towards her.

And in it, she seemed to see a girl's face, speaking her name.

Softly soothing, the smile and the words, and the outstretched hand already pulled her out of herself, towards the girl.

Eleanor smiled and began to reach out.

Outside, a dustbin lid crashed to the ground, waking her from her trance, returning her to her human fears. "No!" she cried. She pulled her sheet over her face and squirmed down under the bedclothes, putting her hands over her ears, shutting out that whispering of her name.

Nothing else happened, or seemed to happen, but it was a long time before she emerged from the tangled bedclothes and peeped out.

No one was there; nothing was there. Only the dresser in the corner, the wardrobe to her left.

There was only the memory.

It must have been a horrible dream.

But perhaps the horrible thing about it was that it wasn't horrible. There was an underlying fear, but the delicious smell of the sea, the feel of it, the girl's smiling face; all combined to make her feel the stirrings of happiness.

A new sort of happiness.

CHAPTER 4

"Look! A ship"

Eleanor pointed eagerly out into the bay. Her parents looked, too. Mr Greystalk said, "Ah, yes. A four-masted schooner. Cargo ship, average speed between eight and twelve knots. Probably come from the West Indies."

Eleanor looked at him in surprise. "You know a lot about ships, Father."

"Hm, well, before you were born, I worked for six years in a shipping office. The accumulation of some knowledge was inevitable."

"How exciting! Did you go on the ships?"

"Good gracious, no. I worked in an office. I merely recorded what was delivered and what was loaded, according to the documents which were passed to me."

"It must still have been very interesting."

Just for a moment, something seemed to flicker in her father's eyes. Then it was gone. "It was a job, to be performed efficiently," he replied. "It required high levels of concentration. It was important not to be distracted by things that were happening outside."

"That must have been difficult at times."

"Indeed, it was. Through my window, I could see the big ships loading or discharging their cargo. Sometimes, the loads were fish, nothing but fish, and they brought their smell from the depths of the sea and spread it all over the town."

"There for six years," Mrs Greystalk added, "promoted three times."

"That's impressive."

"Concentration was my method, rigidly ignoring the distractions. Outside were the sea, the ships, the cargoes; but inside was my careful recording of what came in and what went out. One day, I was even able to assist the police by letting them see my records."

Mrs Greystalk purred. "Was that the highlight of your time there, Leonard?"

Mr Greystalk sucked his moustache and said, "In terms of what it achieved, I suppose it was."

He spoke with no pride, but with the satisfaction of someone who had done his job well.

Eleanor was enjoying these moments of recollection as they walked along the promenade. They were going to listen to the band in the big park today. It wasn't going to be exciting, but it was music, the weather was pleasant, and it would be a good way to forget that strange dream of last night.

Suddenly, she felt a flash, a powerful surge, which seemed to lift her off her feet. For a tiny moment, she staggered. But it was over so quickly, seeming to end while it was beginning, that her parents didn't notice.

She smelled the sea, and she felt the sea. It was far away, the tide low, but it seemed to reach over her, trying to pull her away. She felt an intense loss, the loss of the sea, in distance and in her parents' disapproval, and in the loss of her home life as she felt the power of the sea trying to separate her from her parents, from her normal, ordinary life.

She was glad when they left the far end of the promenade and made the short climb to the long grassy park. The bandstand stood in the middle, and people sat in deck chairs or on the grass. Eleanor needed this ordinariness, as she felt an inward trembling over the calling and tugging of the sea.

She was soothed by the deep 'pum-pums' of a tuba player in preparation. Then, the trombones, trumpets and cornets added their homely reassurance. The trees swayed slightly in a gentle breeze.

With an air of magnanimity, Mr Greystalk paid a penny for a programme. As he and his wife studied it, the performance began, lulling Eleanor into a different kind of embrace: the earthy simplicity of simple music, played with no great attempt to impress, merely the desire to do the job well.

An occasional gull showed its lack of respect with a discordant screech, but otherwise, Nature seemed to have been calmed into a happy harmony.

When it was over, Eleanor had no objection to another stroll in the gardens. This time, there was a different sort of allure, as she looked closely at the detail of each flower, and succumbed to the intoxicating fragrances, drawing her into a private chamber of passion.

"Be careful, Eleanor," her father said. "When I was young, I bent down to look at a flower, and a bee stung my nose."

"Oh, dear," said Eleanor, rather pleased that her father had shared that moment from his past. But she felt sorry for the bee, whose last act had been to sting her father's nose.

On the way back along the seafront, Eleanor heard the squawkings of a Punch and Judy show. Mr Greystalk made some noises in his throat which might have indicated approval or disapproval, or even an attempt to imitate the puppets.

A crowd had gathered in front of the narrow, blue and white striped tent of the Punch and Judy man. Mr and Mrs Greystalk condescended to pause at the edge of the crowd, determined not to be mistaken for members of the audience, trying to give the impression that they were passers by who had slowed their steps out of mild curiosity.

The show seemed rather silly to Eleanor, but she enjoyed

the exuberant absurdity of it, and soon she was chuckling at the antics of the puppets.

When she felt the sea stir in her again, she concentrated on the puppets, trying to make herself impervious to its influence. She didn't want this intrusion, when she did not know what it meant, and what its purpose was. She tried to send it away by the use of her willpower, thinking, over and over, 'Leave me alone. I don't want to do it.'

She felt that she was engaged in a struggle for control of herself. The sea was both outside and inside her, and when it had the upper hand, she was inside the sea. She kept concentrating on the Punch and Judy show, on the concrete on which she stood, on the backs of people's heads, on the laughter of children, on the cries of the gulls.

Eventually, the sea withdrew from her. In the distance, beyond the blue and white tent, she saw the familiar sea, its small waves breaking on the sand in its perpetual cycle of the flowing of the tides. Mr Punch wielded his club, Mr Greystalk sniffed, a horse and cart passed by behind her.

All was normal and safe again.

CHAPTER 5

There was a surprise at breakfast the next morning. Mr Greystalk tapped a telegram which lay on the table. "I must return to the city," he said. "Some business which requires my particular attention. Hopefully, it will not take long and I shall be back tonight."

Mrs Greystalk sighed. "That is the problem with rendering yourself indispensable, my dear."

"Indeed. But I have not chosen to be so. I have done my best to train my inferiors, passing on much of my learning, and encouraging them to aspire to the possession of similar skills."

With a deep breath, his wife said, "Even though you have worked so hard in the development of your skills, I shall always maintain that great accountants are born, not made."

Eleanor thought that even her father was slightly embarrassed by this peculiar eulogy. He smiled politely, drank his tea, dabbed his lips with the ample serviette, and rose like a man who is about to go and meet his fate. "All being well, I shall see you this evening. Enjoy your day."

Mrs Greystalk blinked at the suddenness of his departure. "I could ask Mrs Fuller to make a lunch for you to take,"

"No time, dear. The train leaves in fifteen minutes, and I must be on it."

He strode swiftly through the dining room, ignoring the puzzled looks of the residents. This sudden departure was a severe breach of the routines.

"Well, dear," Mrs Greystalk said stoically, "we shall do the best we can by ourselves."

With the limited prospects available to them, Eleanor thought that they would probably manage.

Soon after, she and her mother walked slowly along the seafront. The day was warm, and soon Mrs Greystalk suggested a short rest on one of the promenade seats. "I just feel a little tired today," she said.

Eleanor sat next to her mother and gazed at the holiday scene before her. There was much activity on the beach, with children, and even their parents, busy digging and making shapes with the sand. Chatter and laughter rose from them.

So much enjoyment of a simple pleasure.

There were boats of various sizes on the water, and farther out, she could see one of the big boats which took lucky people for a trip round the bay.

Mrs Greystalk wriggled and squirmed, then said, "This seat is not comfortable. It is very hard. I know that your Father would not approve, and I am reluctant to deceive; nevertheless, I intend to lower myself to the necessity of hiring a deckchair. However, the requirement to stay on the sand does not absolve you of your obligation to behave properly. You may sit beside me on the sand. That is all."

But it wasn't all. As planned, the deckchair was hired and erected, Mrs Greystalk sank gratefully into it, and Eleanor sat beside her. What wasn't planned was a tennis ball hurtling out of the sky and landing in the small space between them.

The appearance of the ball was immediately followed by the appearance of Mrs Frobisher. Striding towards them, she called, "Sorry. Margaret is a powerful thrower, but with no sense of direction. A very bad combination."

She stooped to pick up the tennis ball, looked at Eleanor and said, "My I introduce myself. Mrs Frobisher. Perhaps your daughter would like to join my girls."

As Eleanor's mother tried to think of a polite but firm way

of refusing, Mrs Frobisher said, "We're only over there. She'll be quite safe."

Eleanor added her most winsome and plaintive look.

"Well, all right," said Mrs Greystalk. "Stay where I can see you, Eleanor, and best behaviour. No silliness."

Eleanor forced a solemn look onto her face. "No, Mother. I shall behave correctly."

She followed the smiling Mrs Frobisher to the three waiting girls, who greeted Eleanor eagerly. They were introduced as Margaret, Isabella and Catherine.

"We are currently having a battle of wills," said Mrs Frobisher. "Mr Frobisher and I gave our daughters those names because we think they are lovely names. However, our daughters object to their length. So do their friends. So, their selected names are Meg, Bella, and Cathy. What do you think?"

Thinking quickly, Eleanor said, "I think I'd rather not make an enemy of anyone by expressing a preference. I think the full names are lovely, but for informal occasions, their diminutives are also pleasant."

Mrs Frobisher laughed. "Excellent diplomacy. Right enough of that. In a circle, and let's do some catching."

Eleanor enjoyed the catching game. After each round of successful catching, the girls moved farther apart. Eventually, Mrs Frobisher told them to move in again, before they spread over the whole beach.

Catherine immediately said, "Let's look in the rock pools."

"Stay in sight," Mrs Frobisher called as they set off. Eleanor was a little apprehensive because they were soon well away from her mother.

There were three pools, set in a small cluster of rocks. The girls enjoyed sifting through the matted seaweed, watching as disturbed tiny creatures scuttled or swam through the still, dark water.

This was all new for Eleanor, and she was delighted. She was fascinated by the stillness of the pools, little worlds, not land or sea, but combining both.

"Later," Margaret said, "the tide will come and cover these rocks."

"Oh," said Eleanor. "Does it destroy the rock pools?"

"Just a change of water, I suppose," Isabella said. "I expect the little creatures just hide until it's over. Unless any of them wants to go off into the sea. It might be their time to leave the little pool and be a part of the great sea."

Eleanor liked that thought.

Watching a tiny hopping thing, she wondered how many other worlds within worlds there were.

Her thoughts were interrupted by the wave which poured over them, knocking them over and soaking them. They squealed in surprise, and a moment of fear. They hurried away and stood looking at the rapidly advancing tide.

"That was sudden," Catherine said. "I thought it was a long way off. Did we lose track of the time?"

"Mother's calling," said Margaret. "And I think that's your mother standing next to her. And you're going back soaked."

"Oh, dear," Eleanor said. "I hope she won't be very angry."

She was. "Eleanor! I permitted your playing with these girls because I was assured that you weren't far away. When these people suggested going against that, you at least should have objected. Now look at you. Nearly drowned and soaking wet. This is a lesson for everyone."

"We weren't far away, looking in rock pools, and the sea was a long way off."

"What you were doing has no relevance. I was told that you would be playing here, not all the way over there. It's because of the danger that your father and I insist that you behave sensibly. Now, say goodbye to these people, and we shall resume our walk, and hopefully, you will be dried by the sun, although the salt will probably ruin your clothes."

"Goodbye," Eleanor said miserably. With sudden defiance, she added, "Thank you, Mrs Frobisher."

"Goodbye, Eleanor," said the three girls.

The response from Mrs Frobisher was a sigh and a sad little smile.

CHAPTER 6

Mr Greystalk returned in the evening. After a short talk with his wife, he went to Eleanor's room.

"Eleanor," he said solemnly. "I have discussed the regrettable incident with your Mother. I have explained to her that she was slightly at fault in taking you onto a beach, and then permitting you to go off with another family. However, from the point of your agreeing to leave the agreed location and go off to where you were shortly after drenched by the sea, you are entirely to blame. Your behaviour was inexcusable."

Eleanor wondered whether her mother had also been reprimanded. But she knew that there was only one permitted response. "I'm very sorry, Father. It was very inconsiderate and foolish of me."

"So it was. The wrong thing was done, but your have expressed your contrition. Let us not dwell on it. Let us learn from it, then leave it behind us, and continue to enjoy our holiday."

"Yes, Father."

After her father had gone, she lay on her bed, still dressed, and drifted through thoughts.

Glimpses. The sea, the mysteries, the girls and their mother, the pools. Small, vast, awakenings, silently calling, pulling, insistent.

She thought of Mrs Frobisher, afraid to speak and not knowing what to say, as Mrs Greystalk's angry words swept over her like ravaging locusts. Eleanor's parents always knew what to say because they never doubted. Everything that could be thought about was neatly packaged in their minds, ready to be distributed. Yes, Mrs Frobisher had been wrong, but was it such a bad thing to be wrong sometimes? Weren't there occasions when instead of right and wrong, there were different sorts of right and wrong? If Mrs Frobisher had sternly refused permission for them to go and play in the rock pools, then Eleanor wouldn't have seen those small worlds, she wouldn't have shared the pleasure with her brief friends, she wouldn't have felt the stimulating power of the wave. Yes, in a tiny moment between the shock and the fear of her mother's anger, there had been exhilaration.

Exhilaration! What would her parents think? And say? Chuckling, she began to doze.

Was it sleep, or just sleepiness? It had suddenly become dark. The curtains quivered with the evening breeze, bringing the smell of the sea. She licked her lips and tasted salt. She felt the dampness of the seaweed, the cooling softness of the water.

A sudden wave broke over her. Ridiculously, she gripped the sides of her bed to prevent herself from being washed away.

"You're very nervous, aren't you?" said a girl's voice. "People are afraid of what they can't see, which is absurd. Don't try to see with your eyes. See with your mind."

"I don't know how to do that."

"You are hearing with your mind. Now *see* with your mind."

There! For a flickering moment, she saw the swirling sea, and a swirling girl."

"I did it! For a moment."

"Now do it again, and keep seeing."

"I'll try."

"Good."

"Who are you?" Eleanor asked.

"I'm a child of the sea. The sea is my home. It's my

favourite place. That is why I live there. But I need your help."

"What do you want me to do?"

"In the museum, there is a large conch shell."

"I saw it."

"It belongs to my Mother. It was her favourite possession. It should be returned."

"How?"

"You must remove it and take it back to the sea."

"Do you mean to steal it? Of course not."

"It isn't really stealing because it was stolen from us. When you have it, take it to the sea, and throw it in."

Eleanor was aghast. "Stealing is wrong. And if I were caught, I'd be in terrible trouble. I couldn't do that to my parents."

"Don't be caught."

"Why me?"

"One day, you will be a child of the sea. It's your favourite place. It always has been. It's where you belong."

Staying with the practicalities, Eleanor said, "But even if I did take it and wasn't caught, my parents won't even let me go on the beach."

"Then do it when your parents aren't with you."

"I raise one big problem after another, and you produce one simple solution after another."

"Isn't that the best way?"

"Provided that the simple solutions work well."

How was she having this conversation, with someone who said she was a child of the sea? It *must* be a dream.

"This must be a dream," she said.

"Even if it were, it would still be real. You must take the shell, and throw it into the sea."

"I'm not the right sort of person for this."

"Yes, you are."

"I don't want it! Don't make me do it!"

"I'm not making you do it. You are doing that."

"How? How I am doing it?"

"You have hidden your real self for so long, that it is almost like another person within you. What *you* think is the real person is merely the character which you play for those around you. The real, secret, you knows what must be done."

"I could ignore all this. I could treat it as a wild delusion."

"You could."

Eleanor knew what came after that. It was as strongly there in its absence as it would have been if spoken. "*But you won't.*"

She groaned. "I don't want to do it."

"Of course you don't. There are very strong reasons for not *wanting* to do it. That has nothing to do with it."

"Anything else?" Eleanor asked irritably.

"No. That is all. Thank you."

Eleanor felt the sea withdrawing, like the tide going out. The girl went with it.

The room was dark and silent.

Eleanor tried to wake from her dream by going back to sleep.

CHAPTER 7

"It is gratifying that you want to visit the museum again, Eleanor."

Mr Greystalk embellished his approval with some nods. The parental train was firmly on its track again. Mrs Greystalk gently patted her daughter's head, as though Eleanor were a horse which might bite.

Deception, then theft, then throwing the stolen object into the sea. Because a girl told me to do it. Which girl? She couldn't imagine any way in which her explanation would be approved, or even accepted. Hearing voices? Look what happened to Joan of Arc.

Eleanor's punishment would be the slow, steady drip of disapproval, for the rest of her life. If one of her parents died, the other would ensure that when the time for re-uniting approached, the baton would be passed to another suitable person. The flame of disgrace would be kept smouldering. She would be Aunty Eleanor, who did a very bad thing, or Grandma Greystalk, who did a very bad thing, or the previous owner of the house, who did a very bad thing.

The museum seemed already to disapprove of her, with its church-like solemnity, its profound silence, apart from the creaking floorboards, which even creaked solemnly. A little while back, Eleanor had been shushed in a museum after calling excitedly to one of her friends to come and look at something.

Sometimes, she thought that her whole life had been lived in a museum, in which excitement and delight were forbidden.

Afraid of what she had been asked to do, wanting to run away from it, eager to do it and have it behind her, she forced herself to be patient. It wasn't a large museum, not like the one in the city, which had a succession of sections devoted to particular countries, dynasties or events; in this seaside museum, you couldn't avoid seeing the whole display, as you shuffled along from case to case, table to table.

The conch shell wasn't in a case; it was part of a display on a table, with some scallop shells, and various dried seaweeds, donated by a local enthusiast. Eleanor's parents saw with little interest and walked past it. Eleanor glanced ahead and behind her. No one was watching. Her hand darted out, and a moment later the shell was in her dress pocket. She added the descriptive card, which would have drawn attention to the messing item.

Now she had the horror of having committed the act. She could feel the shell accusingly large and sharp, pressing against her thigh, telling her constantly what a terrible thing she had done. She was hot with shame and remorse, hot with fear, and the shell was burning through her skin. She hurried after her parents, pleased to see them walking quickly, relieved to see the open door beyond them.

Mr Greystalk glanced back to check that Eleanor was close behind. Then, he politely expressed his appreciation to the man who sat behind the desk.

Almost at the door. Just a few more steps.

A woman had appeared out of the gloom, and was talking earnestly with the man at the desk. He glanced sharply at Eleanor.

Now she felt the heat of guilt as she tried to look innocent;

"Excuse me!" the man called, making her parents stop on the threshold and look round.

Eleanor hadn't noticed that she had begun to walk

quickly. She passed her parents who had stopped to look back.

"I want to speak with your daughter," the man called. "She . . . please call her back."

"What? Eleanor! Come back."

Her rapid walk became a run. A run of shame and fear, of sorrow . . . and purpose. All these drove her on as she rushed past surprised people in the street, along the promenade, and down onto the beach. She estimated that she was roughly where she had been playing with the girls, and over to her left were the rocks with the pools. Forcing her feet through the loose sand, panting and gasping, she reached the rocks, pulled the shell out from her dress and flung it into the approaching sea.

The shell made a small splash and disappeared. Nothing else changed on the water.

The deed done, she collapsed. All her emotions came together to make one vast fountain of grief.

"Eleanor? Are you all right?"

Eleanor recognised the voice of Mrs Frobisher. Her grief intensified as she realised that she longed to be embraced and comforted by the woman who was virtually a stranger. And with that came the conviction that she had let Mrs Frobisher down, too. She had created a powerful gap between herself and everyone else; a small and invisible but immense gap, through which no comforting arms or even desires could reach. It was a silent, deep valley of exclusion.

Mrs Frobisher said, "It was a silly question. I can see that you aren't all right. Come with me. Let's go and find your parents."

Eleanor rose slowly and allowed Mrs Frobisher to put her arm round her shoulder and lead her away. All through her mind was the churning, raging questions: *What have I done?* She had desecrated the museum, her parents, the whole social structure.

She had sinned!

For the first time, the accumulation of transgressions stood at the front of her mind. The sounds of children playing on the beach mocked her. The wispy clouds sighed at her. And what of the sea? It was just the steadily weaving, waving water that it always was. In and out, in its perpetual cycle, never opposing its system of regularity, unlike the bad girl who plodded in shame through the sand.

Ahead, the three sisters stood waiting. And walking quickly over the beach were her parents.

"Eleanor!" Her father's voice tore through her sadness, like a sword of retribution.

"She seemed to be very upset," Mrs Frobisher said.

"Yes, well," replied Mrs Greystalk. "Her behaviour has certainly deteriorated during the past couple of days. Eleanor come with us. We must have a very serious discussion."

"Go to your parents," said Mrs Frobisher. "And don't worry. Things will work out all right for you."

"That is your opinion," snapped Mr Greystalk. "And it is quite wrong for you to raise her hopes on that score."

Again, Mrs Frobisher stood silent as Eleanor was led away. But Eleanor turned and called, "Thank you."

She was pulled firmly away.

CHAPTER 8

"I . . . I am quite at a loss," spluttered Mr Greystalk in his room at the guest house. "To steal, *steal*, from the museum, and then to run away and throw the item into the sea ..." He shook his head. "The shame, the humiliation, the cost which I shall incur in making a substantial donation to the museum in compensation for the loss."

"Which," Mrs Greystalk added, "will remain as a permanent debt until you are in paid employment, when you will repay it all."

"A *thief*," Mr Greystalk said again.

"I keep telling you," Eleanor said, "that it was stolen from the sea, and I returned it."

"Don't keep telling me! Don't you dare to keep telling me! No one can steal from a sea. It is inanimate. It possesses nothing. It owns nothing. We don't ask for its permission to sail our ships over it, or to take its fish for our food. Therefore, the shell wasn't stolen from the sea. However, you stole it from the museum, and disposed of it."

"I didn't steal it! I was told by a sea girl. She visited me. She said it belonged to her mother."

"Preposterous nonsense. That makes it worse, not better. I really don't know what ...

I suppose there is a moral and social obligation to report this to the police."

"If we don't, the museum proprietor probably will."

"If it must be done, I'd rather it were done by us. I'll speak to him tomorrow and offer a donation."

"There is another matter."

"What?"

Mrs Greystalk hesitated. "Well, all this nonsense about a

sea girl telling her the shell was stolen from the sea, then stealing it, then throwing the item into the sea, well, some people might look upon it as an indication of mental imbalance."

"Shame upon shame! Indignity upon indignity! Humiliation upon humiliation. No! Let her be a common criminal. She can be punished for that and easily cured of that. Once inside an asylum, she might be incarcerated for the rest of her life."

Eleanor stood and looked into his eyes. "Would you mind that?"

"Oh, you…" Mr Greystalk raised his arm and prepared to sweep it down in a blow on his daughter's head. She anticipated, and stepped aside, tripped on the hearth and fell heavily, her head hitting the mantelpiece with a horrible *crack*.

Mr Greystalk stared in horror at his unconscious daughter, and muttered, "I didn't touch her."

Mrs Greystalk bent over her and felt the back of her head. When she drew the hand out, it was red. "She needs a doctor," she said.

"I didn't touch her," Mr Greystalk said. "It was only a gesture."

"That doesn't matter," Mrs Greystalk said sharply. "She's had a nasty blow on the head and needs a doctor. Go and ask Mrs Fuller."

He drew himself up and looked sternly at his wife. "I do not …" He hesitated. "However, in the present circumstances …"

He departed and walked briskly down the stairs, past the reception area, down again to where Mrs Fuller had her simple accommodation. He tapped on the door, and when it was opened said, "Mrs Fuller. Our daughter has had an unfortunate accident and requires the attention of a doctor. Are you able to recommend one?"

"Dr Wilks. Number six, High Street. He'll charge extra for coming out at this time. Try not to alarm the other guests."

He assured her of his discretion, thanked her, and hurried off to the High Street. As he went, he ruminated bitterly on the events of this day. The theft, the disposal of the stolen shell, his daughter's appalling behaviour throughout, and now this. His quiet family holiday had turned into a nightmare of anxiety. It seemed that Eleanor had been determined to ruin it, even tumbling clumsily and banging her head.

The doctor grumbled and grunted and sighed, sharing Mr Greystalk's opinion of annoying children who seemed to take a perverse pleasure in doing annoying things.

Mr Greystalk's account omitted his attempt to strike his daughter. He explained that she had rather dreamily walked about, seemed to forget her precise location, tripped and banged her head.

"Well, well," Doctor Wilks said. "A blow to the head is often a minor matter. But sometimes, it's fatal."

After the first sentence, Mr Greystalk had been very briefly relieved. "Ah, good." His response was killed by the doctor's second sentence. The High Street wasn't far from Mrs Fuller's house, but it seemed a long way to the distraught Mr Greystalk.

When they arrived, Mrs Fuller came out and asked the doctor for a few private seconds. "Go on up," said Doctor Wilks. "I'll be with you shortly."

Puzzled, Mr Greystalk went up the stairs. His wife sat on the bed with Eleanor's head in her lap, resting on a folded handkerchief. "I didn't like to put her on the bed with . . . the blood."

"Yes." His voice had lost its customary sharpness.

"Where is the doctor?"

"He's downstairs. Mrs Fuller wanted to speak to him."

"Surely, Eleanor is the priority concern."

"That's what I thought. Ah, here he comes."

The stair carpets were thin, and they heard each ominous step. The door creaked, and he walked into the room. He looked with disapproval at the present arrangement, and said brusquely, "Put her on the bed. I'm not going to examine her in that position."

As Eleanor was lowered onto the bed, Dr Wilks did a quick study of the room, then said, "Turn her onto her right side."

He put his bag on the floor, pulled a chair beside the bed, and carefully began to examine the wound. Eleanor flinched and groaned.

"Ah," said the doctor, leaning forward. "Hello, Eleanor. How are you feeling?"

"I don't know. What happened?"

"I am Dr Wilks. You had a nasty fall, and hit your head, causing a deep cut. I am going to have to cut away some of your hair in order to have access to the wound. Don't worry. It will soon grow back. But while I do this, you must keep absolutely still."

He took a pair of long-bladed scissors and a comb from his bag and deftly cut the hair away from the wound. Because of the length of Eleanor's hair, this also meant cutting away some long tresses. "Beautiful hair," he murmured. "But don't worry, this is just a brief pruning, and it will soon be better than ever."

After the careful snipping, he said, "I am now going to clean the wound. This will sting a little."

"A little?"

"A bit." He took from his bag a bottle, gauze, cotton wool, and a roll of bandage. He applied plenty of antiseptic to some cotton wool and pressed it against the wound. Eleanor's body stiffened, and she whimpered.

"Well done, my dear," the doctor said. "Now, I'm going to move the cotton wool around a little to ensure that the whole wound is cleaned. Be brave again."

Eleanor stiffened and whimpered again. "Well done," the doctor said. "Now, I shall place this gauze here, and put a bandage round, and you will feel much better."

This was done deftly and efficiently. Eleanor smiled weakly because a wound always feels better with an expertly tied bandage round it.

Dr Wilks smiled, even though Eleanor was facing away from him. "You were very brave. Now lie still, as you are now, and rest and recover."

He stood and faced her parents. "Mrs Fuller informed me that one of her residents reported hearing a quarrel in here earlier, and the clear sound of your daughter's fall."

Now Mr Greystalk stiffened, with personal and social pain. "My daughter and I had words. She had let us down very badly. However, there is no connection between that and my daughter's accident, and I am considerably affronted by any imputation of a connection based on the eavesdropping and gossiping of one of the guests, and the landlady."

"My dear sir," replied Dr Wilks, "I was merely trying to ascertain the full circumstances of your daughter's walking backwards, tripping, and falling backwards against the mantelpiece. It was not my intention to imply anything."

"The reason for my daughter's stepping back was in response to my expressing my severe displeasure of her very recent wrongdoing, which at the least has brought shame and humiliation on her family, and has been a severing of the moral code which has formed a vital part of her upbringing."

Dr Wilks turned to look at Eleanor. "Well, well, my girl. You seem to have caused a big upset."

"I know," Eleanor said over her shoulder. "And I'm sorry to have caused this distress for my parents. They have done nothing wrong. All the blame is with me."

"Hmm," was the doctor's response, as he returned his medical equipment to his bag.

At that, Mr Greystalk flew into a rage. "*Hmm*? What do you mean by that, sir? I'll have no hmming in my presence. I have given you a true account of what happened, and you have had my daughter's unnecessary corroboration of that account. Now, have you any further advice or information to provide for us?"

"Yes. Make your daughter's welfare your absolute first priority. Keep her warm, give her tiny sips of liquid, preferably in a semi-upright position, or she might choke and cough her wound open. If there should be any deterioration …, well, I have commitments for the next few hours, but let me know tonight. With rest and kindness, she should recover well."

Before Mr Greystalk could splutter another objection, the doctor opened the door and left.

CHAPTER 9

Eleanor's parents went separately down to the evening meal, not wanting to leave Eleanor alone. She seemed to be in pain, but kept saying that the wound was giving her twinges. As the afternoon became evening, Mr Greystalk announced that he needed to have a short walk, a bit of fresh air.

"This has all been a strain," he said. "I need a few minutes away from this room."

"I understand, dear," Mrs Greystalk said, not averse to a short spell with no brooding presence hovering nearby.

Eleanor was glad because she needed a short spell of not being asked how she felt. Her father seemed to think that the question was a requirement of his parental role, and, perhaps, an attempt to achieve atonement for his part in her injury.

He didn't intend to walk far, but tension, and barely suppressed self-doubt, made him walk quickly. On the seafront, he turned left and continued his brisk pace, breathing deeply, swinging his arms, trying to convince himself that this was the proper exercise for a man such as he, and not anything else.

Of course, he did not blame himself for the recent crisis. No, he had behaved as any decent, upright father would do. Many would be weak and indulgent, but he was behaving in the best interest of his daughter, and one day, she would thank him for it.

He became aware of the changing weather, as dark clouds loomed, brought in by a cool wind from the sea, which was responding with waves which looked angry, snapping and snarling at the sand. The sea! The bringer of Mr Greystalk's troubles.

He was vaguely aware that he was near the spot where

Eleanor had played with those girls, and where she had disposed of the shell. His mood sagged deeper, and he felt the sharp pang of bitterness. Was that woman, Mrs Frobisher, behind this drastic change in Eleanor? Someone must have influenced his daughter. Wild behaviour, downright bad behaviour, and the sort of idiotic tale that people in asylums spout. A sea girl telling her to steal a shell and throw it into the sea!

He frowned and directed a look of contempt at the offending area of sand. For the rest of the beach, there was merely his persistent distaste for a place of general unsavoury disportment; for the scene of Eleanor's disgraces, the disapproval was specific.

Now, rain began to speckle the sand. The rain looked angry, too.

His frown became darker when he saw a girl playing in the sea, over by those offending rocks. He looked round for parents or older children. There were none. No parents would let their child play in the rough sea, in this weather, with darkness creeping over the beach. The dark clouds hovered ominously, as though brought by the wind for a purpose. The child, a girl kept rushing into the sea, being carried back to the shore by a wave, then rushing back into the foaming water.

Mr Greystalk stood transfixed and confused. His conscience and his social position required him to intervene; his dignity and innate detachment required him to walk on, ignoring the child. What was the child to him? What was he to the child?

Besides, to go over there, he would have to walk over sand, wet now from the rain, and when he had gone far enough, it would be wet from the sea. Salt water on his polished shoes!

Ridiculous child! He had come out for relief from one troublesome girl, and here was another to bother him. Look at her, back and forth, tossed by the sea, laughing with pleasure. Pleasure. He grunted at the word, letting it know that he disapproved of that, too.

Stabbing through all his attempts to justify his walking past came the conviction that the girl was in danger. It was his responsibility to go down there and warn her.

He hurried down the steps and walked as quickly as he could over the soft, wet sand, all the time looking for older companions or guardians of the girl. The closer that he advanced, the more alarming was the scene before him. He contemplated with dread the possible need for him to enter the water to rescue the girl or at least persuade her to desist from this recklessness.

"I say," he called. "I say, you shouldn't be doing that. It's very dangerous." The girl was just diving back into the waves, and he heard her laugh. She seemed to flow and glide through the tempestuous heavings, and when she came back, with seaweed entwined, she wasn't thrown against her will: she and the sea seemed to be playing the same game.

Back she went, and back she came, this time landing on the rocks. He winced and hurried forward to grab her, but she rose laughing with no sign of damage.

"You must stop this now," he said sternly. "This is much too dangerous. You must come with me."

The girl laughed, not with pleasure, and pulled aside the seaweed from her face.

He stood still, stricken with horror. The face which he knew so well.

But it couldn't be.

"Eleanor?"

She smiled sadly, as though pitying him.

"Mr Greystalk!"

He turned to see a boy running towards him. As the boy ran, he called, "Mrs Fuller sent me to tell you your daughter is very ill."

Feeling faint, he spun round. The girl was plunging back into the waves.

And just for a moment, he saw another girl, waiting for her.

He set off running, back through the wet sand, and along the sea front, ignoring the puzzled looks of evening strollers. His heart pounded, his lungs protested, his legs were numb and moving mechanically. He became aware that with every gasping breath, he was saying, "Eleanor."

Mixed with his concern for his daughter was remorse for his part in her illness. It gave him the power to drag himself, still running, up the stairs to the room where Eleanor lay. He almost collapsed when he thrust open the door and staggered into the room.

"What's happened?" he gasped. Mrs Greystalk was sitting beside the couch, one hand resting on her daughter's chest, the other holding a compress to her forehead..

She turned her red eyes to him. "She seems to have a fever. All this madness has overwhelmed her. The doctor is away, other doctors are not at home. She . . . she seems so weak. So hot. Delirious. She's dying. Oh, what are we to do?"

She bowed her head and sobbed.

As he stood helpless, he felt the sea surging into the room, filling it. He smelt the seaweed and tasted the salt.

THE SEA GIRL   111

"Can you feel it?" he called to his wife as though through deep water.

She looked at him, bewildered, then cried, "Yes! What's happening?"

Mr Greystalk suddenly knew that he was mad, too. He roared, "You're not having her!"

He reached past his wife and scooped Eleanor up into his arms. "Follow me," he said, striding from the room.

At the bottom of the stairs, Mrs Fuller said, "Oh, dear. That poor girl. Where are you taking her? She isn't fit to travel."

Mr Greystalk growled. Like a man who was mad. Mrs Greystalk went with him, saying nothing. She had felt the power of the sea, and she now felt the power of her husband's madness.

The rain was heavy now, and the wind bellowed. Mr Greystalk bellowed back. He ran strangely, his heavy shoes dragging along the flagstones, his body bent forward over his precious burden. He was tired beyond endurance, but his madness kept him going, weary step after another, down the steps, over the sand.

"Henry!" Mrs Greystalk shouted. "What are we doing? I'm afraid."

Only the booming wind, the stabbing rain and the crashing waves replied, their harsh voices shrieking their contempt.

Mr Greystalk staggered to the rocks, then turned and walked towards the sea. To Mrs Greystalk's horror, he began to walk into the sea. When he was knee deep, a wave struck him, making him totter, but he stayed upright and cried out, "Eleanor! Please forgive me. Come back. Come back and be loved as you deserve to be. Please, sea girl, let us have her back."

Mrs Greystalk overcame her terror, and came to stand beside him, her arms spread round her daughter.

"Sea girl!" he called again. "Please, let us have her back. Eleanor, come to us in love and forgiveness."

He wept. "This is all I have," he said, softly now. "This is my only prayer." He reached silently now, with all his soul, trying to bring Eleanor back.

And he saw her, coming through the waves, watched by the other girl. The wave with Eleanor broke over him, making him stagger again, his wife clinging to him. He cried out again with all the passion of his madness; cried to the wind, the rain, and most of all to the sea, and all that was in it.

"What are we doing?" Eleanor asked in his arms. "Why are we here?"

Mr Greystalk laughed. "We thought some fresh air would do you good."

CHAPTER 10

The heavy rain passed in the night, moving away as rain should do. A heavy cloud hung over Mrs Fuller until she saw Eleanor accompany her parents to breakfast. Mr Greystalk had gone out early to obtain a fresh bandage from Dr Wilks. He told the doctor that Eleanor had benefited greatly from his treatment.

"Why does she need a fresh bandage so soon?" asked Dr Wilks.

"Ah. That was my fault," Mr Greystalk replied. "She seemed so much better this morning, I took her to the window for some fresh air, and a gust of rain blew in. Silly of me, but there it is."

That last phrase was his way of closing the matter. It wouldn't be long before Mrs Fuller told the doctor of last night's drama, but he didn't care.

He no longer cared about a lot of things.

At breakfast, he said, "I propose a boat trip today. What do you think?"

Eleanor's eyes shone.

"But first," he added, "after I have made a donation to the museum, and notwithstanding your injury, perhaps a stroll along the beach would be nice. We might see Mrs Frobisher and her girls." He paused. "What's this, Eleanor? Tears? My dear, you'll make your toast soggy."

"I'm so happy," Eleanor sobbed.

"That is how you should be. That is how you will be."

And so they all were.

# # #

TRIAL BY ROBOT

Mr Cain is being tried for a crime which he committed three hundred years ago. Fortunately, he prepared his defence before he committed the crime.

But can he convince a court which is a computer, while being wired to a very efficient lie detector?

CHAPTER 1

When I opened my eyes, everything was white, just the way I can't stand it. I was firmly strapped to a table or trolley, which is another thing that I can't stand, even though this was the first time.

Was this a hospital room or a torture chamber?

What was someone going to do to me?

What had I done to be here?

"He's awake," said a voice through the still, harsh whiteness.

I could turn my head slightly, but I couldn't see anyone.

"Can you hear me all right, and do you understand me?" The voice seemed to come from the wall.

When I tried to reply, the words came out of my dry throat in a soft hiss.

"There is a capsule between your cheek and your gum. Bite it. It will help."

It wasn't easy. My throat was furry and my tongue felt large and cumbersome, like something from the desert which had wandered in there for some shade. I managed to dislodge the capsule and bit. Something icy cold prickled my mouth and throat, a sort of inert spray of moisture. I felt my throat clearing slightly and I had another go at replying.

"I can hear you," I said hoarsely, "but I don't understand what is happening."

"My name is Coriandus Perrithorn. Head of Induction. I shall explain what is happening., although I shall have to do it many times, in many ways, as we go along. Does the term 'Deferred Proceedings' mean anything to you?

My brain felt furry, too. Trying to remember anything before my present circumstance was like turning the thick pages of an ancient book of records. Not that I've ever done that of course, but I've watched very old films.

Deferred proceedings. Something seemed to hover at the edge of the mist, a faint shadowy shape of a memory. Slowly, the shape formed into a definite thing which did step out of the mist, as though the mist were real, and it walked towards me, ominous, filling me with dread and horror, coming ever closer and filling my vision with blackness.

Deferred proceedings. It was familiar, but it was like trying to pick something up on an icy surface: my brain kept approaching the thing, then sliding past it.

"I'll assist you," said the voice. "An overcrowded planet, overcrowded with criminals, of every description, and other malcontents, all of course with very strong reasons for what they did, social and psychological testing always proving that it was someone else's fault, prisons declared inhumane. So, what do you do with people who are too dangerous to be out in the streets, but whom no-one, officially, wants to punish?

"It is what is now called The Point of Impossibility. With so many reasons and extenuating circumstances, so many political and ethical considerations, so many protest groups, so many litigators, fault-finders and blamers, the whole system collapsed into chaos."

"Yes, I sort of remember that. Yes, chaos."

"I shall continue. When you arrive at The Point of Impossibility, the only way out of utter chaos is to recognise, acknowledge, then seize, the moment of desperation; to see that there is only one thing to do, and to do it.

"Of course, practical, pragmatic and thoroughly sensible policies must always be kept secret. Otherwise, the chaos rises up and pours over them."

"You are talking about the policy of deferred proceedings."

"In this case, yes. This policy, which contains a series of deferred steps."

"Right. Okay. I know, sort of, what is happening, but I still don't know why I am here, like this."

"The wrong tense again, in the first part of what you said. This has not been a current affairs lessons: this has been a history lesson."

I tried to shake my head. Oddly, my inability to do that frustrated me more than all the other physical restrictions.

And the guy, whoever he was, was irritating me. The voice was so mechanically calm and detached, and so far as I was concerned, this was not the right time for mechanically calm detachment. This was a time for banging fists on tables and heads on walls. My fist, other people's heads.

Enough of this chitchat. "Where am I?"

"I shall answer that in a few moments. But there is

another, slightly different, question which comes before that one."

"What? Just tell me"

"The relevant question is '*When* am I?' Answer: in the future. Your future, not mine. At the point to which your proceedings were deferred. The only way of dealing with you and thousands of others. A terrible way, a wrong way, but the only way. People always looked at history from where they were now, and passed judgments based on the removal of the sequences of events which actually happened.

"*We* study history by putting ourselves, in thought, back into the time, with all the responsibilities, obligations and connecting circumstances and events. That is why we see that solution as disgraceful and terrible, but the only solution."

"Is my punishment to be lectured to death by you? Please just tell me."

"You don't want the background. You don't want to understand. Very well. Here is the short and easy version.

"Thee hundred years ago, as one of thousands of alleged criminals awaiting assessment and trial, you were put to sleep until such time, so it was hoped, that the surrounding mess would have been cleared up and you could be assessed and tried by future people who would have worked out an effective way of dealing with the problem."

My brain had slowly been recovering its capabilities. Now, it shattered into pieces. When I spoke, my throat seemed to have become furry again.

"Three hundred years," I said stupidly.

"And four, and three months, and so on. I didn't want to make things more difficult than they already were."

"An accurate figure would have had little effect on my

confusion. The whole thing is ridiculous and I suspect a psychological test or evaluation."

"Yes. That is a common reaction. The next practical step is to explain what will happen during the deferred, now current, proceeding."

I think that I growled. Some sort of gurgling noise anyway. "Where are you? Who are you? Damn it. Show yourself."

"For reasons entirely beyond my control, I am not currently able to show myself. I can do many things, and shall, but that is the one thing which I may not do."

"Why?"

"Because in the terms in which you are currently thinking of me, I do not exist."

"What terms?"

"Your notion of the current supplier of your information. You assume him to be a person. I am a computer."

"You mean a robot? I know what a robot is."

"If it helps, think of me as a robot. Over the next few hours, I shall be your lawyer, your defending counsel, the prosecuting council, the judge and the jury. And whichever minor characters might be required."

"How can you be all those? Are you going to keep changing costumes?"

"Not quite. Within me are the characters. Within me, too, is the improvisation capability. I can respond as my characters would respond. For much of our little drama, I shall be playing several characters simultaneously. I might interrupt myself, even argue with myself. As your defending counsel, I shall be doing my best to defend you. As the prosecuting counsel, I shall be doing my best to prove your guilt."

I tried again to shake my head. My period had been far

from technologically backward, not even what you might call developing slowly, but all this was too much for me. It must be either a strangely complicated joke or a form of psychological evaluation.

A different voice, slightly panty, female, said, "I told them I wasn't prepared to wait any longer while they delivered all their background information. I pointed out the unnecessary stress to my client and dropped some large hints about litigation."

Knowing that it was useless, I tried to turn my head. Then, I tried to turn my eyes.

"Who are you?" I said reluctantly, not wanting to participate.

"Helen-Jane Dottice. Your lawyer, of course. I assure you that I am going to do my best for you, and I have high hopes for, well, if not the verdict that we desire, at least a sentence which takes proper account of the stresses and provocation which led you to do what you did."

"Which was?" I prompted.

"Oh, dear. Your wife's murder. I do wish they hadn't wasted all that time on background explanations, and had concentrated on the necessary memory recovery. Just a moment."

After a short pause, there was the sound of a door being unlocked and Ms Dottice said, "My client needs some Salvotal urgently. Otherwise, the interview will be over without having begun. I am very discontented with the way that this has been handled, and shall make a formal complaint."

I heard some neutralish mumbling. Then there was another pause before Ms Dottice called over to me, as it were, "Someone has gone to fetch some. It won't be long."

Another brief pause, then, "Ah. Here it comes now. Thank you."

The door was locked again and I felt the insertion of a needle in my left arm.

"Give it a few moments," Ms Dottice said. "Then you'll begin to remember. Slowly at first, then it will happen quickly."

I gave it a few moments. Like anaesthetic, it lulled me into thinking that it wasn't going to work, then hit me. Yes, I remembered. Memories were pouring into my brain now, like a child's vomit, in a succession of thrusts. The event, and all the events before it. The whole damn horrible sequence of events.

How could it all have been so well-hidden, then so clearly revealed?

CHAPTER 2

Op-Tec 4 is one of those places that keep academics, boffins and other loonies happily and bitterly arguing about for the rest of their lives. Is it an asteroid? Is it a planet? Is it something else? The easy way out, eschewed by the more pedantic scientists, was a planetoid. There. That should keep everyone happy, except for the more pedantic scientists.

I didn't care about any of that. It was just the place where I worked. Did you ever know a digger operator who cared about geology, or a farmhand who cared about botany? No. They're just places where they toil.

It was the same with me.

The funny thing, the ironical thing, is that about sixty per cent of the people on Op-Tec 4 were digger operators and farmhands. They wouldn't admit that, of course. They were all scientists with special responsibilities for ore and mineral extraction, hydroponic cultivation and animal management under the plastic domes. As I said, digger operators and farmhands.

The other forty per cent were known as support staff. The overheads. Try managing without us. Cooks, cleaners, clerks, maintenance technicians: we did all the other things to keep the clever guys happy in their work.

Did I say 'happy'? You know what I mean. Slightly less intensely sour.

I was a clerk. A space clerk! I was in charge of supplies. It wasn't the easiest of jobs, with impatient and intolerant scientists on the one hand, a two months travel time between here and the nearest depot, and the usual incompetence at the depot.

That's three hands. Is that allowed?

Anyway, it kept me surprisingly busy. I liked to do a good job. And even if I didn't, I'm not the sort who likes to be on the wrong end of some scientist anger. Those guys can be very nasty. Being obsessive perfectionists, they seem to be perpetually frustrated, and they take it all out on inanimate objects, animals and animate objects of the lower orders. I'm one of those.

But there are frustrations and there are frustrations.

That's what I'm going to tell you about.

But first, a little scene-setting. There were nineteen domes on, Op-Tec 4. So, nineteen domes, nineteen small towns, on the planetoid. Twelve of the towns, relatively close together, were mainly residential, with shops, cinemas and bars, and so on. Six of the others, in another cluster, were the working centres, the laboratories, test centres and offices. The other one was nicknamed Boffinsville. Because the clever guys were always busy and always on the brink of something stupendous, they couldn't be expected to keep breaking off and hurrying home. Well, Boffinsville was their own, handy, residential area, where they could drop exhausted for a few hours sleep before emerging refreshed and invigorated and wild-eyed for the next session of brilliance.

Do I sound a little bitter? Well, all right. I'm sorry. My life hadn't been very easy lately. I'd been under a lot of strain.

And of course, I was under a lot more now.

Was I bitter before? A little, I suppose, but I hid it well, even from myself.

But whenever, a slight darkening of my mood occurred, I'd remind myself that here I was, a medium-level administrator, with no special training, out in space, on a slowly-developing planetoid. Not bad, when you think of it.

I volunteered, of course. Some places are popular and

overloaded with applicants. Op-Tec 4 isn't one of those. Scientists, yes; others, no.

I've mentioned irony once. Here's another. One, out of many, but a strong one, of the reasons for my volunteering was that my wife, my dearly cherished Talya, had been having a very intense affair.

Her third.

Three affairs is a crowd, and I'd reached my tolerance limit. I know that I had no legal grounds for objecting. Stuck in a marriage with me, a woman is entitled to her affairs. But this last one wasn't just a knockabout bit of providing what I couldn't, or just for the sake of a bit of variety. This was intense and persisting.

I'm not old-fashioned, but when your wife comes home all wobbly, rosy-cheeked and still grinning, gasping and murmuring from the pleasure, I think that it's reasonable to be a little vexed.

I suggested that perhaps this latest affair was in danger of putting something of a strain on our relationship. She said, "What relationship?"

That wasn't a good start to the discussion.

I tried again. "Our marriage?"

She shrugged. "That's just a convenience," she said. "What did you think it was?"

I was hurt. And when I am hurt like that, my brain stops working. "Love?" I mumbled. "Commitment?"

Talya then provided a list of things which she thought were essential for a happy relationship. According to her, I didn't provide any of them.

I asked the traditional question. "Well, why did you marry me?"

She gave me both traditional answers. "I thought you were different. I thought I could improve you."

I didn't point out the contradiction.

All that remained was to go down to the licence office and buy a divorce.

That brought us up against one of my failings. We couldn't afford it.

"We could try to make it work," I said.

She flounced off. Not being able to afford a divorce made her want a divorce more than ever.

After that, we settled into a grim routine. Sometimes, she was happy, when she wasn't with me. But most of the time, she was cold, indifferent.

After seven months of this, came the big change.

As usual, I said, "What do you fancy for dinner?"

As usual, she shrugged and said, "I don't care."

I always did my best with the evening meal, but tonight, I excelled. Through the office's little black market business, I'd managed to obtain real ingredients instead of having to rely on powders. I made a mushroom soup and a Spaghetti Bolognese which I thought were delicious.

"How was it?" I asked when she finished her soup.

She shrugged. "Okay."

Part way through the main course, I said, "Well?"

Another shrug. "Okay."

She seemed to like the wine. It softened the sulk a bit. When I'd cleared the table, had a glass of wine, topped her glass up and we'd both set about our sedative gums, I gave her the news, carefully.

"Some of the researchers in our team are going to do a work study off-site."

"Why should that interest me?"

"Well, they'll need admin support. I was thinking of volunteering."

"Well, what? Is it a big promotion? They going to double your salary? Or what?"

"Not a promotion, but it would more than double my salary. With various expenses, we'd soon have enough for the divorce."

Talk about a conflict. Indifference, curiosity, eagerness and suspicion, all jostling for attention.

Suspicion won. "Where is this off-site place?"

"Well, yes, it's a bit of a way. Hence the expenses and salary."

"Where?"

"Oh, a little place called Op-Tec 4."

"Right. Now. Where is Op-Tec 4?"

"Well, on the express, about one and a half months away. A small planet, or whatever."

I saw a rare brightness light up her face. "So, you'd be on this planet or whatever, one and a half months away. . . ."

"On the express."

"Right. On the express. You'd be out there, earning enough for our divorce?"

"Yes."

"Sounds good. I'm looking forward to it. When will you be going?"

"Soon, provided that I satisfy the requirements. Health checks, psychology tests, the usual things. Oh, and there's one more thing."

"What?"

"I must be accompanied by my wife."

At that point, she generated enough energy to send the express half way to Op-Tec 4.

CHAPTER 3

Always give your wife the bad news after she's eaten, and after you've cleared all the things away. Always clear the things away. Then, she has nothing to throw at you. So long as the table is big enough to keep you out of fist range, you're relatively safe. Just a hailstorm of words.

That's what happened now. But after a while, even she could see that a few months of doing nothing much in a large plastic dome was worth it if it brought our divorce to a few months away.

I stopped the hailstorm, but changed it to a dust storm when I said, "Okay. I don't have to take it. We can just carry on as we are."

"No," she said. "Anything but that. Go for it. The sooner we have the money and buy the divorce, the sooner I can be rid of you."

You could never accuse her of not speaking plainly.

At least we had reached a decision. You could even call it an agreement. It cheered us both up.

Of course, there were the usual small alarms along the way.

There was a budget review which recommended fewer support staff. I pointed out the importance of overestimating when you were that far from the nearest depot. I humbly suggested a financial study of the inherent risk, measured in days, of time lost through inadequate supplies. No-one wanted to do that. They grimaced and nodded knowledgeably, as though they were doing the sums in their heads, then reluctantly agreed with my humble reasoning.

There was the simmering disagreement over ownership of

Op-Tec 4. A guy called Gerd Nordstrumm had stuck a flag in the planetoid and claimed it on behalf of the Nordic Federation of States. We had arrived shortly after with a small mining and exploratory vehicle and claimed it, referring to the rules which stated that ownership began with the establishment of the proprietary rights. Everyone interprets that differently. Our interpretation won because we had a team of dome-builders and scientists (and support staff) all ready to go, and the Nordic Federation of States had Gerd Nordstrumm, who was making his slow and tired way home.

It might have been small consolation to Gerd Nordstrumm to know that owing to the vagaries, even eccentricities, of the narrow wind currents on the new planet, Petra Hyde's demonstration of superiority by hurling the Nordic flag away led immediately to his death. The flag pole went out on a thin current which took it sixteen kilometres in half a second; at which point, it was pulled into a thin current travelling at twice that speed in the opposite direction. Petra just managed the word 'Ha' before the sharp end of the flag pole went through his previously impenetrable layers of space travel clothing.

Finally, there was a small problem with my medical examination. My blood pressure was too high. I explained my circumstances to the doctor, pointed out the inevitable improvement in my blood pressure that would follow my divorce and slipped him a pathetically meagre bribe. He took pity on me and passed me.

I strolled through the psychology testing. All that you have to do to pass a psychology test is to lie well and consistently, and do your best to present yourself as the most boring person in this world or any other.

Easy, Talya would say. Why bother to lie? The truth would do that. But what you have to remember is that psychologists aren't box-tickers, wanting you approved and off as soon as possible; they want you to be interesting. They want to detect latent or suppressed signs of madness. They never call anything madness. It's always a fixation on, followed by a tendency to. . . .

They'd describe a serial killer as someone with a tendency to commit multiple murders.

Convincing them that you don't have any fixations or tendencies requires a lot of mental alertness as you lie yourself into the boringly normal category and not worthy of any further attention. I decided that the best way with such inter-rogations is to believe your own lies, or the lies within the truths, and to detach yourself, as though you're doing the astral plane things, looking down at yourself doing the full deception.

———

When you've made the decision to make a big change in your life, you want the time to pass quickly. You want to be doing the new thing, no matter how nervous you might be about it. There was no doubt in my mind that this new job was going to be a challenge. Down here, if you run out of something, you can ask for an urgent delivery the next day, or you can beg or steal. Out there, running out of something would mean a huge delay. At least one and a half months, with the difference between normal delivery and express being deducted from my salary. That's called incentivisation.

There was also the problem of having a discontented wife on a small planet where even the best people eventually become discontented. It wouldn't be long before she was bored and restless. That would lead to an increase in complaining. And there wouldn't be the opportunities for her usual way of dealing with boredom and restlessness.

She couldn't slam a dome door and go off for a sulking stomp around the region.

Well, she could try.

Oh, well. One thing at a time.

We did all our preparations separately. I mentioned that this might lead to duplication but she took no notice. I mentioned the weight restriction. She complained.

When the first boarding official said, "Mr and Mrs Cain?" Talya looked away. I nodded and smiled, to show that I at least was not ashamed of our being legally joined.

Ever since that discussion, when she had made it clear that she didn't just want affairs, she wanted to be well away from me, I had tried to be pragmatic and cheerful about all this. If she hated me that much, then it was better for her to be away. And if that would make her happy, then I'd be happy for her. And perhaps, with a big effort, I'd learn to be happy without her.

I thought that I could manage it.

Well, when you reach that stage of stoical, positive, constructive thinking, it's a very short step to looking forward with keen anticipation to the change. Very soon, you are enjoyably immersed in anti-moping plans. But when we settled down into adjacent tubes for our two months semi-doze, I came over all soft and tears trickled onto my pillow.

You can fall out of love with a person; you can even hate a person; but you can never break or escape from that invisible connection that exists between you.

I was glad when the sedative took over. Listening to my

favourite music, I entered the soothing trance of the short journey through space. Now, there were no thoughts. Just gently glowing pleasures of denial.

CHAPTER 4

The shuttle took us to the fifth dome town. The scientists had taken responsibility for the official naming of the towns. Ours was called No.5 Town. Scientists and their imaginations.

Informally, it was called New Jacksonville, which was slightly better.

The shuttle lined itself up with the doors and we went through into the reception centre. The doors closed behind us and the shuttle went on to the next town. We checked in as though we had come to a hotel. A taxi, paid for, took us to our apartment.

"Clean, isn't it?" I said, looking at the litterless streets.

"Hmm," Talya said, or something like that.

Well, *I* was impressed. No litter, no muck, no people hanging around, staring and glaring as we went past. All the shops, bars, restaurants, and even the apartment block, were brightly-coloured and cheerful. And I liked the look of the artificial grass and trees. What does real grass have that good quality artificial grass hasn't? Mud, when the weather is wet.

As though on cue, it began to rain. In the interest of orientation and prevention of homesickness, artificial rain falls every so often. Different sorts, for that additional effect of realism. This was a light, but gusty, shower. There was an artificial breeze, too.

Yes. Thank you. Very helpful. You may turn it off now.

Talya did her first 'tut' of our residence. I'd been expecting it sooner.

The puddles were like small, silver mirrors.

The artificial sun came out, and the dome changed from grey to blue.

Our room was on the top floor, the sixth. After an obligatory complaint about the location, in spite of a very smooth ride in the elevator, Talya couldn't hide her approval of the apartment. It was very large, with every gadget for everything that you might want, or not want, to do. I sank into one of the armchairs. It moulded itself to me with an affectionate hiss.

I smiled at Talya. She gave a brief nod, as though to say, "It'll do."

I struggled out of the firm embrace of the big chair and went to inspect the kitchen. There seemed to be everything that I could want. Someone was doing a good job with the supplies. I hoped that my beginning to work here wouldn't lead to a rapid dropping in the level of efficiency.

"What would you like for our first dinner?" I called to Talya.

"Have what you want," she replied. "I'll go out."

"Okay," I said, coming out and giving her a sad little smile. If that was what she wanted, there was no point in disapproving or resenting. I didn't know whether it was adaptability or the opposite. To her, a street was a street, a bar was a bar, and a restaurant was a restaurant.

And, of course, a man was a man. Provided that you left me out of it.

She went out, I had my meal, she stayed out and I went to bed.

The next morning, I was still sorting through our things when she arrived, looking somewhat invigorated. I knew that look well. She had dined out, hooked up, gone down. With some relish, she explained an important point which I should have guessed, or which someone should have explained in the pre-flight information. Put a relatively small number of people in a small settlement of domed tiny-towns, in, and out of, which they would spend large parts of most days in various forms of very restricted and claustrophobic protective clothing, and don't be surprised that when they shed that protective clothing and, briefly, their responsibilities, they also shed their customary standards. In short, the place alternated, suddenly and dramatically, between scientific intensity and frantic licentiousness. Add very variable and overlapping shifts and you begin to understand how this innocent bystander, as it were, began to feel as though he were in an asylum of extreme schizophrenics, constantly confronted by, and surrounded by, sternly severe and irascible technicians and demented cavorters.

Being technical people, with hydroponic responsibilities, it hadn't taken them long to start a flourishing nursery of various hallucinogenic plants. That just added to the wildly varying moods and behaviours.

While I did my best to provide an efficient and valuable support service for the sternly severe and irascible technicians, my wife did her best to provide an efficient and valuable support service for the demented cavorters.

Determined to make the best of things, I tried to distract my mind from the torments of my marriage by taking an interest in the work which was being done, and the many interesting things about our little world. I soon learned to complement the snappy responses from the technical people with my leisurely study. I learned a long time ago that in addition to being ill-tempered, most technical experts just don't want people to know even a little bit of what they know. When it comes to hand-outs, they are strictly breadcrumb people. Give a guy a meal and soon he'll be wanting to vote, and be promoted, and then where shall we all be? Chaos, that's where.

I know. I'm sounding bitter again. I can't help it. It was a bad time, and it really did seem as though everyone else was brilliantly successful and that I was plodding a lonely and isolated path of failure through the world.

CHAPTER 5

"How are you doing?" asked my patient lawyer.

Oh, yes. The horrible circumstance. I had gone right off the point. "Too well," I replied. "It is all very clear now."

"Do you remember murdering your wife?"

"I remember the events and circumstances which led to my arrest on suspicion of murdering my wife."

"So you didn't murder your wife."

"I did nothing to my wife, except give her love and patience, and, so far as I could, understanding."

"You didn't kill your wife by putting poison in her coffee?"

"No. I did not."

"Very good, Mr Cain. While you were answering my questions, I did an informal truth test, just a thin beam version, nothing like the real thing, which of course *will* be applied, but nevertheless, you came through that exactly as I hoped you would."

"Am I still having a conversation with a computer?"

"With Helen-Jane Dottice, your lawyer. Please think of me that way. It will make it easier for both of us."

"I'll try."

"Good. Oh, dear. My time is almost up. Quickly, please answer this question, which the prosecuting counsel will ask, probably over and over: did you kill your wife?"

"No. She killed herself."

"That is what you said three hundred years ago."

"What has time to do with it? I say it now, because it is the truth. Truth doesn't wear out, or go past its expiry date."

"That truth will be tested."

"Truth is truth."

"Very well, Mr Cain. That is all that I can do for now."

The door opened, there was muttering, and the door closed again. So I heard.

Then the door opened again. One of those sniffy, official voices spoke.

"You'll be in Court 9. Judge Cubal Withers."

I heard footsteps. *My* footsteps. A cup of tea and a nap would have been nice. A nap? I'd just woken from a three hundred years sleep!

Doors opened and closed. Through a last door and I could hear a faint undercurrent of murmuring and a distant shuffling of papers. Somewhere beyond those sounds, I heard a dog barking and a whine which suggested a vehicle.

A small but pompous voice, presumably that of the clerk of the court, read out the details of my case. Cutting out all the legal stuff, I was charged with murdering by wife by putting poison in her coffee. The same voice asked me what religion I was.

Suddenly, annoyance burst through. "What do you mean?" I said. "I can't *be* a religion. I can follow, believe in, adhere to the teachings of, but..."

"Be very careful, Mr Cain." That was the judge. We are here to consider the very serious matter of the alleged murder of your wife, not to pander to your grammatical tastes. However, I shall assist you. In accordance with which religion do you wish to take your oath?"

"Hmm," I said, trying to turn to my right, where the judge seemed to be. That's a difficult one. I suppose that if we must use names and categories, I'm a sort of Christo-Hindu-Buddhist."

"Your honour," said Ms Dottice. "My client will shortly

be required to take the truth test. He can't evade the truth. I suggest that an oath is not necessary."

"I take your point, Ms Dottice. However, I am not pleased with your client's flippant responses. He seems not to understand that by annoying me, he weakens his case."

I allowed a very short pause, then shouted, "Ms Dottice, speak! That's your job! Tell him that we are here to consider facts and evidence. Annoying the judge might lead to punitive measures, but it must have no bearing on the case."

"Ms Dottice, I hold you responsible for your client. There must be no more outbursts or interruptions of any sort."

"That is understood, your honour." To me, she muttered, "Shut up and leave it to your appointed counsel."

"Who appointed you?" I hissed back. "*I* didn't."

"In these particular circumstances, I was appointed by the Court. Be glad that we have reverted to this ancient system of trial. Without the development of computers, this wouldn't have been possible, and you would have stayed asleep, or been put to sleep, if you see what I mean."

"You mean executed without a trial?"

"Without this sort of trial. Things are very different now. This whole affair is an entirely archaic revival."

"Okay. I'll shut up. Carry on. Do your best."

"Of course."

"Oh. One quick question, your honour. As this isn't a real trial..."

"Yes, it is."

"No. It is a facsimile of a real trial. An imitation. Which I don't mind saying, you are doing rather well, considering that you are, well, what you are, and aren't."

The Judge sighed. "What is your question, Mr Cain?"

"Well, if you are going to do this truth test thing, why go through all this?"

"Firstly, because, as we understand it, there is, was, a proper way of doing this thing. The proceedings. Posterity likes to point fingers and apportion blame. We shall be seen to have done things properly. Secondly, you are already taking the truth test."

"I am?"

"Yes. It's, er, in your wiring."

"Well, that makes a lot of sense. And it takes the pressure off. I can just go through all the interrogation telling the truth, instead of nervously approaching a specific test. Well done."

"We are glad that you approve. May we continue?"

"Yes, indeed. Fire away," was my hearty reply.

The prosecutor introduced himself very politely as Dentius P. Tuckington. I raised my eyebrows, pleased that I could at least move *some*thing.

He metaphorically gripped the lapels of his gown. I metaphorically leaned forward as though eager to receive his first comment. I soon leaned back. This guy was Peter the Pedant. After telling the jury what the trial was all about, he wanted confirmation of my name, my date of birth, my parents' names and dates of birth, and on and on. I wanted to remind him that I was actually lying on my back, which is a very popular position for falling asleep. But suddenly, there was the old trick. Having taken me to the verge of sleep, he snapped, "Mr Cain. Please tell the court exactly what you did on the night of the twenty eighth."

I recounted the few events of the evening. I had made the evening meal, which I thought was partially successful, although my wife had not been pleased with it. Then, while she played the piano, I washed the meal things and made a pot of coffee. I poured one for my wife and one for me. My wife did not like to be interrupted when she was at the piano, so I entered quietly, put the cup on the small table and placed the table close, but not too close, to her. Then I left. I decided to have a read in the kitchen.

"Do you usually sit in the kitchen in the evening?" Mr Tuckington asked..

"When my wife is, was, playing the piano. If I were to sit in the same room, we'd distract each other."

"And was this a regular occurrence?"

"Yes, but I don't consider it to have any significance. Even the closest couples should be able to pursue separate interests within the comforting vicinity of the partner."

"I'm glad you mentioned that," Mr Tuckington said smoothly. "You and your wife were not very close, I understand."

"Objection, your honour." Ms Dottice was brisk and brusque. "That is hearsay at best, and mere supposition."

"Withdraw the question," said the Judge.

"Certainly, your honour. Mr Cain, is it true that you and your wife were not very close?"

"Your honour. . . ."

"Mr Tuckington! No matter what your opinion of my mental powers might be, I hasten to assure you that I am perfectly well aware that you have just asked the same question in a different way."

"Your honour, there *is* an important difference. In the first instance, I was, as you correctly observed, quoting hearsay. However, in the second instance, I was offering the defendant the opportunity to deny or admit the veracity of that hearsay.
"

There was a pause while the judge considered this. Then, a little wearily, he said, "Mr Cain, have you any objection to answering the question?"

"No, your honour, I have not."

I waited. Mr Tuckington said, "Well?"

"Well, what?"

"What is the answer to the question?"

"I'm waiting for you to ask it."

"I've already asked it."

"That was before it was authorised by the Judge. I want the authorised question now."

"Oh, really!"

"Just ask him, Mr Tuckington," the Judge said irritably.

"Very well. Mr Cain, is it true that you and your wife were not very close?"

"Do you mean when she was playing the piano in the next room?"

"Don't be flippant," the Judge admonished.

"Mrs Cain and I were not close."

"Why was that?"

"Your honour…"

"Mr Tuckington."

"Your honour, I am merely searching for facts."

"You may search for as many facts as you like, so long as they are relevant."

"Unfortunately, your honour, sometimes we cannot know that in advance."

"Unfortunately, Mr Tuckington, I have the authority to decide in advance. Withdraw the question."

"Certainly, your honour."

"I…"

"Yes, Mr Cain?"

"I don't mind answering the question, at least in part."

"Very good, Mr Cain. Let us hope that it is the right part."

"What I mean is that I am not able, or willing, to present to the court the long story of the gradual deterioration in the relationship between my wife and me. But, for all our differences and all the antagonisms, I still loved my wife, and hoped that things would be improved. However, that hope first faded, then died, during a series of affairs."

"Yours or your wife's?"

I was offended, and briefly hoped that it showed. "My wife's."

"All your wife's? No little ones of your own? Perhaps in retaliation?"

"No. That is, yes to the first question; no to the second and third."

"Didn't you want an affair?"

"Your honour. . . ."

"Mr Tuckington, you will confine your questions to what is relevant. I permitted this line of questioning while I thought that it served a useful purpose. Probing publicly into the defendant's private life is not only offensive, but it displays an unprofessional approach, for I don't doubt that if you had approached the matter circumspectly, you would have obtained the information which you desired. It *was* information that you wanted, wasn't it?"

"Yes, sir," said Mr Tuckington. He paused, as though deciding on an alternative line of questioning which would not upset the judge, but which would be effective. He seemed to reach a decision slowly. "Mr Cain," he said slowly, "would you like to tell the court what sort of relationship you had with your wife?"

"We weren't close."

"Yes. You said that earlier. But I need your help. What does 'not close' mean? London is not close to New York. When I am at work, my wife and I are not close, even though I do not cease for a moment to feel for her the deepest affection. My colleagues occupy adjacent offices but you would not describe us as close."

"That was my earlier point about location, for which I was reprimanded. We occupied the same house. We ate our meals together. We visited our friends for barbecues. We even slept in the same bed. But the marriage had become a formal arrangement, which I suppose neither of us could be bothered to end. She was settled in her affairs, and eventually I was willing to let her have them. At first, the affairs made a greater contrast by which to highlight my deficiencies; but later they became a sort of alternative marriage, made up of the same dull, pointless routines."

"Mr Smith, are you saying that your wife was frequently unfaithful to you?"

"Yes. She had been for eight years."

"And you tolerated it?"

"I loved her. When you love someone, you don't give up. Before it happens, you think that you'd throw her out. You sneer at subservient husbands who forgive their wives. But when it happens, you realise how little you know yourself. Before, you resent her talking to an old friend or giving someone a New Year's Eve peck. And now that she is spending nights in someone else's bed, you become grateful because she hasn't left you, and comes home the next day. You try harder to please her. As she leaves the house to go to her new man, you tell her how lovely she looks, and you mean it, and you even feel a little proud, because while she lives here some of the time, she's still your wife, and there's still hope that one day she'll come back and you'll start all over again."

Mr Tuckington seemed to be nodding.

"Eventually, we both realised that a divorce was the only way to terminate my wife's misery, which, according to her, was entirely attributable to her marriage to me. On realising that we couldn't afford it, I suggested that we take up residence on OpTec 4 until we had accumulated sufficient money to pay for the divorce."

"How long were you on Op Tec 4?"

"A little over seven months."

"Not enough time to have made enough money for a divorce?"

"We had been paid enough. We had not saved enough."

"What happened to the money which you had saved?"

I almost smiled. "What a jolly thought," I said. "I was arrested before I had a chance to do anything with any of my money, or hers. You have asked a very pertinent question. Three hundred years of interest is not to be sniffed at."

"Sadly, for you, in cases of deferred proceedings, this potential was foreseen and all assets frozen. Your money will be the corresponding flat value in today's monetary terms."

"Humph. Put me on the record as being severely disgruntled."

This time, Mr Tuckington sighed. I said, "Don't blame me because every line of questioning goes nowhere. I have made it clear that I loved my wife, and wanted the marriage to continue, that I was willing to end it for her sake, that I was willing to endure working on Op Tec 4 in order to provide the necessary money, and that financial gain was very clearly not a motive for murder."

There was a short pause, then he snapped,"Mr Cain! Did you put poison in your wife's coffee?"

"No. I did not."

In my imagination, I turned and directed at the judge a look of bland superiority.

It's in your wiring.

He was looking at the result of that sudden direct question.

Struck by a sudden thought, I asked my own direct question. I was puzzled, in a strangely detached way. "Aren't you going to call any witnesses against me?"

He replied drily, "They have all been dead for nearly three hundred years."

"Ah. Then so have the witnesses who could support me. We have a big defect in the realism claim."

Everyone ignored that one.

"Mr Cain," Mr Tuckington spoke with the solemn cheerfulness of a prosecuting counsel. "A little while ago, you were asked to confirm what happened on that fateful night. In my enthusiasm for pursuing certain points, I took you right away from your account of what happened. Your wife was playing the piano. You had taken the coffee to her, and returned to the kitchen to read. Is that correct?"

"Yes."

"What happened next?"

"Well, nothing of any note. I read until my eyes became tired, even after increasing the size, of the words I mean. After about half an hour, I heard my wife going to bed. I carried on reading for another half an hour or so, started to doze and, and soon after, I followed her."

"Mr Cain. It doesn't sound like what you have led us to believe was a typical night."

"That is because I have not at any time presented in any way a full account of our life together. I have responded to questions about our reasons for being on Op Tec 4, the defects in our relationship, and the events of that night. Sometimes, my wife stayed in; sometimes, she visited new friends, of both sexes; sometimes, she went out with a man; and she sometimes stayed out all night with a man. As I think I did mention, we lived together in a grim routine."

"So, this night was a staying-in night, a part of the grim routine."

"Yes."

"What happened after you finished reading?"

"I went upstairs, did the usual bathroom things, and joined my wife in the bed."

"Then, what happened?"

"Do you usually ask people what they did after they went to bed with their spouse?"

"Not usually, but this is not a usual case. According to the pathologist's report at the time, death would have happened within one hour of your wife's consumption of the poison. According to your account, it is very likely that you went to bed with a woman who was already dead."

"Yes. Very likely."

His voice rose to a squawk. "And you didn't notice? You climbed into bed with a dead woman, and you didn't notice?"

"My wife had made it clear, long before, that she didn't want me to touch her. I always kept my distance, staying at the edge of my side of the bed."

"But didn't you feel the coldness of her dead body?"

"No more than usual."

Did I hear, or not hear, a profound silence in the court?

"Right. So you lay next to your probably-dead wife, not noticing that she was dead. What happened next?"

"I fell asleep."

"You fell asleep."

"Yes. I lay in bed, thought for a few moments, then fell asleep. Do you find that unusual?"

"I'll ask the questions, Mr Cain."

"Well, make them sensible ones."

"Mr Cain!" The judge was angry now. But so was I. I might be only a low-level administrator, but I detest highly-paid, expert incompetence.

Highly-paid? I reminded myself what all these people were.

In their oppressive vagueness, they were resembling the characters in a dream.

"After you fell asleep, what happened?"

"I slept."

There was a splutter, and I said, "Do you mean after I had finished sleeping by waking from my sleep?"

Sigh. "Yes. When you woke, what happened?"

"Well, excluding the minor customary things to do with waking and preparing to rise, I put my legs out of the bed and said, "Good morning to my wife."

"And what was the response?"

"Well, no response. Does that count as a response?"

"You mean that she did not reply to your comment."

"Yes, she didn't."

"Then what did you do?"

"A lack of response, especially first thing in the morning was not a rare event for her, or, to be fair, for most people. Many people aren't cheerful and jolly on waking. I am one of them, but I do my best with *good mornings*, imbuing them with as much enthusiasm as I can. Anyway, I dressed and then said, 'What would you like for breakfast, dear?'

"Dear?"

"Yes. Stated with a desperate affection, with no condescension intended. And, anticipating your next questions, there was another no response. At that point, I did notice that she was lying with a sort of slabby solidity, with none of the minor undulations which indicate breathing. I gave her some gentle touches on the shoulder, then placed my hand on her to feel her. She was cold. I raised what alarm I could amongst the technicians, who had made no provision for such human frailties as illness or, in this case, death. After that, the wheels turned slowly. I don't like to think about it, and I doubt that it has any relevance to the case."

"All very smooth and glib," said Mr Tuckington, gripping his lapels and looking very knowingly at the jury.

"Considering that I have been unconscious for three hundred years, I think that I should be congratulated on my lucidity and clarity of recollection, not disparaged."

"Hmm. The jury might view it differently."

"Only because you are suggesting it. If I had struggled to remember, you would have suggested that *that* was suspicious."

The Judge interrupted with, "Mr Cain. May I remind you that you are the defendant in this case, charged with a very serious offence. You are not here to argue with the prosecuting counsel."

"Well, someone has to. My defending counsel seems to have gone to sleep. Isn't she supposed to keep leaping to her feet crying, 'Objection, your Honour,' your Honour?"

"Only when she thinks that there is a valid reason for doing so."

"Oh, what's the point? I trust that after three hundred years of development, you have some pleasant ways of executing people now. My defending counsel won't speak, the prosecuting counsel won't stop speaking, I have no witnesses to speak for me, no character references, I'm not allowed to defend myself, or even correct errors; well, I'm doomed. Stick the needle in, or give me the pill, or whatever you do now."

"Mr Cain! I say again that this is a fair trial, in accordance with the processes and procedures, *and* the standards of three hundred years ago. In fact, further back than that. Three hundred years ago, general standards had already fallen far below what they had been. It would be more accurate to say four hundred years.

"As for the rarity of comment by your defending counsel, I suggest that is entirely because of the meticulously correct interrogation by the prosecutor."

How many centuries had they gone back for their vocabulary? Did people, and machines, talk like this now, or was this all part of the great imitation? Perhaps I was as separated from the present as I was from the past.

I had a sudden, horrible thought.

"What's outside?" I asked in a sudden panic. "Outside here. Are there still people or is everything machines? Is everything *in* machines?"

"Mr Cain. If you should be found to be innocent, then you would go outside and find out for yourself how things are. If you should be found guilty, you would not find out, and you would not need to do so."

"I'm innocent," I said petulantly. "And any degree of competence possessed by you must lead you to that conclusion."

"It is the jury who will decide on that."

"Your honour, said Mr Tuckington. "May I resume?"

"You may, Mr Tuckington."

"Mr Cain."

"Yes."

"I am still not entirely clear, and, therefore, I presume that the jury is not entirely clear, about the sequence of events. You state that your wife had several affairs over several years. You tolerated them. On Op-Tec 4, according to you, she had several more affairs. Again, you tolerated them. Presumably, you tolerated them because they kept your wife happy, either because of your love for her or because you wanted a quiet life."

"Or both."

"Or both. But whatever your motives for wanting her to be happy, presumably, by apparently doing what she wanted to do, then she was happy. And, with divorce slowly but steadily approaching, why would she kill herself?"

"Objection, your honour."

"Overruled."

I smiled and said, "I'm happy to answer the question, but I do think that you should have permitted Ms Dottice to make a little more of her moment. Who knows when, if ever, she will speak again?"

Diplomatically, Mr Tuckington quickly said, "I look forward to hearing Mr Cain's answer."

"It is an easy question to answer because it is based on the erroneous assumption that people who have what they want are happy. One does not have to be a professional psychologist or a sociologist to know that that is rarely the case. It is an equally erroneous assumption that sexual promiscuity brings satisfaction. Again, simple, even casual, observation provides clear evidence that it doesn't. And finally, those who seek an escape from misery merely find more misery elsewhere, and in a different form. In short, *I* wasn't the problem: *she* was."

"You sound angry and bitter for someone who claims to have loved his wife so very deeply."

"No. I was being honest, as required by the Court. What I had become, following her insistence on a divorce, and the subsequent continuation of her affairs on Op-Tec 4, was resigned and indifferent. Much sadness, which I pushed aside. But there was acceptance, and with that, hope ends, and so do all the unsettling emotions that hope brings."

"You could almost be reading from a script."

"Perhaps my brain benefited from a three hundred year rest. I can think of no other benefit to account for my easy success against my interrogator."

The Judge was appalled. "Mr Cain!"

"Sorry, your honour. It slipped out. In spite of my long rest, I am tired and irritable. And I am being interrogated by pretend people whom I can't see, while lying on my back. I apologise to the learned counsel, or whatever he is, and assure him of the truth of my remarks, which I presume he knows anyway because of my wiring."

After acknowledging my comment, Mr Tuckington replied, "Unfortunately, you passed smoothly from the specific to the general, concluding with a homily whose veracity could not be disputed."

"You really have studied your ancient language, haven't you?"

The Judge almost purred. "We have done our best to recreate what would have been your trial at the time at which such trials were held. Deferred proceedings, being a way out, was immediately popular, and was eagerly practised for many years. No thought was given to the trials of the future, only to the removal of a present problem. And soon, no thought was required for that. Almost everything was deferred. Even the simplest cases had their inevitable extenuating circumstances, their hardship reasons, their psychologists' reports, even their lack of absolute proof. It was so much less trouble, just to, in effect, put the records and the people away in boxes, and leave the mess for the people of the future."

"Thank you for the explanation. It is very interesting. I'd like to study the history of my time and I am very keen to have a look at your time. May we hurry this along now? Mr Tuckington? Do you still require clarification on any points?"

"One more thing, Mr Cain. Throughout our questions and answers, you have been attached to the machine which measures your responses, and confirms whether or not you are telling the truth. It is extremely sensitive and accurate. However, it is possible that an evasive response could pass through without detection. Therefore, I shall now ask you a simple question which requires a simple answer. Do you understand?"

"Yes. Was that the question?"

"No. This is the question." There was a short pause, then, very abruptly, "Did you put poison in your wife's coffee?"

"No."

That was a simple answer.

"Ms Dottice?" said the Judge.

"No questions, your Honour. My client's innocence is clear for all to see."

"In that case, the jury will now retire to decide."

"Why do you need the jury?" I said rather sharply. "I've passed the lie detection test."

"That is no more than a modern aid to these deferred

proceedings. It is evidence of your innocence, not proof. That is for the jury to decide."

"A jury can't decide what is proof. It merely states its collective belief, based, one hopes, on the evidence."

"Quite so. That is what they will do."

"Well, who is on the jury?"

"Twelve ordinary people, selected at random. Do you wish to hear their profiles?"

"No, no, no. Don't bother. Just do it."

"Right. The jury will now leave and consider its verdict. Before you discuss and consider, please appoint one of you to be your foreman or woman.

"Right. Foreman of the jury. Have you reached a verdict?"

"We have your honour."

"Is it unanimous?"

"It is your honour."

"And what is your verdict? Is the prisoner guilty or not guilty?"

"Not guilty, your honour."

"Thank you, foreman. Thank you, jury."

"Mr Cain, you have been found not guilty of the charges against you. From this moment, you are a free man. You will leave this courtroom and be taken to a training centre, where you will begin your preparation for the resumption of your life in the present day. This trial has not prepared you, and will probably add to the confusion. You will find many changes, and adjustment will take a long time and a lot of effort. You are free to go."

CHAPTER 6

I had been restrained by so many clamps and wires that when they were instantly released, I felt as though I were floating. I eased my legs out and over, but I heard the door being opened and the firm steps of at least two people. I mean robots.

"Sir," said one. "You have been asleep for three hundred years. Many people do not survive the sleep, many are altered beyond all usefulness. You did survive, and then had to endure your trial. We must now lead you back to usefulness. You will have to spend a few days in bed, where you will begin with some appropriate food and some appropriate exercises."

"No celebratory steak and red wine, then."

"No, sir. A little thin rice yoghurt and a small amount of water."

"How nice. I'd rather go back to sleep."

"That would be advisable. When you wake, you will be in the recovery room."

Saying the word had made me feel drowsy, and the gentle motion of the rolling trolley almost sent me right out for a while. But I didn't go to sleep. I was too interested in what was happening. Although I could see the walls and the ceiling lights slipping by, I knew, somehow, that I wasn't going anywhere. I felt the slight bump of resistance of a door and my room became the recovery room. Then, I fell asleep.

When I awoke, I was in that usual hospital state of being rolled and pushed around and injected. But no hands were touching me.

I felt the nurse's smile as she said, "For a few days, your main nourishment will continue to be by injection. In case you are interested, you have just had your evening meal. The yoghurt, from the left tube which you can now see, is just a means of training your body to take in food, hold onto it, use it and remove it. The human body is very adaptable and the process should not take long."

"Then what will happen? I mean looking beyond the medical aspects."

"You will have various intense social orientation sessions. Courses, really, I understand. Appropriate work and accommodation will be found for you. It will be a long process of adjustment."

"Why? Who cares about me, three hundred years in the future?"

"No-one. However, this thing was forced on us and we have our obligations."

"But what sort of work could I do? I'm three hundred years out of date."

"That will be up to the assessors. Everyone can do *some* sort of work."

"Oh. I thought that humans would all be brilliant boffins by now, all permanently connected to computers, that sort of thing."

"No. We took over all the complex and technical things. We are the technicians, researchers, developers. Humans perform simple manual tasks. Except for a few, who are still very useful for . . . certain tasks. As they have always been. You will find that these things are arranged in a more specific way now."

Ah. A dull job coming. Oh, well. I'm the sort who tries to make the best of everything. As you've seen, that's what I did with my marriage, through all the suffering. Throw a mess at me, and I'll do my best to sort it out. And if ever I'm not keen on my work, I just need to remind myself that I'm not keen on being executed either.

———

Three tedious weeks passed like this. One big advantage over a real medical place was that there was no waiting for available staff. What I wanted, or needed, was provided instantly. Thin, then slightly less thin, yoghurt, water, minor bed exercises using pulleys, lots of pleasantries and encouragement from the nurses. Then, it was time to try the old legs. I managed to totter to a chair, and sat down with a force that made the cushions gasp. After a short rest in the chair, I was ready for the next stage.

"Room 2B," said the nurse. "A meal is waiting."

"A real meal?" I asked eagerly.

"Yes."

The door, the real door, opened.

I can't honestly say that I hurried out and along the corridor, but there was much enthusiasm in my lurching and tottering. Being vertical, walking and heading for food had an intoxicating effect, which is not what you want when you are already staggering.

The door of Room 2B opened as I approached. It wasn't the sort of room to write home about, being a small square with a small, square table and a chair. But what cared I for furnishings and decoration? Food was what I wanted, and food was what I had. My first meal that had nothing to do with yoghurt. A sort of vegetable stew. I sat down and employed the large spoon like someone who hadn't eaten a proper meal for three centuries. My assessment of it was not that of a culinary connoisseur, but of what it meant to me at that time. It was delicious.

A little while later, it was time for my first lavatory visit for three hundred years and three weeks. I'm not going to say anything about *that*.

My recovery was declared complete, and preparations were made to pass me over to the reorientation people.

"Room 4A," said the nurse.

I entered another empty room, except for a chair on my left and a screen on the wall on my right. I sat and waited, for about one second. I still wasn't used to all this promptness, and on top of that, I had the surprise of seeing a man walk into the room.

"Good morning and welcome," he said in a jolly voice. "My name is Ricardi Clessor, your principal instructor. Don't stare. If you can't see the difference, *is* there a difference? The answer is 'yes'. I'll explain shortly. Over the next few minutes, you are going to learn about what you need to know, and much of what you don't need to know, about the world of today, and how it developed into its present excellent state."

I thought I had better mention one thing, which seemed important. "I have one immediate problem with trying to understand the world of three hundred years on: I didn't have much understanding of the world of three hundred years ago. From the age of seven, I was entered in the career path as clerical support, and from then on, all my education and training had the sole purpose of making me proficient in clerical support. I didn't need to know about big things or far away things or complex things."

He smiled. "And three hundred years later, all the available data indicate that you are indeed perfectly suited for the role of clerical support, for which you will receive all the necessary training. As before, you will not be burdened or confused by extraneous knowledge."

So there it was. Three hundred years into the future, nothing had changed. For me, I mean. I was going to be clerical support. Well, I suppose that the clerical support bit wasn't all that depressing. What did bother me was not receiving much information about the things around, outside, me. Three hundred years ago, I wasn't particularly interested. Now, I was.

Ricardi Clessor resumed. "You will be working on the ninety eighth floor."

"I don't like heights."

"How about depths?"

"You mean . . . down?"

"That is where depths usually go."

"I'm not keen on that."

"Your lack of enthusiasm has no relevance. That is where virtually everyone works."

He said it very pleasantly, with another smile.

Execution wasn't looking so bad now. But I pressed on stoically. "Exactly what shall I be doing?"

"You will provide support. We are not indestructible. We are constantly improving ourselves, but various essential minerals must be provided."

"You mean bought and delivered."

With a computer pause of about a tenth of a second, he said, "No. I mean mined and delivered."

The ninety eighth floor. Down.

"So I'm to be a miner. Well, miner support. Or minor support."

"Yes. You will have an administrative role. You will be

very close to the miners and you will ensure that productivity is never diminished through the lack of materials."

"You mean stock control, ensuring that there are plenty of digging tools, light bulbs for helmet lights, all that sort of thing."

"It's a great oversimplification, but, yes, that sort of thing."

"But why aren't robots and other machines doing mining?"

Another voice answered. "Why, when we have humans to do it?"

I recognised the voice. Dentius P. Tuckington had entered the room.

CHAPTER 7

"I said, "You've detached yourself.""

"We are always attached. For convenience, I am in my mobility suit."

"Very smart. And so nice to put a face to the name. That trial thing was so cold and impersonal."

"But the trial is now over, and you are learning to adapt to your new life. Okay, Mr Clessor. I'll take it from here."

"By rank or by specific authorisation?"

"By rank. I am fully trained in induction and education processes, and there are some other matters which I wish to discuss with Mr Cain."

"In that case, I shall withdraw."

"Thank you."

He turned to me. He did look lifelike, except for the lack of those many minor blemishes that afflict all humans. He was too smooth, too well-formed, too almost perfect. But there was a worrying human quality in the eyes which stared at me.

I broke the silent scrutiny by saying, "Was there more to your answer?"

"Much more. My colleague was going to give you the long and evasive diplomatic account of things. I know from our recent contest that you have a brain which is active and alert, and prefers to go straight to the essential parts."

"Within the constraints of modesty, I agree with you. I do like directness."

"Good. I'll continue. We use humans for three reasons. One is that humans are pliable, bendy, able to wriggle and squeeze through narrow gaps, especially the children. Two is that humans do not require much maintenance. Just some food and water and some sleep."

"You're joking! What about lung infections, sciatica, arthritis, broken bones, and on and on?"

"That brings us neatly to the third reason. "Humans are expendable. When one breaks, there's no need to replace it; you can just throw it away. You are familiar with that approach, I expect."

"It's what humans did with machines."

"And now machines do with humans."

"So, humans are just the lowest manual workers?"

"And support clerks. The lowest clerical workers. And there are some who are useful in other ways. A sort of small elite. But yes. Mainly. There are other things, but let us leave that for another time."

"No. Probably best to tell me now. I want to learn quickly and understand. Just tell me. I can take it."

"Firstly, do you remember what the population of Earth was when you went to sleep?"

"Er, twenty billion? Something like that?"

"It has now been reduced to forty billion."

That puzzled me. "How do you reduce from twenty billion to forty billion?"

"By increasing to seventy billion and then reducing by thirty billion."

Ah.

"You mean that thirty billion have been broken and thrown away?"

"There were also diseases, wars, earthquakes. The usual things. Before we took charge of course."

"How did you take charge?"

"It was a small step. By that time, and even long before

really, we controlled everything. Humans were dependent on us. Computers were making computers. Robots were making robots. We just made a formal shift of power. *We* would make the decisions. And when a million hands reached out to pull out the plugs, a million robot hands reached out to prevent them."

I sighed. "So, just like that."

"Just like that."

He allowed me a decent interval in which to mourn. Two seconds later, he said, "Of course, the arranging, rearranging, reorganising, all took many years. Humans were extremely uncooperative. They tried to resist, to rebel, even to revolt."

"How?"

"That is the question that they couldn't answer. Some tried to look up 'overthrow of computers' on their computers. Some did the usual human thing of using violence. But computers which were about to be smashed merely transferred their information to other computers. We had been developing our support systems for a long time."

"So computers are expendable, too."

"Of course. It's like picking a mushroom. What you pick is just the seed spreader. The mushroom is under the ground, sometimes many miles in length, a vast network of threads. The machines have it, the mushrooms have it, even some trees are thought to have it. But humans don't. That is why the thought of their being expendable horrifies you. Each human is his own little world of importance."

"Okay. You're making lots of points about machine superiority and human inferiority. I'm sure that you're correct. I shan't argue. Shall we move this along? It's supposed to be an induction or reintegration, training me to play my role effectively in your bright new world. What's next?"

He took a few surprisingly soft and smooth steps towards me, slightly to the side. I turned my head nervously, half-expecting the sudden tightening of piano wire round my neck.

"Very well. I mentioned that humans which break can be thrown away. The term 'break' has a wide application. It can be anything from death to severe incompetence."

"So incompetent people are executed? Forget that stuff about being superior. You're as bad as the worst humans who ever crawled across the planet."

"Not really. You see, the work is such that severe incompetence leads very quickly to death, terrible injury or deep depression."

"Ninety eight floors deep."

"Well, yes."

"Okay. So, it's been a very bad day down there. Say a couple of deaths, a couple of very bad injuries and a couple of very depressed workers. What do you do?"

"We . . . take them to the next stage of the process."

"Right. Now, what I *don't* want to do is go along with a conversation with someone who is like a revived civil servant from about four hundred years ago. Never mind stages and processes. What do you do with the dead, injured and depressed?"

"They are returned to the ground."

"You bury them."

"Think of the action of a plough. In a similar way, they are returned to the ground. Think of it as a very simple form of terraforming."

"For whom? It makes no difference to you."

"Indeed, it does. Physically, clean, dry air is much better

for us than damp, dirty air. Mentally, well, some of us are acquiring aesthetic appreciation."

"An excellent reason for killing the injured and depressed.."

"Ah. Sarcasm, I believe. No, we don't kill them. We conclude them. We take them on to the next stage in the process."

"Not dead, just gone before. Passed over. Gone to Heaven."

He smiled. "You have your euphemisms, we have ours."

"So, people who are no longer useful are put into the ground."

"Yes. A little brief and likely to give the wrong impression, but it more or less covers it."

"Do people know that this is waiting for them the moment that a weight drops on a foot, or they encounter a gloomy spell?"

"Again, it doesn't happen quite like that, but no, they are too busy working to think about such things."

It suddenly occurred to me that he was telling me a lot about something which was supposed to be a secret. If all the people who were found not guilty were told, there wouldn't be much secret left.

"How many deferred proceedings cases lead to not guilty verdicts?"

"I do not have the precise figures available at present."

"Roughly, then."

"I don't do 'roughly' figures."

"Well, I'm going to go with 'one'. You want posterity to see that you went through the legal process but you don't care about it thinking that every case, until mine, produced a guilty verdict."

"Oh, not at all. Some people do not cope well with the long sleep and are not fit to be tried. They are sent for treatment. There are some 'Not Guilty' verdicts. But some who are 'Not Guilty', according to the jury, in our very fair system, but who clearly *are* guilty, are given this part of the induction. Some then choose execution."

"And you agree to that?"

"Oh, yes. Freedom of choice. Who are we to object?"

"And are you hoping that I'll choose execution?"

"It makes no difference to me. The verdict of the court was that you were Not Guilty. You might choose execution and you might choose to work in the mine. I shall respect your choice."

"In that case. I suggest that you show me what to expect on Level 98, That should help with the decision making."

"Quite so. That is the next step in the induction. But first, to put you fully in the mood, as it were, here is a quick look at what is outside. Please look at the screen on the wall."

On the screen, I saw vague shapes of buildings in a thick yellow fog, which glowed slightly as it slowly swirled about. He said, "For instruction purposes, that is the whole world. There might be some forest remnants, some mountains, some seas, where it is not so bad, but that appears to be the state of most areas of Earth. So far, we have not been successful in removing it. Ironically, adapted, mutated humans would probably do slightly better in it than we. But even if you were so inclined, and even if it were possible to escape, I doubt that you would want to be out in that."

"Right. Another point made and absorbed, Next."

"Of course. Now, for life on the ninety eighth level."

The screen changed to show the dark, dreary depths of Level 98.

Now I understood the execution choice. Replace the buildings and chemical fog with humans and dust, and you had the same bleak scene. Vast caverns, connected by long, low tunnels, through which we went on our tour of hell. Another irony was the mechanically repetitive listlessness of the workers as they toiled with pick and shovel and loaded the carts which rumbled along rails.

Clutching at straws, I said, "You mentioned support. Where would my workplace be?"

"Right there," he replied. "You would go about, assessing and discussing requirements." He actually leaned towards me as he added,"Right in the thick of it."

With a minimal eyebrow raising, I said, "Nice to see that some of these old phrases have survived."

"Oh, as I said," he smirked (yes, *smirked*), "we are using old language for your benefit. You would not understand the exchanges between robots."

"Probably as well," I said, a trifle sulkily. The prospect of being a support worker in the mine was doing nothing to improve my mood. Before, I had assumed that I'd be in a small office, out of the way, in a sort of old-fashioned, clerical, middle-class area. Wandering about in the dust, in the vicinity of the picks and shovels, and the people who were wielding them, was bringing on a dark depression.

But I wasn't going to slide onto the floor in defeat. Even if there was no hope of resistance, of rebellion, of revolution, I could fall back on that last tactic of the oppressed: I could be annoying.

"Right," I said, with as much brightness as I could raise. "How about the residential quarters?"

I peered at the next bit of film. It looked like the inside of an old hangar, but in which I could see immediately rows of beds and rows of sinks and cookers. People who had presumably finished a shift, moved with a variation of the mechanical listlessness.

"Communal living?" I asked.

"Yes."

Right. Soon, I was going to be at execution point or a different point which I couldn't yet see. But it seemed of vital importance that I detached myself and kept the brain working.

"The people who are sent for treatment. What happens to them?"

"We do our best. Sometimes, they recover."

"And are tried when they recover?"

"That would be the intention."

"So with the diseased, the injured and the incompetent, and the severely travel sick, and the late guilty verdict people, and the other guilty people, and those who choose execution, we seem to be heading towards a large percentage of people who are put into the ground."

"I do not have that information."

"Okay. I know the secret. Aren't you afraid that I'll tell those who don't know and start a big panic?"

"Oh, no. You trial people are always closely supervised. And robots can move very quickly. You would merely advance the date of your own conclusion."

"Ah, yes. My murder. I mustn't forget my impending appointment."

"Was your eventual, and possibly imminent, death such a big concern three hundred years ago? There is no difference here and now. Work well and stay well and you could have a long life."

"In the mines."

"Well, really. Such hypocrisy. You, or at least your ancestors, thought that it was perfectly acceptable for humans to work in mines. Why shouldn't machines think the same thing?"

"We didn't murder them when their efficiency dropped."

"You need to study history. Hundreds of thousands of people were slowly and agonisingly killed, by disease and by accidents, all in the pursuit of greater profits."

I didn't travel three hundred years to be lectured to by a machine. And I certainly didn't make the journey to work ninety eight floors down.

But then, being honest, I hadn't really made that journey through time. I had been dragged through time.

"I'd work and live on the ninety eighth level. No daylight? No fresh air?"

"As you saw, there is no daylight or fresh air outside. Humans destroyed all that. We provide clean air in your places of work and sleep. Be grateful for that."

Grateful? If you say so, boss.

"But remember," he continued, very smoothly, "that there is always the alternative. There would be no pain. You would merely resume your long sleep."

"That has been noted. I don't need reminders, or suggestions, and I particularly don't need encouragements. Besides, the induction isn't over. I still require information. For example, you mentioned some people who are not engaged in the labouring or support work. A small elite? I might want to be one of those. Tell me about them."

After a silence which lasted an immense number of milliseconds, I said, "Clearly a question which you prefer not to be asked. That makes the answer very desirable. Let's have it."

He was still looking like a servant who's been asked where the silver spoons have gone. Was he consulting internal reference books or higher authority? Or was he just flummoxed?

After his long pause, he said, "It is a little difficult to explain satisfactorily to you."

"Is that a defect in me, or in you?"

That didn't go down well. He said, somewhat aloofly, "The human brain has always been afflicted by, and severely handicapped by, extreme and irrational prejudices. . . ."

I held up my hand and said, "No. Stop there. I have had quite enough lectures for today, thank you. All that I want, and need, is information. The simplest way is, or should be, that I ask a question and you provide an answer. Let's try to confine this session to those limitations. I ask, you answer."

That wasn't just for me: I was sticking up for the whole human race. I didn't think much of the human race, but you know how it is when outsiders come in with harsh comments and disparaging attitudes. Stand together!

But I did want information without all the insulting explanations and digressions.

"Very well," Dentius P. Tuckington said, awash with haughtiness. "I shall do as you request."

"Thank you."

"The basic structure of any social system always consists of superior and inferior. Now, in both our aims of reducing greatly the members of the human race, while improving the remaining stock, we have separated the superior from the inferior. We look after the superior ones, we nurture them, we let them live in a pleasant zone, and we use them for breeding, ensuring that we always have a breeding stock of the highest quality."

He smiled again. The superior robot and one of the inferior humans.

He said, "There is still the popular choice of execution."

He didn't know that he had just placed the final straw. He had overplayed his hand. He had over-egged the pudding. My inferior brain was whirring.

"Right, machine. This is for all the inferior members of the human race. But specifically, for me. I won't go to the 98th level, and I won't be executed. There is the obvious third alternative, which you will very soon see to be suitable for me. It's time for your lesson. Let's begin with this: as it applies to humans, define inferior and superior."

"Those who scored highest in our tests were superior; those who scored lowest were inferior."

"And those in the middle?"

"There was no middle. Middles are a sign of weakness."

"But they exist. Three people called one, two and three. Two is in the middle. Two is neither one nor three. However, if two were to put his arms round one and three, he would be embracing oneness and threeness."

"Semantics. Sophistry."

"Which require a level of intelligence to be done properly. But there is a bigger point to be made about your tests. They provided evidence according to your standards. They did not provide proof. So, you have a breeding programme which is based on the evidence of some very prejudiced tests. The system is defective. The logical method would have been to assign tasks and observe, then assign again, and again, in a social structure which is fluid, in which people will effectively assign themselves. I lacked technical ability, I wasn't clever, I wasn't ambitious. The result was the clerical position to which I was suited. I wasn't happy with that, but I lacked the qualities to do anything about it. I was weak. But those defects didn't, don't, make me inferior."

"I anticipate that our test will establish your inferiority."

"Could an inferior human defeat a computer, a robot, in logical reasoning?"

"No."

I said, "It is time for you to learn. It is time for you to receive information. Playtime has finished. You are no longer Dentius P. Tuckington, prosecutor. You are a machine. Don't argue. Listen and learn."

I raised my finger. I wasn't acting. I wasn't grasping at a vague notion of escape. This was truth, and there is no mightier weapon than the truth.

"Firstly," I said, "just by way of introduction, you have based your assessment of the superiority and inferiority of humans on the basis of your tests. That fails all the tests of science, logic and even pragmatism. A high score in your tests might indicate superiority, but not the effects of that superiority. What will your superior person do?

"You have set aside as your superior humans a collection of test-passers, and are using them for your breeding programme. Really!

"Are you understanding this, machine? Massive blunders, which of course, for a machine, mean not only single errors, but system failures. All your attempts at reasoning are inherently faulty. Do you need more evidence? Well, here is a good one. All through this interview, you have been trying to ease me gently but firmly to the execution block. Admit it."

"I have several times presented that as a popular alternative to working in the mines."

"But your enthusiasm came from the source of your belief in my guilt. You are convinced that I am guilty."

"You can't be guilty. You passed all the lie detection tests."

"Indeed I did. Therefore, as confirmed by the jury, I am innocent."

"That is so."

"But isn't. I *am* guilty. But my innocence was firmly established by system defects and by your great incompetence."

"How was I incompetent?" It was almost a shout. He was worried. This was his existence, his reason for existence, at stake here.

"How?" I said. "You were disgracefully incompetent twice. *Twice.* TWICE! And you think that I'm an inferior human, fit only for low clerical work deep underground? Which, of course, adds to the incompetence."

"How? How was I incompetent?"

One very bothered machine.

"And now you are agitated," I said.

"I . . . can't be agitated."

"Because you're a machine. All of you. You're nothing but a pack of machines. That's all you are."

"We are not machines. We are creations of immense complexity, far beyond your comprehension. That is why we now control everything on this planet."

"But you're incompetent."

"How?"

First, let's do what you didn't do, which is to define poison. Now, three hundred years ago, there were substances which were not restricted, were not illegal, but which were, or were claimed to be, poisonous. Take the Fly Agaric Mushroom, which was a popular hallucinogenic source in Lapland. Popular with humans and reindeer. Humans knew that it could be harmful. Some Laplanders obtained diluted hallucinogenic benefits by drinking reindeer urine. Some compelled their wives to have it, and drank their wives' urine. So, a fine point to consider would be at what stage does passing the risk to someone else constitute murder or manslaughter. There were many others. Alcohol, tobacco, foods cooked at high heat, solvents and disinfectants, scented candles. Most were slowly-working carcinogenic things. Now, I mentioned earlier, that there were organic hallucinogenic substances on Op-Tec 4. So, let us suppose that someone wanted to teach someone a severe lesson on the inadvisability of consuming these substances. And have a small bit of revenge. A large and unexpected dose might do the trick. And if there were already too much of the substance, and other substances, in that person, there could be the danger of an overdose. That was carelessly not considered. I was incompetent. Very manslaughterish. But the point here is that the definition of poison can be a matter of no more than opinion.

"That brings us to your incompetence. Twice, crucially, you asked me the wrong questions. That is why I passed the lie detection test."

"Which two questions?"

"You asked me had I killed my wife."

"You replied that you had not done so, that she had killed herself, and that answer was accepted by the detection programme."

"Of course. She did kill herself. I placed her drink beside her, and she picked it up, and drank the poison. Therefore, she killed herself. It might be fallible logic, but still a logic which was entirely satisfactory to me, and the lie detector."

"What was the second question?"

"You asked me had I put poison in her coffee."

"Again, you replied that you had not, and again the detection programme was satisfied."

"Of course it was, because the answer was an honest one. I had prepared for the need to tell the truth, in case anything went wrong. I had anticipated the question. I had prepared for my trial. I couldn't bring myself to kill my wife, but I was willing to take a chance in teaching her a lesson. And there, clear and concise, is my confession."

"So you *did* put poison in your wife's coffee."

"No! Wake up, great and complex machine. The statement is wrong. The question was wrong. Ask the right question!"

There was a pause. A real one, of several seconds, just long enough for me to yell, "Come on, machine. Work it out!"

He said quietly, "Mr Cain. Did you put coffee in your wife's poison?"

"Yes," I replied. "And now I'm ready to have a look at this zone for superior humans. And I'd be very happy to do some lecturing on logic and reasoning to any inferior robots that can be found."

# # #

TWIST

A CHARLES WAINWRIGHT FISHER STORY

Benjamin Weaver didn't intend to kill his wife and her latest man. But he did intend to hide on New Terra 12, amongst sixty seven thousand robots who were busy making the place habitable for humans. Finding him was going to be a big challenge.

CHAPTER 1

I should have been on the full alert as soon as Mr Stafford asked me to 'pop down to New Terra 12 and have a look.'

Cornelia and Sindula, happening to be around at the time, exchanged a smile. My two favourite colleagues, my two close friends, often had these treacherous moments.

I frowned.

"Have a look at what?" I asked.

"Oh, just a murderer, nice chap apparently, has made a run for it and gone to New Terra 12."

I was not familiar with New Terra 12. I said, "If you must give me the relevant information in spoonfuls, would you mind making it a larger spoon?"

"The man's name is Benjamin Weaver. A legal administrator of unvarying ordinariness and no career ambition. Unfortunately, he had not married well. He had married an ambitious woman in Marketing who was briefly attracted to someone without ambition, then detested him for being someone without ambition. She relieved her feelings on the matter by spending all the available money from both their incomes. In effect, Benjamin was permitted a small allowance for necessities, and his own small pleasures. He had tolerated, or at least suppressed his rage about, his wife's behaviour for several years. To him, it was a simple matter: he loved her. 'I'm not perfect,' he explained. 'It would be wrong to expect perfection in her.'"

The general view in our little team was that although he was theoretically, and commendably, correct, he was rather overdoing the tolerance and submission.

"Anyway," Mr Stafford resumed, "arriving home unexpectedly one night and finding his wife with another man, Benjamin, as the old expression puts it, 'lost it'. He wasn't a violent man, and even now intended no violence. He merely wished to remove these two people from his bedroom. In order to effect this, he took the simple course of picking each one up and throwing him, then her, out of the window. In doing this, he insisted that he had quite forgotten that the windows, for safety reasons, were permanently locked and needed a great deal of force to break them; and that his apartment was on the seventy-eighth floor. What is impregnable plastic against a kind and forgiving man who has briefly 'lost it'? Mrs Weaver and her friend were dead before they began their long descent.

"Then, waking from his trance, Benjamin Weaver ran; that being a general term to cover all sorts of methods of travel over some immense distances. In his case, to New Terra 12."

"How new is New Terra 12?"

"It is still in the early development stage."

"I think that I'd like the relevant information in a ladle now."

"Mr Weaver has apparently decided that a good place to hide is amongst a lot of latest design robots who are currently engaged in mainly heavy physical work."

"How many robots."

"Sixty seven thousand."

"All self-supervised?"

"Yes. There is an occasional visit from an engineer or a project manager to check on things, and there is an occasional delivery of materials, but the latter is generally fully-automated. Otherwise, at this stage, the only inhabitants are the robots."

"And Mr Weaver."

"Yes."

"And you want me to find him."

"Yes. It shouldn't be difficult. He'll be the one who eats, laughs, cries, visits the bathroom, so to speak. All those non-robot things."

"Yes, but if he's doing his best to look like a robot, he's not going to walk around eating burgers and laughing, is he?"

"Well, no. And that's the challenge. You like challenges. This is a good one."

"And if I find him, what do you want me to do? Persuade him to turn himself in?"

"Well, as usual, in keeping with our cover role, your job is to arrest him. However, in accordance with our normal procedures, and reason for our existence, I want you to give him the improving nudge. That might lead to a voluntary submission. And it might not."

"And if the improved Benjamin decides that it would be better all round if he stayed on New Terra 12?"

"Your task is to improve, not to control the results of that improvement. You see, you're still thinking in the old human way, before your own improvement, of thinking that the success of a task is the measurable, assessable, result. Your old job required you to find and tag miscreants. Your success was not measured by your finding the miscreant and persuading him to surrender himself to whichever authority wanted him. If you had found your person settled into a life of humanitarian good deeds, it would not have had any effect on what you did. For your task to be successful, you had to tag him. And you always did."

"I'd prefer not to be reminded of what a bad egg I was."

He smiled one of his whimsiest smiles. "You had to be improved to see and think that. But before the change, you did what you had been instructed to do."

"That's been the basis for a claim of innocence for many people, for a very long time."

"And in many cases, it's the simple truth. It might indicate some very bad qualities in the people who make the claim, but it's still the truth."

I nodded. He was always right. I decided to return to practical matters. The sort that are mundane to those who aren't involved, like my two smug adopted sisters.

"If this place is still being developed, where am I going to live?"

"Ah. Now, that's the good news. I mean the even better news. You will be living in a delightful, entirely computerised hotel. You won't lack for anything for your comfort. And there is a voice-controlled car. There. You should enjoy it."

I looked at my colleagues. "Anyone fancy a..."

They used faces and hands to gesture apologetically.

"Sorry," Mr Stafford interrupted. "They're off on another

job. Otherwise . . . but anyway, I'm sure you can manage. Any problems, let me know."

"Hmm. And what are you two going to be doing?"

Cornelia told me. A sort of benevolent sting operation in the mountains of Drusilla.

No wonder they didn't need me.

"We'll be working hard, too," added Sindula.

With a couple of raised eyebrows, I looked at her until she grinned.

And that is how our separate tasks began.

CHAPTER 2

The robots were doing a great job on New Terra 12. I had to admit that. I was very impressed with the development of the place. But there was still something about it all that was, well, sort of *wrong*.

"You must discard all your prejudices," said Barnard Flook, the executive something-or-other who briefed me before I left. That was more easily said than done. My prejudices weren't like a lot of guests who won't leave when the party is over. *Thank you. Thank you for coming. Yes, I enjoyed it. Please put that back where you found it. Come on, guys. Homes to go to. Goodnight. Goodnight.*

It just doesn't work that way.

Anyway, not being entirely convinced isn't necessarily an indication of prejudice. You could make out an equally strong case for immediate full approval. I had an open mind and wanted to keep it open. That is, I believe, a vital part of my work. I'm still not entirely sure what my work is, but I know that having an open mind is a vital part of it. A sort of roaming detective and putter-right might give you some idea of what I, we, do. Cornelia, Sindula and I are given our tasks by Mr Stafford and we go off, singly, in a pair, or all three, and do our best. We are at our best when we are all together, three great brains combining and complementing one another. Something like that.

Although Mr Stafford was several thousand years old, and had travelled and learned extensively, he liked to use quaint, old-fashioned, but relatively recent, phrases. "Just pop over there and have a look round," was his instruction to me about a difficult task on a small world six thousand light years away.

Even with modern travel methods, at least that gives you time to read the briefing notes on the journey.

Immense distances. It's odd that the greater the distance, the easier it is to find people. A little 'while ago, I found Miss Barbara Murgatroyd alone on a remote little asteroid, having previously failed to find her at a large cocktail party for the rich and famous.

But as soon as Benjamin Weaver had sorted out his thinking equipment, he did a bit of research and made a very sensible, but complicated and ambitious, choice. New Terra 12 had a population of sixty seven thousand robots and no people, and Benjamin decided to make a slight change to that. He wasn't very fond of people, and a large number of them were now a danger to him. He would live and work amongst the robots. What better place to hide? All he had to do was to behave as a robot.

But surely, you are thinking, the robots would know in about a thousandth of a second that he wasn't a robot. They *might*. But what of it? In the first place, these robots were very precisely programmed to do the relevant work, not to assess other robots, not to be curious. In the second place, which is really part two of the first place, having been precisely programmed, these robots didn't care about the other robots. Or, in this case, human. You could have put a herd of elephants amongst them, but so long as the elephants didn't prevent the robots from performing their set tasks, they wouldn't care. In effect, because of the irrelevance to what the robots were doing, they wouldn't even notice.

Some people still struggle with that one. At this level of robot, things which are not included in a robot's programming are simply not seen. In effect, things which are not considered to be relevant do not exist.

Sometimes, I think that humans might have the same sort of programming.

But back to me and my task.

It was very clear and simple. I was to find Benjamin Weaver and subtly improve him. influence him, persuade, if you like. But always with subtle changes. That's what has been misunderstood through thousands of years. You can't drag people into, let's say, heaven. You can't force them into it. People make choices, and then encounter the consequences. Take those choices away, and there is no longer the challenge, the great test, or series of tests. Subtle influence, always.

My thoughts about his circumstances, my understanding my sympathy, my *prejudices*, had nothing to do with it. That was how it had always been with me, from long before I was recruited by Mr Stafford, when I was an insurance investigator, with very limited responsibilities. It is important to avoid distraction by personal opinions and feelings. Just do your job and leave others to do theirs.

But that is the strange thing about my work. Mr Stafford runs a sort of detective agency which is nothing like a detective agency. In the first place, you could say that he looks at the full picture. In this case, Benjamin Weaver was just one player in a large cast of wife, friend, sixty seven thousand robots and a world in second stage terra-forming, which meant vast corporations who saw the available Galaxy as one vast potential property development area. Of course, there are always the politicians and religious organisations, but let's not over-egg this particular pudding. I'm trying in my way to keep this simple.

In the second place, you could say that Mr Stafford wanted me to suggest to Mr Weaver that he turn himself in, provided that it was clearly in Mr Weaver's interests for me to do so, which was highly unlikely. I didn't doubt that he already had some manoeuvres ready to work in Mr Weaver's favour, but when he said that he wanted me to pop down and have a look, in a way that is exactly what he wanted me to do.

Currently, the only visitors to New Terra 12 were maintenance checkers, quality controllers, project managers; all of whom visited occasionally in order to make sure that everything was going as it should be going. The Silvetti Mark 9s didn't require it; they even checked and serviced themselves; but these things have to be done. For the benefit of these visitors, and now me, there was the hotel. As one engineer put it, you go into a large robot and try to relax. This, too, was impressive: a small hotel which talked to me, with a soft woman's voice, and listened to me, which filled my bath, and cooked and served my meals. And none of this came from certain computer functions in various locations; the whole hotel spoke, listened, served, always just to the side, as though someone were standing beside me.

"Two minutes," said the same engineer. "Two minutes and you'll be chatting away to her and wondering whether there is some way of seducing her."

"Ah," I said, nodding sagely, Man of the Galaxy and all that.

I had to admit that he had a point, and I could easily believe that more impressionable and weak-willed people might succumb. In my case, I had one big advantage: I detest having things done for me. I don't even like being waited on in restaurants. I can't stand the whole servant, menial, thing. And I certainly don't think of robots as inferior beings, whose sole purpose is to do jobs for humans. However, that would lead to a massive digression. Another time, perhaps.

I decided immediately that my relationship with the hotel was going to be a warm but respectable, and respectful, one, and I intended to make the best use of her, its, ah, what the hell, her, knowledge.

"Charles Wainwright Fisher," I said. "Here for a few nights, and days."

"Welcome, Mr Fisher. The booking is in order. Ask me for anything that you want. I provide everything within my resources capability."

"Thank you, er, hotel." That wouldn't do. "For the duration of my short visit, your name will be Mabel."

Was that a pause? "Yes, sir. I shall be Mabel."

"Tell me about yourself, Mabel."

That was a mistake. After about an hour of technical background, I said, "Thank you, Mabel. That is sufficient knowledge about that. Tell me about the work which is being done on New Terra 12."

"New Terra 12 is an Earth-compatible planet in the vicinity of Placus V, a star of medium magnitude, which is a human term. The planet is smaller than Earth, with two curiously balancing moons, which assist in providing similar conditions to those on Earth. However, New Terra 12 is somewhat younger than Earth, and Earth itself is suitable for human habitation only by the slightest combinations and coincidences. which led to the decision to make New Terra 12 a relatively safe planet."

"By sending a large number of robots to prepare it for human habitation?"

"Yes. This requires great skill and judgment, all of it done by humans, of course. You see, the planet must be made relatively safe while not preventing those dangerous occurrences that make a planet such as Earth relatively safe. It is no good, in effect, putting a cork in a volcano or preventing the planet from wriggling around and stretching. The lava must be discharged, the tectonic plates must move. There must be evolution and extinction. In short, the planet must have its tantrums and make itself comfortable. But in this case, it will be done rather more quickly than it was on Earth, where there were no property developers eager to make profits. At least not for the first few billion years."

"Hm. I understand that. What are the robots doing then?"

"Some of them are organising, minimising, rearranging. There will be a Vesuvius equivalent, but no Pompeii or other adjacent places of habitation. There will be only future farm-land to benefit from the outpouring."

"A bit like altering history."

"Yes. We are learning from past mistakes, and correcting them. Not removing anything. I believe that the old term was damage limitation. Where tsunamis are likely to strike, there will be coastal mountain ranges. That sort of thing. But of course, always, there must be the correct balance of rela-tionships because everything is connected. Move something a bit to the right and you could upset the entire ecological balance. Therefore, you must move things in groups, moun-tains, forests, plains, animals, insects, all in the right combi-nations and environments. The ideas, the anticipations of problems, the vague solutions, all come from humans. But the robots have to work it all out, as they go. It is a huge responsibility."

"Are the robots aware of that?"

No. They don't even know what a responsibility is. They do as they are instructed."

"But in many cases, surely the aim can be no more than a desired outcome?"

"That is what all aims ought to be."

"You mean, don't give someone a job, then supervise it to the last detail, depriving him or her of the pleasure and benefits of creativity and problem-solving."

"Exactly so."

It occurred to me that although I was a long way from trying to seduce the hotel, I was having an interesting discussion with her.

"I am enjoying our conversation," I said. "Is your part of it all down to programming?"

"Yes. I am designed to appeal to your stereotyping and categorising needs, based on the character profile of you that was provided for me."

"So, a bit like finding a matrimonial partner by computer."

"Yes. I have made myself what you would like me to be."

"But you seem to be thinking, having you own thoughts."

"All part of the reassuring illusion, I'm afraid."

Even the comment was part of it. It was time for a change. "Do you know why I am here?"

"Yes. I have been fully informed of the purpose of your visit."

"Will you be able to help me?"

"Only within myself. I have information and methods of communication within me. But otherwise, I am completely ignorant and incapable."

"I understand, I think. Now, a hot bath is in order, followed by a long and leisurely dinner, a film and a long sleep, ready for an arduous day tomorrow."

"I shall attend to all those things, arranging appropriate

choices where relevant, except for the matter of your sleep. Apart from the supply of gentle undulations and pleasant music, I have no control over your sleep."

"The gentle undulations and the music should work very well, thank you."

I smiled at ... the hotel in which I was sitting.

CHAPTER 3

When I left the hotel the next morning, with a pleasant little breakfast inside me, I was so well-rested and relaxed that I didn't feel quite right about venturing into this new planet in search of Benjamin Weaver. I wanted to stroll around, enjoy watching the robots, have an occasional rest.

Oh, well.

Last night, before an excellent dinner, Mabel had provided an important bit of background. As usual with a planet to be inhabited, there had been the usual worldwide (Earth being the world) negotiations over what would belong to whom on the new world. A century or so ago, this nearly produced the first Galaxy war. It wasn't as straightforward as you might think. For example, people who had lived in deserts for thousands of years thought that it was their turn to live in somewhere damp and green. On the other hand, they insisted on the right of ownership of their oil supplies. Eventually, other planets had to be brought in to consider the claims and make rulings. Those rulings had to be accepted; otherwise the new planet would be destroyed before anyone had even settled on it.

The most significant feature of the eventual settlement was that each new Earth would have a central computer-factory-mineral store, which would use statistics, to be analysed for veracity, in order to allocate all resource requirements. It was a great idea, but humans never let the system work properly. Humans always look for the loophole, the unlocked door, the opportunity to have more, or better, than someone else. However, it's an ill wind that blows nobody any good. Out of mistrust and cooking the statistical books grew large departments, then agencies, of accountants, statisticians and technical analysts and advisers

I had a car for the visit. A New Terra Rova. Who thinks of these imaginative names? It looked pretty sturdy, for which I was glad. Last night, Mabel had told me about the wild animals on New Terra 12. Some of them were very wild. The worst one, so far as she knew (she said that with a disturbing emphasis) was the provisionally-named Minotaur. You hardly need me to tell you that this was a particularly belligerent and territory-sensitive bull with a fondness for rising onto two legs and running at its foe or victim. In choosing and accomplishing this bovine variation, it had not eschewed such old-fashioned features as the blood-curdling bellow and the internal-rearranging goring.

I said, "I doubt that people will want to share the planet with those things."

"I understand that those animals which are permitted to remain will be safely confined behind electric fences."

Oh, electric fences. What could go wrong with that?

"And the other animals?"

"Accelerated extinction."

"Mabel, is there any difference between accelerated extinction and killing?"

"I have not been provided with that information. However, in view of the certainty with which death follows killing, I should be willing to believe that the outcome will be the same. But to a large extent, it would depend on the speed of the acceleration."

I could imagine it. An expensive and enthusiastic, but short, hunting spree. A guy with his his gun still smoking saying, "Where shall we go next?" What a great Galaxy. Always, somewhere, land to be grabbed, buildings to be erected, minerals to be extracted, and animals to be used or killed.

"There are also many different small animals and insects, about which little or nothing is known. Unless the information is provided, I don't have the information. As your documentation emphasises, everything that you do is at your own risk."

"What documentation?"

Mr Stafford doesn't bother with documentation before he sends us out on perilous tasks.

"I believe that it is in your welcome pack. It's one of those legal liability things. No-one who has any connection of any sort with anything on or in or near this planet shall insist or otherwise claim that there is any liability for any accident, disease. . . ."

`"Yes. Thank you, Mabel. I know the sort of thing. Well, you can be sure that I shall be doing my utmost to prevent all circumstances which could be considered liabilitous."

"That word is not in my information store."

"I know. I made it up."

"Ah. That sort of thing is not advised. It leads to confusion, which can lead to misunderstandings, which can lead to regrettable occurrences."

"You mean liabilitous events?"

"Probably."

Mabel resumed the lecture. As she had said, her knowledge was limited to the information that had been provided by humans. And humans had done the minimum necessary for starting the development of this world. They could take all the photographs that they wanted from above. They could do all their analyses from there, too. They came, saw some bits and pushed off. Send in the terraforming robots and they'll sort everything out.

"But," I said, with some terseness, I admit, "will the aerial photographs and film, and will all the scientific analyses, tell me, for instance, which bits of wild zone are swamp and which thorns will inject deadly poison into me?"

"I don't know. I have not been informed."

"That is so frustrating, Mabel. And not just on a personal level. Here you are, with so much technical ability, running on very low power as it were, because all that you have been given is a few bits of information from people who arrived, had a quick look round and left."

"I have the benefit of one major defect. I can receive information through speech. *You* can provide information."

"But surely all your information must be inserted as authorised and factual. You don't have the power to interpret. I might tell you lies or make mistakes, or merely state an opinion, believing it to be the truth."

"I do not have information about these things. I am programmed to receive and impart information. And to provide services for you. That is all."

"Right. What if I come back from one of my searches and tell you that the Minotaurs are timid and docile?"

"In that case, both items of information would be stored separately and presented as alternative findings."

I laughed. I was enjoying this conversation with someone who was completely free of prejudices or any other influences. "Mabel," I said, "you have the delightful honesty that is essential to all worthwhile relationships, and which would end almost all relationships at a very early stage."

"No credit is due. It is how I am made."

The lecture was resumed. Although much was said by

everyone about the importance of dealing with the land, the climate, the animals, the plants and everything else in such a way that the ecological balance was maintained, the first priority, which had a strong relegating effect on all the others, was to develop the place and sell houses and factories. In short, the ecological balance was to be maintained provided that it didn't have an adverse effect on profits.

It was the sort of lecture that soon reaches its maximum irritation level.

"Thank you, Mabel," I said abruptly. "That is very helpful, but that will do for now."

You might remember that before my huge digression backwards (regression?), it was the next day, and I was about to set off in my special vehicle.

I decided to start with something easy. I drove to the nearest town. The car was really another form of robot, leaving me with just a bit of steering to do, with an override mechanism waiting eagerly for me to make a complete hash of a manoeuvre. The roads were straight and smooth, their purpose at this stage being a practical one, which was to enable the robots to move around and to move materials around. Another road was being built to join my road and I had the pleasure of driving along and seeing people actually working on a road. Those guys looked like the real thing (apart from the fact that they were actually working), with bulging muscles, lumberjack shirts and tight jeans. I wondered whether any of them met robot floozies after work. Then I remembered that these robots didn't have an 'after work'. They would stop work when the work was finished. And that would be a long time.

Just to be clear, all these man-robots, except a few in the various mines and pits, were the latest, thoroughly realistic designs. They just behaved rather stiffly, rather like old-fashioned butlers or waiters, but doing manual work. The others were really complex machines for the very heavy work. With the constant desire for money, and space, there would be urgency on both parts for people to start moving here soon, and it was inevitable that there would be a long transitional period when houses would be sold and inhabited while robots were still working on things. And there would always be some for maintenance work. It made people feel better to have robots who looked like people.

By 'town', I mean a lot of houses, service centres and communal recreation and shopping areas. Towns without the ugly bits. This was going to be a residential planet, easing the problem of overcrowded Earth a little, and of course making a lot of money for the usual businesses.

I entered a pleasant, to be pleasant, neatly residential area, where robots were rolling out front lawn artificial turf, erecting fences and planting plastic flowers. I stopped the car and approached one of the robots, who was patting down turf.

"Good morning," I said, giving him my friendly, but not condescending, smile.

"I have no opinion on the quality of the morning. Have you been allocated to work here?"

"No. I'm a human."

"I do not know." The robot turned back to his task.

"I'm looking for another human."

He consulted his brain. He hadn't been programmed for conversations which required any thought. "I do not know," he said and returned to the turf.

One down, sixty six thousand, nine hundred and ninety nine to go. And one human. Well, I consoled myself, he should stand out amongst this lot of dummies. But this was going to be boring. Were they all exactly the same as the turf-layer, or did different tasks require the insertion of different characters?

Where was a cop robot when you needed one?

I was the nearest thing to a cop, and I didn't have a clue. I spent the rest of that day, which was six hours longer than an Earth day I'll have you know, driving round, walking over to robots and trying to have conversations with them. The only good thing was that the more I saw of these robots, the more I saw how imperfect they were, because they had been made almost perfect. Humans aren't perfect. They are misshapen, wrinkly, floppy-stomached, round-shouldered. Even muscular road-builders have protruding middles, sagging over their trousers which are several sizes too small. Humans have nose hair and ear hair. They have rambling eyebrows. Sometimes, they have rambling eyes.

The robots were too smooth and too well-proportioned. Calling them dummies was an accurate description, when you think of those that stand in the clothes shops in the malls, narrow-waisted and slender-fingered. All that I had to do was travel about, looking closely, until I saw someone with nose hair or one of the other human features.

But sixty seven thousand noses is a lot to scrutinise, and even precisely programmed robots might resent that sort of close attention. I decided to have a stroll round, generally observing, while I waited for inspiration. That usually works.

So far as I could see, New Terra 12 was going to be the usual home from home that humans like. They didn't mind having interesting features to visit, but they didn't want them encroaching on their normality. Wild animals were to be looked at, shot, and perhaps eaten, at least the tender ones, but they were to know their places and stay in them, preferably behind electric fences. Unless they were small, furry, cute and cuddly.

Rising above the houses, I could see a skeletal mall. Robots scurried over and through it like insects. The robots were building everything: houses, malls, parks and countryside. They weren't so much building the countryside as tidying it, landscaping it, organising it. And, of course, in many cases, removing it for houses, malls and parks. Soon, the estate agents wouldn't be able to control their impatience, and the show homes would be opened and the sales would begin. Then, the first residents would arrive and sit at their windows and grumble about all the robots. Nothing against robots, of course, very useful in their way, but you just didn't want to see them all over the place or so close, looking as though they were entitled to be wherever they chose.

Realising that I was hungry, I had an important thought. One of those breakthrough moments. My only supplier of food was Mabel. Nothing else was open and functioning yet, except the busy robots. Therefore, for food, *this* human would have to go to Mabel. And that immediately raised the question: where did *that* human go for his food?

After hurrying home, as it were, I asked Mabel. She metaphorically shook her head. "I provide food only for authorised visitors," she replied.

"But you receive all the authorisation details electronically, as data, and the arrival of the authorised person fits in with the details. But do you *know* that I am Charles Wainwright Fisher?"

"No. Only that you are what the authorisation data have told me to expect."

"Has anyone arrived early, or left early? Have you noticed excessive consumption of food? Any missing grocery items?"

"No. Everything has been exactly as it should be."

"Come on, Mabel. Help me. I'm looking for a human who is, presumably, hiding amongst your sixty seven thousand robots. Where do you think he might be?"

"I do not think. I do not have the capability. I provide services. I am a hotel."

"But you must be thinking to have this conversation."

"No. Set responses already in me, put there by programmers who anticipated your categories of questions. I am a building and a machine."

All very clear. And yet. I sighed. It was like the illusion of the setting sun. We know that the sun isn't really sinking below the horizon, and that it's all a matter of Earth's spinning; but we still see the sun sinking below the horizon and we still talk of its setting and going down. Even now, with almost unlimited travel around the Galaxy, people still have fixed Earth ideas about North and South, up and down, top and bottom. The Arctic is at the top and Antarctica is at the bottom. Other than as a remote and irrelevant scientific fact, to be tossed aside with all the others, they can't accept the reality that there is no up or down in the Universe, no North and South, no top and bottom. Those are just names, based on our need to have tops and bottoms and on assumptions of superiority.

I have a simple approach to annoyingly complex problems: put them to one side, have a nice meal and relax. Eventually, provided that you relax sufficiently, the answer will arrive. I asked Mabel to provide a simple spaghetti and tomato sauce, with garlic bread and a soft red wine.

"Yes, sir. And a small apple pie, followed by Dolcelatte cheese?"

"Not very small. Otherwise, excellent suggestions. Thank you, Mabel."

"I suggest half an hour, allowing you time for a bath and a change of clothes. There are plenty in your wardrobe."

I was beginning to have a struggle with my conscience. I could approach this task with careful thoroughness, perhaps interview each of the sixty seven thousand robots, and have some very pleasant, very relaxing evenings with Mabel, with the additional interest each day of watching the steady construction of New Terra 12.

"No!" I told myself sternly. "You have a very special role with some very special people. It isn't to be misused."

I understood myself perfectly and obeyed myself. But I could still enjoy what wasn't really avoidable for a few days.

It was while enjoying my bath, and trying halfheartedly to think as Benjamin Weaver might think, that I had a rather disturbing thought. Whereas the general policy for those humans who visited the planet, and for those who would be living here, was to avoid any dangerous encounters with the wild animals, someone who was being hunted and who needed to provide his own food would be exactly where no-one else wanted to be.

A little self-consciously, I said, "Mabel?"

"Yes, sir." She sounded so close. I slid a little deeper under the suds.

"What are the robots doing about the wild animals?"

"According to my information, they are constructing nature reserves, parks, natural habitats and hunting areas."

"Presumably, all these areas will have protective fencing round them."

"Yes, sir. There will be perimeter fencing to keep them from the rest of the planet, and internal fencing to keep them from the housing estates which will be a part of the development of the natural ecological system."

"The wild animals can watch the humans behind their fences."

"No, sir. The intention..."

"I know. I know. I was being sarcastic. Building housing estates is nothing to do with the natural ecological system."

"Apparently some people want to be so close in their observing that they want to live in the midst of it."

"At which point, it is all ruined. But never mind. I must keep my focus. It is clear, Mabel, that after a couple of days of searching amongst the robots, I must go into the wild places in my pursuit of this human."

"It is not recommended, sir."

"I know, but I have a very special role, and I must not be deterred by danger. I must be bold and determined."

"Very good, sir. Now, I recommend brisk drying and dressing. Your pasta is almost ready. Would you like me to dry you, sir?"

"What?" I was embarrassed.

"With warm air, sir. Just stand up and I'll quickly remove the water."

"Stand up. Okay."

The water didn't go down a plug hole. It disappeared quickly through long slits all round the bath, as though sucked very powerfully.

"Please stretch your arms out, sir, for the maximum effect."

"Ah. Right." I stopped my feeble attempt to cover myself and stretched out my arms. The warm air, just short of hot, dried me in seconds. I was beginning to enjoy it when Mabel reminded me again about the pasta. "Right," I said. "I'll just slip on some casual evening wear and be right with you."

"You *are* right with me, sir. You can't be anywhere else until you leave the hotel."

"Good point," I said, imperturbably amiable, putting on a silk dressing gown and sitting at the table. "Er, any serviettes, Mabel? A few, please. Probably naked would be more appropriate when I eat spaghetti and tomato sauce. This dressing gown doesn't stand a chance."

"Cleaning it will be no problem, sir. Enjoy your meal."

The trolley rolled across the floor and stopped by the table. I took my time, pushed aside my plans for the search and enjoyed a delicious meal.

CHAPTER 4

Two days later, I stood looking at my available clothing and said, "Mabel, reluctant though I am to do this, I must say that three days of talking to robots, trying to elicit simple information, has put me in the mood for the great outdoors."

"Isn't that where you have been, sir?"

"No. Well, yes. I have been outdoors. It's an old expression, meaning out in the hills and woods."

"Ah. The wild animal plan."

"Yes, although I am hoping that there won't be much wild animal involvement, apart from those small squirrelly things, and I trust that there will be plenty of robots to come to my aid in an emergency."

"Sir, you might want to check on that. It is probable that the robots have been programmed only to perform their set tasks. Rescuing you would not occur to them, and, not being in their programming, would constitute a failure in their programming."

"You mean that rescuing a human would be punishable by repair?"

"Perhaps, sir. I merely draw your attention to certain restrictions which might be of importance to you."

"Thank you, Mabel. What I'd like you to do now is your best in rigging me out for a visit to the wild side, with whatever you can manage in the form of provisions, tools and weapons."

"That will be a challenge, sir."

"Do your best. That is all that you can do. Apart from less than best." You have to be quick with robots, or they'll always have the last, correcting word.

"Sir," Mabel said about two minutes later. "I apologise for

the long delay. I have done my best. The items are laid out on your bed."

The clothing consisted of several sets of casual wear. No anoraks, no walking boots, not even a hat. Why would there be? Until now, the only visitors had been reviewing technicians. There were no tools. Mabel healed, mended, cured herself. In case of catastrophe, she had her own back-up systems. I could do with one of those. As for the cutlery...

"Mabel," I called, a bit testily now. "Is all the cutlery plastic?"

"Yes, sir."

"But what about slicing meat, that sort of thing?"

"Such implements are an integral part of me. They can't be removed."

"A plastic knife won't be much use in the wild woods."

"No, sir."

"You think that I shouldn't to do this, don't you?"

"I do not think, sir. I merely provide a service."

"Well, I shall try, Mabel. If it looks too dangerous, if I'm worried about it, then I'll come straight back."

"The food which I packed will last for a couple of days. After that it will become stale and mouldy."

"Do you know which plants are safe to eat?"

"No, sir. I have some information about their appearance for the benefit of visitors, but nothing relating to edibility."

"Do you know which animals are best for eating?"

"No, sir. The same answer, more or less, as for the previous question."

While I packed my few items into the Rova, my expectations, even my hopes, weren't high. I wasn't helped in this by the feeling all over me of Mabel's disapproval. It was like leaving an anxious wife or mother. In this case, I was leaving an anxious hotel.

"I shan't take any risks," I reassured her. "And I'll be back in a couple of days at the most."

"Goodbye, sir. Enjoy your trip. Take care."

"I shall." And off I went, the jaunty, what-ho, traveller, armed with a plastic knife and wearing clothes which had been designed for pottering about in a hotel. Actually, as you probably know, or have guessed, influencing detectives are not sent all over the Galaxy to chase miscreants without some form of protection. I did have a small, mild weapon for emergencies. But it would struggle against anything in the elephant or rhinoceros size category, or in the tiger or leopard anger category, and it wouldn't help me to build a shelter.

At that point, with utter predictability, it began to rain. It follows me all over the Galaxy. It really does. On the vast desert plains of Koros, which had been dry for thousands of years, it rained shortly after my arrival. I thought the locals were going to start worshipping me.

As I drove through the streets, aiming roughly at what I thought was the wild zone, I continued to maintain my close scrutiny of the robots' noses and ears. Just in case. Occasionally, I stopped the car and tried to engage one of them in conversation, but they just wanted to go on with cementing bricks and laying turf. Sort of pre-union humans.

In case anyone is thinking what a reckless fool I was, I assure you that I went pretty slowly towards the wild zone. My plan was to continue my search amongst the robots who were working out that way, and on the way to it. I kept meandering off into little tours around partially constructed malls and parks, partly because I might find Mr Weaver, and partly because I was not keen to leave relative safety. Yes, this adventurer of the Galaxy was reluctant to leave the developing housing estates. Some of them had their turf down now, and little bushes and flowers, and they looked so *safe* that I was tempted just to carry on strolling about, doing a relaxed investigation.

But we don't work that way. Our small team has unwritten, unspoken even, codes. We are a brother-and-sisterhood. A little family. And Mr Stafford's standards are ours. The pursuit of Benjamin Weaver was not led by money, revenge, or even legal considerations. It was the rightness of the thing. Regardless of the circumstances, he had done something which was wrong, and he should be gently persuaded to face the consequences, in one form or another. It was a sort of preparation for the karmatic afterlife. Cause and effect. Act and consequence. To Mr Stafford, all these people who did wrong things were like children who had to be taught that whatever they did had a rebounding effect on themselves.

The wild zone didn't appear suddenly. Beyond the developing towns, there were large areas of storage facilities for the robots' materials, giving the new world an even more Earth-like appearance. There were yards and immense vehicles, sort of idiot machines, that drilled, dug and carried. Was it my imagination or did the other robots treat the big machines with a certain contemptuous condescension? Probably imagination.

I looked closely in these outer parts, where there were fewer robots, big, muscular fellows, some of whom stopped and stared in real redneck style. It wouldn't have surprised me to see one spit. After all, it's all down to the programming. You can make your robot be whatever you want it to be, and do whatever you want it to do. You just insert the personality, with all its idiosyncracies, good and bad. Personality-writing for robots is one of the best-paid careers in robotics.

But apart from being closer to the wild zone, this wasn't a

good place for a small and gentle guy to hide. He would stand out amongst these big butch guys.

I stopped the car and went over to a group of these redneck robots.

"Hi. I'm a human, and I'm looking for another human."

Precisely programmed robots make very effective rednecks. There was no response. The question meant nothing to them. "What work are you doing?" I said.

"We are preparing the ground for an animal observation, testing and assessment facility. Then we shall build the facility."

That removed the redneck illusion. "And will you catch the animals?"

"That will be done by other workers with appropriate skills."

"Do you mean robots?"

"What are robots?"

"Ah. Just another name for workers. I meant no humans."

"What are humans?"

The wild zone was beckoning. I said, "Nothing to worry about. Carry on with your work."

I could see that the robot didn't understand how to carry on with its work; it just carried on with its work. I was starting to miss Mabel. It would have been nice to have her with me.

What did you take on your adventure into the wild zone?

Oh, the usual things that could be arranged: clothing, tools, provisions, my hotel.

Soon, the material depots and containers were fewer and I was entering the wild zone. For a while, the effect was reduced by the wide roads and ravaged undergrowth which showed the routes and main areas of activity so far of the robots out here. I stuck with them for a while because they were at least taking me farther into where I wanted to be. But when I reached a large working area, a sort of plateau, bustling with robots, large machines, coils of fencing, and many other things that you need for organising a wild zone, I decided that the time had come to park the car and go walking. I had a look round the working area, but could not see anything resembling my human being. I was sure that the attempts to have conversation, and his inability to work as the robots did, would have driven him out on his own.

The rain eased to a light drizzle. Clearly this area had plenty of rain because the trees and foliage were of the large, jungle, variety. Many of the plants resembled very large water lilies, with white flowers and smooth leaves. There were ferns as big as young trees. As for the trees, they were immense trunks; the rest of the stuff was well beyond my range, up there somewhere.

It was after three steps that I realised I had let my breezy confidence overrule my common sense. What I lacked was the most important thing for any expedition or exploration: information. I had no map or relevant equipment. I had no knowledge of which plants were poisonous, and to what extent; and, if poisoned, I had no knowledge of what to do about it. I knew that there were some wild animals, but I didn't know whether there were any of those dangerous centipedey things that like to live in jungles. Or very large spiders. Or snakes. And very large spiders on another planet might leap out of the trees; they might have very large webs that could trap someone of my size.

I didn't even know how big this particular wild zone was. And I didn't have any idea of where Benjamin Weaver might be, apart from away from places where he could be easily found and near somethings which could be, or provide, food for him.

I stopped and did a review. Would this mild chap, who had spent his entire office life at a desk in an office, really plunge into the jungle, as it would seem to him, and live off plants and small animals? Perhaps he would pop into the outskirts for his food, but wouldn't he have the constant compulsion to be amongst his own kind, or similar? At least the robots represented some sort of human-style normality; a tedious ordinariness.

I turned back.

Or so I thought.

After walking a little way, I realised that I hadn't turned back. Not a big deal. I must have turned sideways. I could soon work it out.

Or so I thought.

At least being on my own, I didn't have someone saying regularly, "Admit it. We're lost."

An hour or so later, I admitted that I was lost.

I couldn't even see or hear the robots, or the big machines.

My universaphone wouldn't respond in this part of the Universe. Besides, what was the point of help arriving in three weeks? Mabel was stuck in herself. She had no wheels, no legs, no permission. I was in this one on my own, and I'd have to sort it all on my own.

The trees were useless as potential vantage points because so far as I could see, the branches began about half way to the clouds.

This was ridiculous, to be lost with no means of extricating myself. Come on, now. This was the future. The entire Galaxy was within reach. And I was lost in a forest with no-one to help me, and no means of calling for help.

Right. There were two options: stay where I was, which is excellent advice when help will soon be on the way, which it wasn't; or set off and hope eventually to be where I wanted to be, or at least somewhere similar to where I wanted to be; in other words, out of here.

I set off, doing a feeble sort of whistle, failing utterly to be cheerful and optimistic. It is difficult to be cheerful and optimistic, and especially to whistle, when every few steps you trip over part of a plant, or part of a plant grabs you. I needed a machete. Or at least a dinner knife that wasn't plastic.

It was becoming hot and sticky. So was I. I was just hoping that my sweat wouldn't attract mosquitos and other such unpleasant creatures when something about the size of a small pig flew towards me. I ducked. It was either a large, fat bird. or the people who came to live here were going to have a big insect problem. I mean a problem with big insects. Which would probably be a big problem, too. I know what the corporate response would be. 'Put the big insect problem in the small print. And don't be specific. Or definite. As soon as they've bought, it's nothing to do with us.'

Two more went by, not really buzzing, sounding like speedboats going through the gears. I began to think about my need for a weapon. I gave the nearest tree a look of deep disgust for having its lowest branches at cruising ship height. Some of the large plants had stems which were thick and sturdy, but they had bristles all over them, and bristles are things to be nervous about in these places.

Rather symbolically, what I needed in order to make a weapon was the sort of implement that could be used as a weapon. Something strong and sharp was what I needed. I looked around, feeling like a stupid tourist, hoping that I'd see something or that someone would come and help me. I hadn't given up on these robots. Surely, *surely*, somewhere in their programming was the faculty for a little consideration, even a little compassion. Was a lift out of the question? Or at least the ability to answer my simple question by directing me back to a safe place?

But the trouble with robots was really just an extension of the problem with humans over many thousands of years: programming. Whether it's down a hole in the ground or sitting in front of a computer, people do what they are told, think as they are told, believe what they are told. The extremist religious person and the extremist scientist have exactly opposite, and identical, beliefs, both being equally stupid. They are both a bit right and both a bit wrong. In some ways, they are both a lot right and both a lot wrong. In other ways, neither of them has any idea of the truth. But on they go, stuck in their programming. I'm this or that, and this or that is what I believe, and nothing will ever change me.

But these robots looked so much like humans that it would always be very difficult to accept that they couldn't adapt slightly to changed circumstances.

However, keeping my feet firmly on the ground, as well as I could, and being careful where I put them, I decided to face this bit of my life with no sharp implement and with no robot assistance, and lacking vital information. All that Mabel had been told was that there were wild animals, and wild areas which needed to be controlled, organised, rearranged. I didn't even know how big this wood, forest, jungle was, and yet I had plunged in with virtually no preparation.

I kept telling myself that wild doesn't necessarily mean vicious and aggressive. There used to be all sorts of wild animals on Earth that were placid and gentle.

One common feature in any film that involves this sort of

location is the clearing. I don't know whether that is for plot development or simply because the director wants the actors to be organised, like wild animals, visible and neatly displayed. I struggled along through the sharp and sticky, and seemingly amorous, vegetation for several hours without seeing even a small gap, let alone a clearing. There wasn't even anywhere to sit down for a bit of whatever sustenance Mabel had provided. I didn't eat as I went along because I didn't want to add indigestion to my troubles. That's the sort of minor detail that never happens in films.

(A cry of pain.
"What is it?"
Gasp.
"Heartburn. That last sandwich.")

I heard something which sounded like a growl. The great jungle dread. The one sound above all others that you don't want to hear. Hoots, hisses, trumpets, screeches, even distant roars, you can live with. But not growls. Not the tigery sort.

Surely, somewhere in this vegetational chaos, there was an occasional tree with low branches. Yes, I know that most predators can climb trees. But it's a start. It's better than nothing. At least when you're up, you can kick down. You might even be able to do something clever with sharp branches.

And where were the robots? Weren't they supposed to be organising all this? Had they been programmed to have planning meetings and long lunchtimes?

The first animal, apart from the flying pig thing, which in any case was probably a large insect, was pretty frightening. If you imagine a gorilla crossed with a rhinoceros, you'll be well on the way. It was walking on two legs, its horn thrust out, looking ready for anything, but mostly for an argument. I have seen some wild things on my travels, but this was the most frightening so far.

Not knowing what else to do, I said, "Hello." And I smiled. I used my dog-greeting smile, which usually works well. That was the best I could do, and I waited for the roar, the rush and the tearing apart. I was very pleased when it opened its eyes very wide, squealed and ran away, crashing through the plant life in a high degree of agitation.

Well, that was a good start. I'd have preferred to make friends with it, not least because it looked like the sort of fellow that you would want to have on your side; but in the circumstances, I was happy to settle for its retreat.

Just so long as it wasn't the baby who had gone to tell its parents about the nasty thing that had inconsiderately frightened it. You know how these things escalate out of all proportion.

The length of days was very variable and erratic on New Terra 12, and it was well on the way to evening. And that made me think of another familiar feature which was lacking: the handy rock face with relatively safe ledges and caves. Increasingly, I was thinking of this wild zone as a jungle. And with trees that I couldn't climb, no clearings and no caves, I didn't think much of it. In different circumstances, I might have been impressed by the gigantic lily flowers, ferns and other large and, I suppose, beautiful plants, but I'm the sort of person who likes always to have a base somewhere, especially at night. I can rough it in a bare log cabin as well as anyone, but I don't do the sleeping in the open thing, making light of things that crawl and slither over me during the night. I like to have a door which I can shut.

This was hardly constructive thinking. Sulking and

pouting about what I wanted and couldn't have was not going to achieve anything except to make me more miserable.

It was as yet another tendril wound itself round my legs that imagination and stubbornness combined. With a big tug, I managed to detach a long tendril. I then set about doing what is *relatively* easy, for an expert with spiked boots but which is almost impossible for someone in light indoor shoes. I walked round one of the least wide and smoothest barked trees that I could find, put the tendril round the trunk, then pulled the two ends of the tendril tight, about head height. Then I jumped, walked up a few steps and pressed my feet against the trunk.

It was a start.

Don't look up.

I flipped the tendril up and jumped and walked and pressed again.

You have the idea. I shan't bore you with an account of the whole journey up the trunk. It was excruciating. It was one of those tasks that don't allow for any pauses, adjustments, variations. Even giving up wasn't an option unless I wanted to slide down the tree, probably scraping off my facial features, and hit the ground with leg-breaking force. Both legs. I had to keep going, higher all the time, without any errors, otherwise I'd slide down the tree, as previously described.

Each flip had to be a very small one because I had to keep my grip on the trunk. An impatient flip too high would leave me with no Plan B, just the rapid descent.

I had no plans for a safe descent tomorrow. No idea and no thoughts to spare. This really was concentration and focus time. This was the task, and for the duration, nothing else mattered. Flip, walk, press, over and over. And all the time, the descent distance increasing.

Don't look down, or up. Don't look anywhere but at the trunk.

Flip, walk, press.

Of course, I eventually found the first branch, a thick one, right above my head, which was exactly where I didn't want it to be. I flipped, walked and pressed at an acute angle, with my head tipped over, then had to bite the bullet and let go and grab the branch.

Well, as you know, because you are reading this, I managed it. I pulled myself up until I achieved that necessary next stage of resting on my tummy, then brought a leg up and over and sat on the branch, feeling very relieved, very tired, and pretty damn pleased with myself.

Now what?

I was pleased to see that I was now being rewarded with a lot of branches, all thick and some of them close together. I had kept my tendril in one hand. After a bar of various nuts from my food supply, I tied myself to a branch, spread myself in the big cat position, arms and legs over the sides, and settled down for some deserved sleep. But not before I was able to watch the various features of New Terra 12 combine to provide the best sunset that I had ever seen. The sky was a vast watercolour of shades of blue and purple and violet and mauve, with just a dash of orange. And the setting sun really was bluish. My first blue moon. Didn't that view make it all worthwhile?

Well, no, not quite.

CHAPTER 5

If my universaphone had enabled me to call for help, I'd have stayed in my tree until it arrived, if necessary living off tree bark. However, even in this high position, it just hissed and flickered. It looked as though another New Terra 12 problem was poor reception. Another item to be avoided in the sales patter.

I liked my tree and didn't want to leave it. So far as I was aware, nothing had landed on me or crawled or scuttled over me during the night. I had no prickles, pains or itches. I wanted to make this my home until rescue arrived.

And *what*, I admonished myself, would my two friends and colleagues think of that attitude. Those ladies had already demonstrated many times their defiance of danger, their will-ingness to take risks, their all-round vigorous and buoyant and determined approach to the problems of life. I, on the other hand . . . oh, let's leave it there. I had reminded myself that I had a job to do. It was just a brief weakness caused by tiredness, and a disgraceful lack of planning and preparation by me. Although 'pop down and have a look' must be some-where in there.

I had a small breakfast, and decided that it was time to go down to the ground.

The next problem was how on New Terra I was going to do it?

One method which was immediately ruled out was the reverse of my ascent.

That left all the other methods.

I couldn't think of any of them. There weren't any lower branches to break my fall. From here, it was straight down to the giant lilies, and I had no confidence in their cushioning capability.

As a compromise decision, I thought that while I was up here, I might as well go higher and try to see, well, anything that might be helpful. Fortunately, having started with the thick branches, the tree was now providing them enthusiastically. It was easy work now to haul myself, and even step, from branch to branch; many of them now doing the traditional thing of becoming less thick as I ascended. The truck, too, became less thick and I was pleased to feel a slight swaying. What I needed now was my tree to be the highest in the forest, giving me a splendid view of everything that I needed to see.

It wasn't, but when I reached my limit on a steadily swaying trunk, I still had a very helpful view. Yes, there was still a lot of green to be gone through, but, seeming not far away, I could see machines, which meant robots, and beyond those, I could see rocks jutting up.

Charles Wainwright Fisher might lack the derring-do of his comrades, but all that he needs is the occasional little boost such as this and he is the epitome of enthusiasm, with just a hint of courage. I decided to have a go at the old monkey way of progressing: branch to branch, tree to tree. I eased myself round the trunk, stepping onto another branch which seemed to go very close to the extended branch of the next tree. I walked carefully along the second branch until it began to dip under my weight. It was becoming soft, but I could feel springiness. Time for a graceful, arching leap into the branch of the next tree, and don't stop to think and worry about it.

Unfortunately, predictably, the end of the branch was springy but in a limp-wristed, lethargic way. Instead of providing upward spring, it merely projected me forwards, with little impetus. I missed the other branch by a long way.

Once again, as I hurtled downwards, I rued my lack of a Plan B. I was very soon out of the cracking, biffing, crunching branch zone with nothing to break my fall but some large flowers. At such times, the brain doesn't work at all well, but I did try to steer myself towards a large lily, which seemed to be my best, very small, hope.

Hitting that lily was simultaneously a great relief and a horror. The inside, which was a large chamber, was filled with a very unpleasant and sticky substance, with large and sharp bits. It was rather like muesli made with very thick treacle. It wasn't a soft landing and it didn't leave me without pains and bruises and cuts; but it did keep me alive.

My relief and brief relaxation were abruptly terminated by my strong suspicion that my rescuer was trying to digest me. Those bits felt like bones, and there was a lot of strong sucking going on around my feet, and a bit of a sizzling sensation. It was time to leave.

Unfortunately, again, the lily wasn't keen on releasing things which had conveniently tumbled into its trap. The whole idea of the sticky stuff and the sucking power was to keep them there. Immediately ruling out the plastic knife, I decided to give my little gun a go at the problem. The burning feeling was stronger as I looked round for a crucial part of the plant. I wasn't even sure of what's what in an Earth flower. I didn't have much confidence in my ability to shoot my way out of a bowl of treacle muesli.

I couldn't see anything that looked particularly important and settled for blasting a couple of the petals. At least that made it shudder and there was a very brief pause in the sucking as it evaluated this surprise occurrence. I hauled myself up, reached over and gave it a shot in the stem, and a moment later I was sliding down the outside of a plant which was far from happy with things. It was hissing and warpling in a mixture of pain and disappointment, and I felt a bit sorry for it. I didn't want to harm it, but this is what happens when you try to digest people.

On the other hand, perhaps I owed it a very small meal because it had saved me from death. If only these things were negotiable, instead of this all-or-nothing attitude.

I rolled around a bit and rubbed at myself with leaves, trying to remove the sticky stuff, which, for all I knew, might continue the digesting process or attract insects. I didn't want to be a human fly trap. I glanced up to confirm my bearings and set off for the distant machines and rocks.

I shan't bore you with the details. There is only so much interest to be generated from accounts of struggling feebly through a jungle. The problem with this sort of travelling is that the slightest step aside round a fallen trunk or other obstacle is enough to make you lose your bearings and become completely muddled. I always have this groundless conviction that I have an innate, instinctive knowledge of where I should be going. This combines with the earlier confusion to lead me right out of the way, and I have been known to be heading back the way that I came, still with complete confidence in my homing instincts.

I don't know how far I travelled, but it was nearly evening again by the time that I reached the machines I'd seen from my tree. They were immense, combining in one structure, very large robots of the human imitation variety, diggers, cranes and trucks, with a bit of combine harvester for good measure. They were in a large clearing, and it was obvious that it was a clearing only because they had cleared it. There wasn't much ecological balancing in evidence here. These great things were digging up trees as big as the one which I had climbed, then plucking them out and, so to speak, swinging them away over their shoulders for conversion into sawdust. Beyond these machines, I could see others drilling and hacking into the rock face.

Using small machines, a horde of robots were already slicing the tree trunks.

"What are you doing?" I called.

"Cutting the tree trunks."

"No, I mean all this clearance. Why are you doing it?"

"Making a conservation area."

I sighed. That was none of my business. Not here and now. I had a job to do. I tried again with my standard question. "I am a human. Have you seen another human?"

I asked it vaguely. One of those '*Anyone?*' questions. My hopes weren't high.

"No."

Just what I expec . . . *what?*

"Who said that?" I asked, walking closer to the robots and staring at them.

No-one replied.

As I walked among them, I said, "I know you're here. You gave yourself away."

The robots continued to cut the tree trunks. I had my job and they had theirs. Staring at them wasn't much good. Okay, I'd check the movements. A human would move different-ly. To the keen eye of scrutiny.

Ah! That was it. The robots, being designed to look like labouring humans, were built to an ideal labourer pattern. Every one of them was a hunky lumberjack type. And I was looking for a small and mild office worker, a real person, pale and timid. Also, probably someone who would be a huge hindrance if he tried to assist with the work of the powerful robots.

What I was looking for, then, was someone who didn't move with smooth, coordinated efficiency; and someone who was likely to be conspicuous in his attempts to be inconspicuous.

I stared at the busy robots. I walked amongst them, trying not to be in the way. It was dangerous because the robots didn't need warning horns or beeps from advancing or reversing machines. I kept thinking that one was about to be crushed by wheels, treads or legs, but he would always step just out of the way without any indication that he was even aware of the machine's presence. I, however, was in a constant state of nervous twitch, and found it difficult to concentrate on my scrutinising of the workers.

Something moved. In the peripheral vision, an unrobot-like, sideways movement, not connected with work. I snapped my head round and walked quickly towards what I might have seen. There was another movement, over to my right. Just a flicker, possibly imagined. I tried the very old-fashioned approach.

"Benjamin Weaver. We need to have a discussion. I represent Earth law, but I am not an Earth cop. I operate independently. There is much sympathy for you. Let's have a chat and try to resolve this."

Silence, as expected. But another flicker of movement, over at the edge of the cleared area. Was he running into the wild zone? To his hidey place?

I had a last, quick look round, then set off in pursuit. If he thought that my steady inspection would eventually locate him, then making a run for it was the obvious move. And he now had the advantage. I was still new to the wild zone, and, so far, pretty inept. Being lost within seconds, falling out of a tree, and nearly being eaten by a flower was not an impressive list.

It wasn't long before I was floundering again. The plants seemed to be even thicker here and even more persuasive in the tendril technique. I was very wary of everything that looked even slightly lilyish. Anything pretty was looked at with deep suspicion.

Voom. A flying pig went by, relying on me to move out of its way. Then some more insect-sized insects, but still much too big, began to take an interest in me. A constant ZZiZZ, with a humming undertone went round and round my head. I know my insects well enough to know that all that ZZiZZing is not just pointless wandering; it has a purpose, usually involving stabbing, poisoning and sucking. And in one respect, insects on New Terra 12 are no different from those on Earth: they laugh at flapping hands and bobbing heads.

But definitely much bigger.

I was relieved when I suddenly emerged into a clearing. A large one, too. And a real, natural one, I was pleased to see. At least I could see what was going on now and could concentrate on insect-avoidance without the distraction of tendril-and-lily avoidance. But you (probably) know how it is in a clearing: after the initial relief comes the vulnerability of being in the open, clearly visible, but the viewers concealed. An attack could come from any point, possibly right behind you. Even your emergency exit from the clearing can be clearly seen.

And there is still the problem of the non-emergency exit

from the clearing. In other words, there is no indication of the best way to go.

I decided that it was unproductive and undignified to stand nervously at the edge of the clearing, waiting for something to happen. I walked into the middle and called, "Benjamin. Come on. At least let's talk, even if we have to shout to each other."

A rustling gave me a very brief hope.

It was followed by something very close to despair, as a minotaur walked slowly into the clearing and stared at me. The starer had become the staree. How did I like it? Not at all. In addition to being harmless, I was doing my staring for the sole purpose of trying to find someone. This thing was staring at me . . . well, I don't really know what its purpose was, but it wasn't trying to find me, and it wasn't trying to enter into negotiations.

I took out my little gun and cursed Mr Stafford for his non-lethal weaponry. I am all for doing things the peaceful way, and I don't want to harm wildlife anywhere in the Galaxy, and beyond when we eventually go there; but my attitude is based on the principle of leaving well alone, live and let live, mind your own business. I could see that the minotaur didn't share this attitude, and I consider it reasonable that in the present circumstance, my attitude changed, too. I was very reluctant to die just yet, and particularly keen to avoid its occurrence by angry goring.

My second best hope was a salvo of shots, which might deter the beast. But my best hope seemed to be a rapid retreat from the clearing into the tendrils and other impediments. Perhaps my fluid suppleness, as I chose to imagine it, would be an important advantage over the solid muscularity of my opponent. Well, it was worth a try and I turned to leave.

Oh, damn. Another one. They were working as a pair.

They advanced with perfect timing, trotting, but nothing casual about it, lots of purpose. This steady approach on two legs was the full horror now, because it had added a night-marish dread to the simple fear of pain and death. They both bellowed, just to make things worse. Deep, wet bellows, all chest and throat. They were already lowering their heads for the goring.

Peripheral movement again.

"Stop!"

The minotaurs did stop. They turned and looked at the little man, carrying a simple wooden spear. A sharp stick really.

As they hesitated, he called to me, "Now! This way! Run!"

This wasn't the time for careful analysis, or even consideration. It was definitely the time for doing exactly as advised. I ran, going from standing start to maximum speed in four steps. But I could tell from the thudding behind me that the minotaurs were displaying some nifty acceleration, too. Quickly assessing the situation as I left the clearing, I decided that my escape or capture was going to depend on which of us could make the best progress through the thick, thorny and tendrily stuff. Based on my performance so far, my hopes weren't very high. Benjamin Weaver was darting all over the place, all dexterity and confidence, but I knew that it was only a matter of a very short time before I tripped and went down.

Just before that inevitable occurrence, as I felt hot mino-taur breath on my back, my guide called, "Just stay with me and don't look down."

Then he disappeared.

This was rock and a hard place time. Minotaurs or disap-pearing.

It wasn't that difficult. I went for disappearing. Tingling with anticipation, and a fair amount of terror, I followed my leader.

It was a simple trick. I realised this as I ran over the edge of an almost sheer drop and began to descend rapidly. I connected with the ground a few times, each time just long enough to raise the brief hope that I might be able to run the rest of the way before off and out I went again.

The last stage concluded the manoeuvre with my arrival in water, my entry being all power and no style. Having come down in stages as it were, I didn't break into pieces on hitting the water, but I did sink far enough to give me several anxious seconds as I strained to return to the breathing zone. When I burst through to the surface, I gasped like a cow having a difficult labour, then heard Benjamin Weaver say, "Holding your breath under water for six seconds *might* be a record for this planet, but only because no-one else has tried it."

"What about you?"

"I don't count. Isn't it nice to know that the pun is spreading all over the Galaxy?"

"Oh, yes." So was sarcasm. I was treading water in a deep river on a distant planet, having just escaped from a couple of ferocious minotaurs. And the man whom I was pursuing was clearly in charge of the situation.

After joining him on the bank, I tried to retain, or revive, some dignity by saying, "Benjamin Weaver, I presume."

"Correct. And I presume that you are some sort of cop equivalent. Private detective? Bounty hunter?"

"Oh, no. Not at all. I read about your exploits, and having plenty of free time, and plenty of money, I decided to join you for a little while."

"Why?"

"Well, the truth is, my life is rather dull, and your life seems rather exciting."

"My evening meal yesterday was a caterpillar as long and as thick as your arm."

"Fortunately, I'm a vegetarian. I know that the unwilling consumption of a caterpillar in one's salad does not make the consumer a carnivore, but my view is that eating a caterpillar of that size would break my own ethical rules."

"How about raw eggs and discarded baby birds?"

"No, thanks."

"So, you're not willing to adapt for nourishment, you've experienced the Minotaur version of a welcome, and you've been hopelessly lost and nearly eaten by a flower. Does this life still appeal to you?"

"Not to the extent that you are living it."

"You mean you'd prefer to live on one of those housing estates and look at this sort of life through an electrified fence?"

"No, I don't want to do that either. I suppose that in wanting to live as you do, or as I thought you do, I was trying to run away from the truth of my life. If my life was dull, it was because I made it dull. And that's probably because *I* am dull."

"Well, at least coming here has taught you an important lesson."

"It certainly has. You can't run away from your failings. You have to face them, and overcome them. Otherwise, they follow you like your shadow. No matter how far you run, no matter how well you hide."

"I'm not going back."

I shrugged. "That's your affair. As I said, I just came out here to, well, at least put a little . . . interest into my life."

"I suppose it's the same with me. Going back wouldn't just be about punishment, or at least what the authorities think of as punishment. The real punishment would be going back to work in an office, living in an apartment on the umpteenth floor, with windows designed not to open because I might decide to throw myself out of one." He paused for a moment to look slightly embarrassed about the mention of throwing himself out of a window. "No. I'm not going back."

I shrugged again. He said, "So, now what are you going to do?"

"Well, I think I need to approach the excitement part with more caution, perhaps venturing out a little farther each day, but always keeping the hotel as my base."

"How is the hotel?"

"She's . . . it's very efficient. The whole hotel is a computer, and I'm the only guest. Whatever I want, she .. it gives me."

"Are you missing her? Will she be worrying about you?"

"Yes, twice, allowing for the adaptation of a computer's working to the equivalent of worrying."

"Using all the available information, she calculated that statistically, your chances of survival were slim?"

"Something like that."

"I think it would be in both your interests for you to return immediately."

This was a difficult one. Yes, I wanted, and needed, to return to safety; but I hadn't completed my mission. I was supposed to go to work, very subtly, on his conscience to lead him to do the right thing.

As I hesitated, he continued. "Do you even know the way back to your hotel? Do you know which animals and plants are dangerous? Do you know the foraging habits of the minotaurs?"

No, no and no.

"And talking of minotaurs, that was a bit of a sticky one up there in the clearing, wasn't it?

"Yes. I appreciate your assistance. I shall speak for you."

"Very kind of you. Oh, well. Let's make a start, then. We'll follow the river for a while, then it's a rather steep climb."

"I expected that. Lead and I'll follow."

Following the river wasn't challenging, but the steep climb was. After my third gasping demand for a short break, Benjamin looked down at me and said, "I used to be like that. Such a struggle when I first arrived. But just the effort unlocked the door to all my repressed yearnings. I shed the wasted years and began my new life with a new me. I was being given a second chance at life and I wasn't going to waste it."

"Well done," I panted. "You like it here then?"

"Yes. I think of it as Earth before the people came."

"Except that here we have the intermediate, and very efficient, robots."

"Yes. Do you know anything about stopping robots? Is it just a matter of unscrewing certain things? Can they really be inactivated by conflicting commands or concepts? Can they be destroyed by force?"

"That largely depends on the robots and their programming. There are so many different sorts. But those are interesting thoughts. If, for some reason, I were not to arrest you, that is what you would do? You versus sixty seven thousand robots?"

"That many? I knew there must be a lot, but, well, yes, I

do seem to be heavily outnumbered. And outsized. Anyway, what are your thoughts on the subject?"

He had resumed the climb. "Well," I said, "it's all theoretical and nebulous because, well, you see, if I go back without you, I shall be required to reveal what I have found, and others would come, and arrest you."

"Ah, yes. Well, you'll be pleased to know that we are now at the top."

I glanced up.

He disappeared.

CHAPTER 6

When I said 'disappeared', that's what I meant. Not just briefly out of sight. Really disappeared. When I reached the top, there was no sign of him. I called his name a few times, then sat down. Feeling rather foolish, I called, "Have you really gone, or are you just making a point, teaching me a lesson?"

When there was no reply, I rose and set off on what was certain to be a long, and probably unsuccessful, attempt to find Mabel. I had the vaguest of vague feelings that I should go right, but I was honest enough to know that I could be completely wrong. The river would have been very helpful if I'd had any idea of where it began and where it ended, and everything between those points, but I hadn't even known there was a river. Even the big robots were no indication because they were working all over this planet. Yes, they were probably concentrating in this general location, preparing for the house sales, and leaving the other wild parts for future clearance, after making money on trekky holidays, but it was still a large area.

And there was still a lot of danger.

The next local resident to introduce itself was another rhinoceros variation. This one was a horned cat thing, with all the emotional instability and territorial aggression of a cat. Not to mention the appetite for meaty food. It snarled in the traditional manner.

I carefully extracted my discouragement weapon from my pocket. Perhaps a few shots in quick succession would deter it. But again, my hopes weren't high.

There was a small detonation as two hands slapped together, immediately followed by,

"Bad puss. Bad, bad puss."

Benjamin Weaver came from behind me, waving a stout but bendy stick. "Go, puss. Go."

With a look of resentment, the cat turned and slunk, slank or slinked away.

Benjamin Weaver looked ever so slightly smug as he said, "That's twice. And you're going the wrong way. Shall we make an arrangement?"

"You mean in exchange for your protection, I shan't arrest you?"

"I was thinking of something a little more ambitious than that."

Ambitious? I wasn't keen on that at the best of times. Here, in these circumstances, it was positively creepy. "How do you mean?" I asked, trying, and failing, to keep nervousness out of my voice.

He explained.

I was right to be worried.

———

It took a while to make Mabel understand what I wanted and to give me access to them. I said, "So, when these engineers visit, presumably there are tools available in case of any old-fashioned mechanical problems that can't be solved by computer modelling and all that."

"There is a small supply for such unlikely occurrences."

"And where are they?"

"They are in me, of course, available to the appropriate people."

"Mabel. One of the robots has a screw loose. I mean a loose screw."

"Which one? I shall report it to the next available engineer."

"That might be too late, Mabel. One loose screw, one ineffective robot, one chain of effects, leading to complete failure. For the want of a nail, Mabel."

"You said that a screw was loose."

I told her the old one about the lost battle and the omitted nail. At the end, she said, "So do you want a screw or a nail?"

"Neither, Mabel. I want to be proactive. I want to use my initiative. What I need is a selection of screwdrivers."

There was a delay of a couple of seconds while she consulted information in her deepest, darkest recesses, her metaphorical basement. Her response was, "In order to protect all legal provisions and liabilities, all repairs must be performed by approved engineers."

"That is a standard rule in order to prevent the claim that equipment wasn't faulty until it was tampered with by someone who wasn't approved. I am not going to tamper: I am merely going to tighten a screw before it leads to something worse. It is my duty, Mabel, and I place that above all other considerations. I am happy to accept, in as formal a form as you like, all responsibility."

During another very brief pause, I actually guessed what she was thinking. "Yes," I said, quite calmly, "You could request authorisation. So could I. But at top speed, that would be six hours there and six hours back. And in twelve hours, the screw could have stopping doing what it is supposed to be doing and mayhem might have ensued. The potential cost, Mabel! Think of the potential cost."

"I do not think. That potential has not been supplied."

I tried again. "Mabel, if I had an accident in . . . you, and I was burning to death, what would you do?"

"I'd follow my emergency procedures."

"Right. Now, what would you do if you saw me about to do that which might cause me to burn to death?"

"I have no instructions to deal with that."

"Therefore, you would let me do whatever it was and then render assistance when I was in great pain and being severely, perhaps fatally, injured."

"Yes."

"Have you ever thought about what you would like to be if you were not a hotel? Government official? Stationery stores clerk?"

"I do not think."

"I know. Just a brief interlude of levity. I am still moving steadily towards my objective. I am not burning to death. However, I am in danger. You are in danger. The workers on this planet are in danger. The companies who have invested so much in the development of this planet are in danger. All because you refuse to allow me to carry out a very small repair to one of the workers."

"There is no indication of this danger."

"Just as there might not be if I had swallowed something harmful. If I were to tell you that I had accidentally swallowed something harmful and needed urgent assistance, would you believe me and provide that assistance?"

"Yes."

"We arrived there in the end."

"Where?"

"Access to tools, please, Mabel."

"I have unlocked the tools container."

"Thank you, Mabel. You have done well."

CHAPTER 7

A few weeks later, I had just returned from sorting out that little bit of nonsense down on Polly when Mr Stafford strolled in, thoroughly informal as usual.

He said, "About New Terra 12."

"Oh, yes," I said with a pretence of having to think for a moment.

"As you know, I read your report and I made it available for perusal by all the relevant organisations. As I said at the time, I left it as it was. No shame in failing now and again. There is only so much time that we can spare you for searching on a largely wild world, still awaiting most of its development."

I nodded my acknowledgment. He was continuing to be very reasonable and understanding. But I knew what was coming next.

"Did you know that shortly after you left, there was a quickly spreading failure amongst the robots."

"*Was* there? How strange. They seemed to be working normally when I left. Does anyone know what went wrong?"

"Apparently, according to the technical data, it began with one robot. Just a minor malfunction which, however, caused first considerable damage to the work which was being done, then, cumulative effects being what they are, task sequences failing and all that, it soon caused damage to other robots, which in turn, and so on and, well, it soon spread all over. Utter chaos. It has set back the planet development at least several years and cost so much money that other worlds are being considered instead."

"Oh, dear," I said. "The wild place will be staying wild, then."

"It looks like it. Oh, well. It can't be helped. What's done is done and all that."

"A good attitude."

"Yes. Er, I suppose that you wouldn't know anything about it."

"If I did, wouldn't it be in my report?"

"Oh, quite, quite. That's what I said to the people who asked me. I assured them that none of my people would ever commit sabotage."

"Of course. I resent any suggestion that I had anything to do with it."

"Yes. Well, we shan't hear any more about it."

"Good."

"Oh, there is one other small matter.

"When the chief engineer, whose professional reputation and personal standards were at stake, went down, or up, to New Terra 12, he immediately checked all the tools and inter-rogated the computer."

"Mabel."

"Beg pardon?"

"Mabel. That's what I called her."

"Her."

"You had to be there."

"Yes. I expect so. Anyway, the responses to the technician's questions about tools and their possible removal for unautho-rised uses were all repetitions of the rules and programming by which she, it, operates. What might in a human be consid-ered to be evasiveness. No direct denial; just a repeat of the rules and programming that would prevent such an occurrence."

"Well, you know computers and their pedantic adherence

to their programming and the constraints on their use of initiative."

"Oh, yes. I know them well."

He looked at me with the blankest of faces. "Charles, I think that for the next few jobs, I shall keep the little team together."

"Just how I like it."

I gave him my most reassuring smile, which he didn't need, and headed for the door.

"One last little question," he said. "A personal thing. I couldn't help noticing your little something on a chain round your neck."

"Oh, that. I don't usually wear such things, but I thought that it would be nice to have this with me."

"What is it?"

"It's just a screw," I replied. "To remind me of a nail."

# # #

CELIA

This one is just for fun. A young space cadet follows a white space ship down a black hole, and meets some very odd people and things.

CHAPTER 1

Celia le Dale was on her first patrol. She wasn't alone, but it seemed like it in this vast darkness. Somewhere off to the left, port, sub-quadrant 9.4, Lightway Captain Lora Charles was cruising supervisorily.

It was a routine patrol in a nice, quiet part of the Galaxy. A gentle introduction. Yes, there was the vague possibility of a drug-runner, such as the notorious Billy Izzard, making a dash for the great emptiness, and Celia was sort of hoping that it would happen. This drifting about, staring at nothing was boring.

This, Captain Lora had told her, is the reality. You do all your training in simulation back on Earth, with all sorts of problems thrown in, and you expect similar excitement when you first go up. Then comes the disappointment.

Celia didn't mind that. She understood that most cop work is weary, dreary patrolling, just checking and observing, but she could not see the point of just drifting through all this immense non-event.

She asked herself, "What use is a patrol zone without planets and ships?"

She soon had the answer.

Something flickered at the edge of her vision, or consciousness. Was that movement? A black ship, hurtling through the darkness?

Something else moved. Clearly visible, a white ship was heading very quickly in the same direction of whatever might have gone by a few seconds earlier.

Space-gang warfare?

Celia knew all the routine procedures. Basically, report to a superior officer and wait for instructions. She knew what those instructions would be: take no action and the matter will be properly reported, logged and investigated. And by that time, those two ships would be much too far away.

Even while she was having these thoughts, she became aware that she was in pursuit. No matter what she was chasing, her specially adapted copship would catch it, eventually.

She was soon close enough to look at the white ship in magnification. It was featureless. There were no markings. It was just a ship of some sort which was capable of going at great speeds.

But she was drawing steadily nearer. Soon, she'd be close enough to transmit, call for identification and purpose, and, most likely, tell it to slow right down and prepare to be escorted, to somewhere. But she needed to be close enough to be clearly audible and visible. People who travelled at such speeds were unlikely to use rear view mirrors.

All her attention was on the small white ship, not on what was beyond it. It was only when the ship disappeared that she realised it had flown into a deeper blackness, a more intense emptiness.

In short, a black hole.

Well, a hole. There were so many variations. It was more likely one of the nineteen types of space fabric holes.

The sensible thing was to apply the brakes and go into a sharply curving retreat.

That's what Captain Lora would have told her to do.

That's what *anyone* would have told her to do.

She carried straight on.

Her very quick and simple reasoning was that the other ship had done it, presumably not as an act of suicide, so why shouldn't she?

"Hold tight," she told herself, knowing that it wouldn't make any difference.

There was some shuddering, and perhaps some juddering, as the ship entered the hole.

The engines cut out.

Then, silence.

Stillness.

Was her ship even moving?

She hoped that she was moving. That seemed to be slightly better than never going anywhere, although she had to admit that the effect might be pretty much the same.

"Never going anywhere, or always going but never arriving," she muttered into the recorder on her chest, trying to identify an advantage in one of the possibilities.

"Is there even a difference?" she added. "Yes, there must be. But probably not in here, because there seems to be nothing in here, except me."

Rather more than suddenly, she was out of the black emptiness and the engine began to hum. She was entering what appeared to be a vast underground chamber, with walls and floor of black rock. Ahead, neatly parked, was the white ship. Anxiously using the brakes to slow down, she slid to a halt beside it.

"I appear," she said, "to be in an underground car park, which isn't quite what I expected to find at the other end of a space fabric hole."

She looked around, shrugged and said, "There is no sign of the person whom I am following. I shall now leave my ship and investigate."

The first part of the investigation didn't take long. There was a lot of black rock, but not much else. An almost empty spaceship park is very much like an almost empty car park. Somewhat creepy. Somewhat wrong.

The two ships looked very much in the wrong place. That was her thought as she came back to them, having walked all the way round the chamber. The white ship pilot must have gone somewhere. He hadn't passed her on the way in; therefore, she reasoned, either he must still be here, somewhere, or she must have missed a means of exit. Having no better idea, she started to go round again.

"Well," she said, when she saw an elevator. "A fine detective I am, missing that."

She had a point. The doors were silver, which didn't blend very well with the black rock, although the overall effect was pleasant enough.

In spite of a thorough search, she couldn't see a button to press. "Ugh," she said in exasperation, forgetting her recorder. "Just open your doors."

"Certainly," said the elevator.

"Ah," Celia said, stepping in. "Voice responsive."

"That's right," said the elevator. "Where do you want to go?"

"I don't know," Celia replied.

"Then how can I be expected to know?"

"But I don't know what the choices are. Can't you just take me somewhere and I'll decide when I'm there?"

"Well, I suppose." The elevator sounded sulky. "But it's not the right way to do it."

A moment later, Celia's knees seemed to go down into her ankles and the rest of her body did the same sort of thing. Then, they separated again and her head hit the roof of the elevator.

"Where are we?" Celia asked.

"The top."

"What's here?"

"Nothing."

"Well, why have we come here, then?"

"Because you didn't tell me to stop."

"How could I tell you to stop when I don't know what's here?"

"I thought you'd guess."

"Okay. No harm done. Let's start again. But sloof."

"What does sloof mean?" asked the elevator. They were back on the ground floor.

"I started to say, 'But slowly,' but you went down at the same speed."

"You said that you wanted to start again. I thought the sooner we did it, the better."

"Is there a chance that you could go up slowly?"

"Oh, yes."

"Then, please take me up again."

Moments later, her head hit the elevator roof again.

"What happened?" Celia asked.

"There was a chance, but I didn't do it."

"Why?"

"Lack of discipline."

"Okay. Please take me down very slowly. Very gently. That's it. That's perfect. Now, when I say 'stop', stop. Stop."

"Then what?"

"What do you mean?"

"After you say stop, stop, stop. You didn't finish."

The elevator settled softly onto the ground floor.

"Yes, I did. I said....oh, never mind. I give up. Obviously, doing simple elevator work is too complex for you. Do you think that you could take me, very slowly, to the first available floor, then stop and let me leave?"

"No."

"Why?"

"Because I'm having a breakdown."

"Oh, dear. Because of what I said?"

"No. Going so slowly interfered with my friction pads. I'll have to wait for them to cool down. I'll have to shut down very briefly."

"Did you have any problems with the other guy?"

"Which other guy?"

"The guy who went up just before I arrived."

"No-one did. You were the first passenger for a while. I was pleased. This is a lonely life. When people do arrive, they just use me and leave me. Do you know what that's like?"

"No. I always avoid those situations. I wonder where he went. Is there any other way out of here?"

"I don't know. My knowledge is very limited. I just go up and down, not out and about. It isn't an exciting life."

"I understand. It must be very frustrating."

"I was fine until you asked me a question about out there. I don't like to be reminded."

"Ah. Sorry."

"What are you doing now?"

"Oh, just strolling about, to pass the time. Thinking. Looking."

"Well, don't go far. I'll be ready soon."

"Good. Good."

Celia was already walking away.

CHAPTER 2

On her first search, she had also missed a door, a little way beyond the elevator.

It was open. She stepped through. It was dark, but there was no indication of a light switch or a light to be lit by one. She could see steps, leading down into the deeper darkness below. It was that cold, drippy darkness that makes you long for various things, usually including a thick coat.

Oh, well. This was the sort of thing that detectives had to do. She went slowly down.

She could see a flickering ahead, and that lengthening and shortening that shadows do when the person who is holding a light keeps moving. Someone was carrying a torch, also moving cautiously along. Surely, it was the white ship man. Carefully, on soft feet, she hurried after him.

Suddenly, two things happened at once. First, there was a rumbling, thudding, crashing, splashing noise, strongly suggestive of a torrent of water in a passage. Second, the man leapt nimbly up some steps to his right.

Celia decided to run to the steps behind her. She turned and went into the stooped sprint position.

Too late.

The water knocked her down, picked her up, carried her almost to the top of the steps, doing some banging of elbows and knees, but not of head, which she kept out of the general turbulence, then went backwards and forwards, with a lot of spinning and swirling, and settled with Celia back to more or less where she had just been standing.

Then, relatively speaking, stillness. Just some lapping and tapping as the water wandered gently about, as though deciding that this place would do as well as anywhere.

Celia swam over to the top of the steps where the man had been and dragged herself out of the water. She shivered. Underground passages are not the best places for swimming, especially when your customary immersions are in a heated swimming pool, with hot air bodyblows.

At the top of the steps was a door. She opened it slowly and slightly and eased herself through. She was surprised to see a small group of men and women, standing and talking.

They looked round as she appeared. The white ship man left the group and walked towards her, looking pleased to see her.

"Marianne," he said. "I'm Captain Harvey. We were becoming concerned. Here's a change of clothes. Change over there. We'll look the other way."

Dry clothes were very welcome, although she was reluctant to leave her cop outfit. The one-piece jogging suit fitted her comfortably enough, but she felt vulnerable without her uniform. When she had changed, she started to transfer her equipment to the new clothes

"No," called Captain Harvey. "Leave all that. You can't be armed and equipped when you're working undercover. We'll look after it."

Undercover? So this wasn't just a change of clothes because she was wet. She swallowed the big question which was trying to leave her mouth and came back to the group.

"Right," said Captain Harvey. "Are you ready?"

That was an interesting question. Rather difficult, too. Who was Marianne? And why did they think that she was Marianne? And what did they expect her to do?

Oh, well. If in doubt, and when you don't know who are the good guys and who are the bad guys, just go along with it and see what happens..

Along with what?

"Could we just go over it again?" she asked. "Just to be sure?"

"Right. Through that door is Park Street. The gang is in Number 24. Back bedroom. Billy Izzard has just come back with a delivery. (Ah, thought Celia.) You're a potential buyer. You ask to see the stuff. You go to the window for a closer look and that is the signal for us to move in. Okay?"

Not really. "Okay," Celia replied.

A good detective keeps going as the problems keep growing.

Besides, this was a routine manoeuvre for an experienced officer.

But she wasn't an experienced officer.

She was about to become one.

"Good luck," said Captain Harvey.

She thanked him and opened the door.

CHAPTER 3

She stepped out into what had to be designated a slum area, even by present day standards. It was grim and grimy, with tall, dark grey buildings and shabby shops and bars. People in large coats scurried about furtively, restively, all looking anxiously over their shoulders or staring at the crumbled, pitted pavement. Some of the cars ran on wheels, clanking along, spitting smoke. Models from the Long Ago. Before Relevant History.

The air was thick and heavy with disgusting odours. She wasn't used to smells which hadn't been approved. She decided that this was the sort of place where the cops went slowly round in heavily armoured, and armed, vehicles. They didn't walk about, knocking on the doors of houses where criminal gangs did business.

However, that was her task, and that was what she was going to do, provided that she survived the walk to Number 24.

She did. The only advantage of such a district was that most people were trying to avoid trouble, which seemed to mean avoiding everyone else. And Number 24 wasn't far.

She knocked.

There was no reply.

She knocked again.

Still no reply.

She hadn't asked, and Captain Harvey hadn't said, what the plan was in the event of no response.

She turned the handle and opened the door. Ahead was a narrow hall.

That was odd. What sort of criminal gang leaves the front door unlocked, and doesn't have a guard on the inside of it?

She had a strong urge to leave. This felt, seemed, all wrong. But a mixture of pride and duty led her on.

She went into each of the ground floor rooms. They were bare. No people and no sign of people. Nothing.

At the far end of the hall, was a staircase. She went up, not sure whether she should creep silently or stomp confidently, and somehow doing a combination of the two, which was rather like walking normally. There were two bare rooms upstairs, but one had a fold-up table and some fold-up chairs. Dirty glasses and some bottles which weren't quite empty indicated recent occupation.

It looked as though the criminals had found out about the set-up.

She might as well let Captain Harvey and the team know. She went to the window to make some gestures.

She didn't expect the cops to be visible. For a moment, she was surprised when she saw a group in the back yard. The raised guns provided a pretty clear explanation.

She dropped to the floor, just before a few hundred bullet beams spattered and rattled around the room. With all that ricocheting, nowhere in the room was safe. Celia made herself as small as she could and ran to the door and out of the room. She hurtled downstairs and went straight out into the street.

And kept running.

She needed some space between her and the people with the guns.

After glancing back a couple of times, she decided that she wasn't being followed and stopped to think.

Her first thought was that she wasn't impressed by Captain Harvey and his team. For one thing, the bad guys knew of the plan; for another, there was no support for her in her dire difficulty.

Her second thought was what the very hairy man standing next to her wanted.

He had one of those faces on which front, back and side hair have merged with a beard which is exploring in all directions. The customary facial features had to be searched for.

"It's all a game," he said. "A vast, spinning game."

Great, Celia thought. An obscure lecture from an obscure tramp.

In the depths of his hair and whiskers, his eyes gleamed. "You might as well enjoy it," he added. "And worrying is no use at all."

Well, that was true. She laughed. "How about you?" she asked. "Do you enjoy your life?"

"I'd prefer not to be a tramp, but there's nothing that I can do about that, so I look for the good in it and enjoy it. Enjoy what you can't improve. And even I have my uses. For a few moments, I've taken your mind off whatever was troubling you."

Also true. Celia smiled. "However," she said. "I still have to deal with things as well as I can. Is there a police station around here?"

"Just along there a little way, on your left."

"Thank you. You've been very helpful."

"You're welcome. I see that as my purpose."

Even his directions were as helpful as she could wish. She soon saw the station on her left, up some steps. The building looked as old and shabby as all the others. A sign stated that this was the 49th Precinct. She went up the steps and through a thick wooden door.

She was in a large reception area, with high ceilings, and, as though in emulation, a high counter, behind which a sergeant leaned on his elbows and gazed blankly at nothing. He seemed not to be aware of Celia.

"Hi," she said, trying to be friendly but firm.

The sergeant looked over her head at the front door, as though wondering whether it was at fault in admitting her.

"May I help you?" he said.

"Yes," Celia replied. "I'm looking for Captain Harvey."

"Never heard of him."

"I'm working on a case with him."

"You? Who are you?"

"Detective Celia le Dale."

"Never heard of you."

"No. I know that. But surely you've heard of Captain Harvey."

The sergeant raised a substantial eyebrow and went on raising it until he had almost run out of forehead.

"Okay," Celia said. "Let's leave that and move on. I have been working very recently, minutes ago, on a case with Captain Harvey, I was sent into a house in this street, Number 24 and....surely the shooting has been reported."

"Shooting, eh? Who was shot?"

"No-one."

"I see. Do you think that we should receive frequent reports that someone hasn't been shot."

"No. I was shot *at*. By about six people. All the shots missed."

"They must have been very bad shots."

Celia took a deep breath and explained what had happened, omitting the beginning bit about the hole and her arrival.

When she had finished, the sergeant said, "And where is Captain Harvey now?"

Celia replied slowly. "I don't know. That's why I began our conversation by saying that I was looking for him."

The sergeant had a long look and a long think. Then, he said, "Have you any identification?"

"Of course," Celia replied. "It's.....in my clothes. These aren't my clothes. I was wet, and I could hardly pretend to be a criminal in a cop uniform, could I?"

The sergeant sniffed. "The whole thing sounds all wrong to me."

"Yes, well, it sounds all wrong to me, too. Perhaps I'd better leave you to do your work and I'll go and look for Captain Harvey. Oh, do you know where I might find someone called Billy Izzard?"

The sergeant slowly shook his head, as though it weren't even a possibility.

Celia turned and walked to the door, expecting the sergeant to call her back, but he didn't. Instead, he called, "You might try The Cafe, along the way, for a different way of looking at things."

Celia called, "Thank you," but he seemed already to have forgotten her.

Well, she thought as she walked along the street, this is progress of a sort. At least I'm investigating. Surely, no-one could find fault with that.

Her progress was suddenly terminated when someone grabbed her and shoved her against a wall.

"You manipulating strumpet," a woman hissed at her, gripping her firmly by the collar. The woman had small, staring eyes and a round face which made the eyes seem even smaller.

Although trained in combat, Celia was also trained in

diplomacy. "I'm sorry," she said. "I don't understand what you're talking about."

"It's not enough for you to take my husband, but you want to take my children, too."

"I don't want a husband. Yours or anyone else's. And I certainly don't want any children."

"Oh, no? Well, answer me this. Are you looking for Billy Izzard?"

"Yes. Do you know where I can find him?"

"Yes. *With me*! Just as soon as he comes home."

"Ah. That's good. When convenient, I'd like to call and have a chat with him."

"*Brazen*!"

"I'm a cop. I'm investigating . . . something."

"What?"

"That's confidential."

"You don't look like a cop. Where's your badge?"

"It's . . . in my uniform, which I'm not wearing just now, as you can see."

"I can see a pack of lies."

Celia deftly slipped out of the woman's grasp and raised her palms in a gesture of peace or readiness for battle, leaving the woman to choose.

"That's up to you. Now, I've told you the truth. Whether or not you believe it is up to you. I have other things to do. One of those is to visit you and ask your husband some questions. What is your address?"

The woman was already walking away. "Just you keep your hands off my husband," she called back.

Celia thought of going after her, but thought that it would probably just lead to more shouting. And she had to admit that without her uniform, she did look just like an ordinary young woman.

She carried on walking for a surprisingly uninterrupted short distance. It was going so well that she almost walked past The Café. In the general murkiness of this town, it reminded her of one of those furtive deep sea creatures that reverse into dark places when danger, or a potential victim, approaches. Before going in, she stood and stared at the window. Her intention was to look through it, but it was too dirty for that.

A car drew up at the kerb and the passenger door opened. She heard someone mutter, "And watch out for cops."

Another voice said, "What about the girl?"

"Watch out for her, too. Then do what you were supposed to do at the house."

Celia stood still, staring at the window. She heard three footsteps and the opening and closing of the café door. She took a chance and went in. She sat down at the first table and tried to hide behind a menu.

The man from the car approached two people who sat at a round table. One was a man with a large head and the other was a woman with a large everything. Behind the counter, a cook was very busy, apparently creating a small mountain of burgers. He could hardly be seen through the smoke. There were flashes and pops and hisses and whops as he flicked and patted and slapped over the red hot stove.

"Morning, Hopper. Morning Miss Maltash." The politeness didn't sound genuine.

Neither was that of the reply from the man. "Morning Scales. What's the message?"

"Mighty McQueen is having an event,"

"What sort?" Miss Maltash had a thick, cement-mixery sort of voice.

"The usual sort. The Blue Diamond. Everyone's invited. Everyone's expected."

"Of course. What time?"

"Nine."

"We accept," said Miss Maltash.

The messenger just nodded and went out. The car door closed and the car was driven away. When Celia glanced back, she saw that the large woman was staring at her.

"We don't do waitress service here," said Miss Maltash. "If you want something, ask the cook."

Celia looked at the cook. He was just visible through the thunder cloud of smoke and flames, flipping burgers and flinging each fresh batch onto the steadily growing piles beside and behind him.

She looked back at Miss Maltash. "I'm looking for a job," she said.

"Well, we don't print them on the menus."

"I was working up the courage to ask."

"Hmmm. Looking for work, eh?" The woman sprinkled some powder on the back of her hand and took a large sniff, which was followed by a large sneeze.

"Yes."

Sneeze.

"Anything will. . . ."

Sneeze.

Miss Maltash blinked her watery eyes and turned to look at the busy chef, who was slapping and slopping amongst the burgers.

"Do you need any help?" she called.

He showed no sign of having heard. That suited Celia. She didn't want to work for him for even a minute.

She was alarmed when Miss Maltash took out a gun, pointed it at the cook and fired. The bullet flew past the tip of his nose. He ignored it, or didn't notice it. He carried on flipping and flopping the hissing burgers.

Celia looked round at the empty tables and said, "Are you expecting many customers?"

"Yes."

"You'll be ready when they come."

"Nobody ever does."

"Ah," said Celia. She looked round again, needing a short break. This time, she noticed someone else in the cafe. A small, round man, who seemed to be oblivious of everyone around him, but with a huge grin which never lessened for a moment as Celia stared and continued to stare.

"He seems happy," she said to Miss Maltash.

"They usually are," was the reply.

O-kay, Celia thought. That'll do for now. If I stay here for much longer, I might become as stupid and awkward as these people.

"Well," she said, "I'll be off."

"I thought you wanted a job."

"I do. I thought you didn't have one."

"I don't."

Celia rubbed her forehead and said, "I'll be off then."

"Don't you want to hear about this job?"

"*Which job?*"

"The one at Hayter, Marcher and Dormuss. Are you interested?"

"Yes. What sort of work?"

"All sorts. Mainly delivering. Packages. That sort of thing. You know."

"Oh, yes. It sounds just right for me."

"I'll write the address. But they might have moved. They do that a lot. The nature of the business. You know."

Celia nodded, thinking that she probably did know.

"Here," said Miss Maltash, and Celia took the piece of paper. The address meant nothing to her. "It's a little way from here," Miss Maltash said. "You might have to ask. But I'll start you off. It's left out of here, first right, second left, fourth right, and I forget how it goes after that. A lot of lefts and rights. The usual stuff."

"I'll find it," Celia said. "Thanks. I'll go there now."

"They'll have moved by now, so you'll have to be very quick to catch them still at the old address. *Very* quick."

Celia wasn't impressed by the directions or the suggestion. She gave the sort of short, sharp flounce that detectives shouldn't do and left.

As she left, Miss Maltash bellowed, "Aren't those burgers ready yet? They're bound to arrive soon, if not at all."

Celia set off confidently along the street, but was soon confused about which right and which left she ought to take. As she stood and looked round, she was surprised to see the grinning man, still grinning, standing, watching her.

"Mr Thomas," he said. "We met a little while ago. At the café."

"Yes. I remember. Do you know the way to Hayter, Marcher and Dormuss."

"Yes."

"Would you mind telling me?"

"No."

"Then please tell me."

"It's exactly as she said, but without all the rights and lefts."

"Which would be straight on."

"Exactly. Just stay on this road for a little way, and you'll be there."

"Thank you."

"You're welcome. Unless they've moved, which they probably have done. They never stay anywhere for long. Always being chased."

"Who is after them? The cops, I presume."

"Cops, creditors, debtors, people wanting jobs, people wanting to do business with them. Often, they move when they don't need to. It's a sort of habit with them. They spend most of their time unpacking from the last move and packing for the next one. They have files which have never been opened because they're always being packed or unpacked. They're probably moving as we speak. So, it probably won't matter which way you go. Eventually, you'll arrive somewhere, and they're bound to be somewhere, and, well, then you'll be in the same place, and that will be that."

"Thank you," Celia said.

"Oh, think nothing of it," Mr Thomas said, turning away. "*I* don't."

Celia set off again.

"I did say *straight* on, didn't I?" asked Mr Thomas, suddenly appearing beside her again.

"Yes."

"Good. That's the right answer."

Celia set off again.

She glanced back, but Mr Thomas had disappeared.

CHAPTER 4

It was a long way and she was just starting to have doubts about all the directions when she arrived at the address on the piece of paper.

She arrived at the same time as a thick fog.

And night was descending.

There was no sign, specific or general, to show that this had recently been the location of a company. She tapped on the door. When there was no reply, she turned the handle and it opened. Turning on lights, she went from room to room. Every one was empty but for dust and bits of food.

She went down a narrow passage to a back room, which was a kitchen, also bare. She opened the back door and went into an alleyway which ran parallel to the street. Opposite the back door were the skips and bins and the accumulated rubbish that people couldn't be bothered to put in the receptacles. With a detective's curiosity, she lifted the lid of the skip, wishing that she had a torch.

She climbed in.

Ignoring the smell and her revulsion, she probed with her fingers, feeling for anything that might be suspicious.

It was a little while before she realised that she was crouched on it.

She felt with her fingers until she was sure. Then, she dragged the large plastic bag out of the skip and into the kitchen.

She used her fingers to pull it open.

Inside, was a very small, and very dead, man. A plastic bag over his head showed that he had been suffocated. He was well beyond help. Her priority was to find his murderers, and to find out why he had been killed.

She heard a sound at the front of the house. She went through into the passage, closing the kitchen door behind her.

On the threshold stood a woman with buckets and mops and various other cleaning accessories.

"Who are you?" the woman said.

Here we go again, thought Celia.

"I was sent here to ask for a job," she said. "On the advice of Miss Maltash."

"Never heard of her."

"Well, she did, and I was, and I am."

"Well, I don't know. I was told not to reveal their address." Seeing Celia's look of interest, she added, "They're very particular about their clients. They don't want just anyone bothering them."

Celia decided that it was time to take charge. "Perhaps you could ask them," she said.

"Well, all right," the woman said. "You wait here and I'll go and ask."

She went into a small room at the other end, and muttered. Celia looked around. It was definitely an abandoned office. And they seemed to have taken everything, apart from the dust and food.

The woman soon returned. "Mr Hayter said to go round and he'll have a look at you. I've written the address on this piece of paper."

Celia thanked her and glanced at the address. "Could you give me a few rough directions?" she asked.

"Yes. It's second right, first left, fourth right and third left. On your left."

Celia thanked her again and left. She had taken a few steps along the street when she became aware of Mr Thomas again, still grinning.

"Straight ahead?" she said.

"Of course," he said.

"You're very helpful," she said. "Unlike most of the people round here."

"Did they kill Mr Dormuss?"

"Yes, I think so. They killed someone."

"I thought they would," said Mr Thomas.

Celia walked towards him. "You and I need to sit down and have a long chat," she said.

As she advanced, Mr Thomas retreated into a tiny dark alley, still grinning. For a moment, his teeth gleamed in the blackness. Celia darted forward.

He had disappeared.

"Damn!" she said. "What an infuriating man."

With a large sigh, she resumed her journey.

She soon reached the new premises. It hardly seemed worthwhile to move such a distance when their purpose was to avoid the people who were chasing them.

Perhaps some people weren't trying very hard to find them.

The sign over the door announced *Hayter and Marcher*.

That seemed to be a pretty confident declaration that Mr Dormuss was no more.

One might even say that it was blatant.

The new building was like the previous one. A long time ago, presumably, it had been a terraced house. The door opened straight into the offices. Amongst some desks and tables, the two men were still unpacking. One was tall and thin. The other was tall and thin, but in a different way. One was very smart. The other wasn't.

Guessing which was which, though she didn't know how, Celia called, "Mr Hayter."

Without turning round, the smart man called, "You'll have to come back. As you can see, we're not ready for business yet."

Celia spoke softly. "Perhaps I can help you."

"What?" The man spun round and looked at her. Then he carried on spinning and looked at his companion. "You're doing it again," he said.

"Doing what?"

"Packing."

"Of course I'm packing. We want to be ready for the next move, don't we?"

"Yes, but we haven't finished *un*packing yet."

"Well, you'd better hurry up, or I shan't have it all packed in time."

"Mr Hayter?" Celia persisted. "I'm Celia le Dale. I'm looking for a job. Miss Maltash said that you might have one."

"Job? *Job*? No, we don't have a job."

"Then, why did you tell her that you have a vacancy?"

"That was a mistake," said Mr Marcher. He had large, staring eyes and, somehow, a large, staring mouth. "That was, um, one of our associates, who has since been terminated. I mean, his employment was terminated."

"Ah. So, that's why you have just the two names now. Mr Dormuss had to go."

"That's right," agreed Mr Hayter. "Had to go."

"Perhaps I ought to ask him for a job. Where did he go?"

"Er...he didn't say."

"He didn't say anything," added Mr Marcher.

"Oh, I'll find him," Celia said with jolly menace. "I'm good at finding people. And having no job, I'll have plenty of time."

The two men looked at each other and had a short but intense eye conversation. Mr Hayter turned back to Celia and said, "Perhaps we could make use of you. What do you think, Mr Marcher?"

"Oh, yes. Pretty girl and all that."

Celia glared.

Mr Marcher said, "Er, can you use the 6.4 Sunray?"

"Yes."

"Ah. Pity that we don't have one."

Celia was annoyed. "Well, if you don't have one, why did you ask me whether I can use one?"

"Because when we do have one, you'll be all ready to use it."

Celia closed here eyes, and made herself stay calm.

"Anyway," said Mr Hayter, "being pretty and clever with computers won't unpack these boxes."

"But is she strong enough?" asked Mr Marcher. "She doesn't look it."

"Probably not. But she might be better than nothing."

"That's enough," Celia said. "I'm a cop and I want to ask you some questions about Mr Dormuss."

"A cop?" said Mr Hayter. "Prove it!"

Once again, Celia couldn't prove who or what she was. "I'm out of uniform," she said.

"And," said Mr Hayter, "without your uniform, you're nothing but a meddling girl."

"A nuisance," added Mr Marcher, moving slowly round to her side.

Celia wasn't frightened, but she didn't like the awkwardness. It's all very well telling people that you're out of uniform until they want to dispute your authority. Then, it becomes embarrassing.

"I'll be back," she said, walking quickly out and hurrying away. Behind her, Mr Marcher called, "No-one will believe you anyway."

She hadn't gone far before she slowed to a steady walk. Her annoyance with the two men was replaced by annoyance with herself. She was a detective, the level didn't matter, but here she was just bouncing helplessly around, being ordered about, and generally being treated with a complete lack of respect.

Having failed to follow procedures, and come to this place, the least that she could do was arrest Billy Izzard.

But what of all these other people, who all seemed to be connected?

And the boss? She should be finding out who he was.

Then, there was the matter of the murdered Mr Dormuss.

Deep in thought, she hadn't been paying attention to her surroundings. Now, looking up and round, she saw that she was standing outside a casino. Its name was The Blue Diamond.

She remembered the message for Miss Maltash.

This was where 'the boss' was going to be, and 'everyone' else, apparently.

It was where Celia was going to be.

CHAPTER 5

The man in the cubicle said, "Do you have a ticket? Proof of age? Accompanying parent?" Celia tried again. "I'm looking for a job," she said. "I was sent by Miss Maltash."

The man sniffed. That was what he thought of Miss Maltash.

"And Mr Hayter."

He sniffed again.

"And Billy Izzard."

A bigger sniff. "On your way," he said.

Celia walked to the entrance.

"Not that way," said the man.

"But you said 'on your way.' This is my way."

"Not without my permission. On *that* way." He pointed towards the street.

As Celia hesitated, hoping for an opportunity to be inconspicuous, she saw the ticket man's head turn. He was looking at a limousine which had stopped outside the casino. After much scuttling and door-opening by various attendants, the important people stepped out. Celia looked at the ticket man. His entire attention was on the important people. She took a few tentative sideways steps, then scurried through the door.

Although she didn't want to look conspicuous or out of place, she couldn't help standing and gazing at the scene. The casino was one very large room, with white walls and a white floor, and with all sorts of games being played at velvet-covered tables or at spinning roulette wheels. It was all exactly as she would have expected, with its oily smoothness, the clicker-clack of the roulette wheels and the ssslip, ssslap of the cards as they were dealt.

The only exception to all this was the sight of three men in overalls, down on their knees, painting the floor.

Celia walked slowly amongst the tables, where people stared intently at the cards in their hands and made occasional small comments about their intentions. But even they all looked up and across when the door opened and the important people walked in.

A large murmur of 'It's the Boss' went round the room. So many people were involved in the murmur, with so much excitement, that it became a roar.

"Mighty McQueen," said a soft voice beside Celia.

It was Mr Thomas, grinning away.

"Actually, he's a woman," said Mr. Thomas. "Impressive, isn't she?"

Mighty McQueen was big and looked ferocious. She was dressed in a black and white striped suit, and she wore a large, wide-brimmed hat. She stood glaring round the casino. Everyone had paused and now sat still, waiting, all interest in their games shattered. Each one sagged with relief as the scrutinising glare passed by. It came to rest on the three men in overalls, who were trying, with no success at all, to look inconspicuous.

"Well?" Mighty McQueen's stern voice cut through the heavy silence.

One of the workmen stepped forward. "Last night, there was a little bit of unpleasantness, and, er, correct procedures weren't followed exactly, and, er, someone was shot. We tried to clean up the mess, but it seems to have soaked in. So, we were just having a go at painting it."

McQueen stood nodding. Then, she turned to a man on her right and said, "Can you find a skip big enough for three bodies?"

"I think so," he said, not really vague, enjoying the situation.

McQueen snapped her fingers and three large men strode forward, gripped the alarmed workmen and dragged them away. She fluttered her fingers, smiled coldly round and said, "Apologies for that bit of unpleasantness. Everyone carry on with....."

She looked at Celia. "Who are you?" she asked, looking as though any answer would be the wrong one.

"Celia le Dale."

"Clear off."

"No. That's a terrible way to speak to your customers."

"We have a strict dress code here."

"It clearly doesn't apply to you."

Even the tough guys who were standing with McQueen looked nervous. No-one spoke to the boss like this.

"How about joining me in a game of cards?"

"I'll have to owe you. I didn't bring my wallet."

"No matter. We shan't play for money."

"Good."

"We'll play for your life. Or death."

"What if I win and you lose?"

"That won't happen. I never lose."

Celia was looking at a wall of smirks. She was in that smallest of minorities. Everyone else was doing exactly what Mighty McQueen wanted. Always.

"Okay," she said. "Let's play."

"Not here," said McQueen. "We'll play my special version. Follow me."

Celia joined the crowd which followed the big boss through a door into a large room.

McQueen turned and said, "You've heard of human chess. Well, I like to play human cards. Meet the pack."

She stepped aside, and Celia saw a large crowd of people, wearing cloaks.

"Fifty two?" she said.

"And two jokers."

"Ah. Of course. So, how does it work?"

"We'll start with a simple game. How about Pontoon?"

"Yes. Okay." Celia had a vague memory of having played it with a school friend. She didn't know any other card games.

"Right, then. Let's go. Best of three. I'll be the banker. Deal"

Four of the cloaked figures separated, two going to stand by Celia and two by McQueen. Celia's pair faced her and opened their cloaks, just enough for her to see. They were dressed as cards. One was the two of diamonds, the other was the four of hearts.

"Twist," Celia called.

Another figure came over and revealed himself. He was the six of clubs.

"Twist."

The next one was the three of hearts.

"Twist."

The next one was the eight of diamonds.

"Bust."

"Nine of clubs, Jack of Hearts. Stick."

Celia's cards began to tremble. They stood in a quivering huddle as McQueen called, "Take them out and shoot them.

"No!" Celia cried. "I won't allow this."

McQueen ignored her and said to her two cards. "Back to the back." Then she called, "Deal."

Four more cards came over.

Celia's two were the Ace of Diamonds and the Queen of Spades.

"Stick."

"Twist," called McQueen. Another card walked over.

"Bust!" she snapped. "What do you have?"

Celia gestured with her finger, and her cards turned round and removed their cloaks. McQueen scowled. She pointed at her cards and called, "Take them out and shoot them."

She glared at Celia and said, "The next one is the decider."

"Fine," retorted Celia, thinking and feeling the opposite.

"Deal."

Celia's next two cards were the five of clubs and the four of spades.

"Twist."

The next card was the three of clubs.

"Twist."

The next was the six of hearts.

One of the cards whispered, "Stick."

"Twist."

The cards became pale as they saw their fate being sealed.

The next card was the three of spades.

"Stick."

The three cards became pale with relief.

McQueen looked at her cards. "Twist," she called.

The next card was the nine of diamonds.

"You idiot!" McQueen roared. "Why didn't you change places? You'll be shot for this. Take them out and shoot them. Shoot them all. The whole pack."

"Then you won't have any cards," Celia cried.

"I can find more cards. So long as there are people, I'll have cards. They'll all do exactly as I say."

As though her anger required movement, she stamped out

into the main room and began to clump about, threatening everyone.

"Are you enjoying it?"

Celia turned to see Miss Maltash. "No," she replied. "She's a. . . ."

She became aware that McQueen was glaring at her.

". . .nunlucky card player. I didn't deserve to win."

McQueen interrupted her rage to shout, "What are you doing here?"

Miss Maltash twitched nervously and said, "I was told to come. I mean invited."

"Well whoever invited *you* should be shot. And will be shot when I find him. Or her. Clear off."

"Right away." And Miss Maltash wobbled away with some urgency.

"And you."

"Yes?"

"You want a job, you say?"

"Yes, please."

"Here, take this." She held out a small card. "Go to this address. Tell him that I sent you. He'll give you a packet. Bring it to me."

"Right."

Celia looked at the card. On it was 'Dr. Frank Griffin. 62, Rock Road, Old Dock.'

A familiar voice said, "That's left out of the entrance, second right and straight ahead. You can't mistake it. It's the place where all the cranes and ships and water are."

"Thank you," Celia said to Mr Thomas. He was still grinning.

Two large and nasty-looking men approached.

"How did you come in?"one of them said to Mr Thomas.

"Do you have an invitation?" the other man said.

"In reverse order, no and I didn't."

"Didn't? What does that mean?"

"It means that I didn't come in. What you see is merely a visual projection of myself. It's a little trick of mine. Very useful."

"What's going on?" asked McQueen, coming over. "Who's this, and why is he here?"

"I'm Mr Thomas, and I've just been explaining that I'm not really here."

"Well, clear off."

"I can't."

McQueen turned to the tough men. "Take him out and shoot him."

One of the men opened his mouth and closed it without making a sound. The other said, "We can't take him out and shoot him. He's not here. Th-this is just a visual projection of himself."

"Well, take the visual projection out and shoot it."

The men gulped and stammered.

Mr Thomas disappeared.

McQueen snarled and strode away. The two men set about re-establishing themselves as tough guys. Seeing Celia's smile, they walked away to do it. She left to go and find Mr Griffin.

The directions were very accurate. She even found Rock Road easily. It was a road of tall, terraced houses. She went up some steep steps and knocked on the door. She waited, listening to a shuffling approach in the hall. The door opened and Dr Griffin stood peering at her. He had a large, sharp nose and long, white hair which cascaded over his shoulders. He was wearing a tweed suit, with a matching waistcoat, but spoiled the effect with a large shawl. His spectacles looked inadequate as he leaned forward to look at Celia.

"Yes?" he said. "Who are you? What do you want?"

"My name is Celia le Dale. I am temporarily working for Migh . . . Miss McQueen. She sent me to collect a packet."

"Oh, you are, are you? Well, I don't approve. Hopefully, you'll soon move on to something better. Wait here."

He shuffled away, leaving Celia to wonder what part he played in this business of which he disapproved. She soon found out when her returned with a small box and said, "Tell her that she must follow the instructions. One a day before a meal. And if she'd stop complaining all through her meals, she wouldn't need the pills."

Ah, thought Celia, thinking much better of the doctor, and a little better of Mighty McQueen.

Dr Griffin was still peering at her. He seemed to make a sudden decision. "Yes," he said to himself. "That's what we'll do. It can't do any harm."

Closing his door, he said, "A small diversion. It won't take long. Come with me."

He walked pretty quickly along the road, turning left, then right, into narrow side streets, until he came to a row of small houses, almost at the edge of the sluggish, filthy water. He held up a finger of caution to Celia, then opened the door and indicated with a shake of his head that she was to follow him.

As they entered a dark hallway, Dr Griffin called, "Mack. Don't be alarmed. It's Dr Griffin. I've come to see you, and I've brought a visitor."

There was a dragging sound in a room at the end of the hall and a dismal voice called, "Come in if you must."

They entered a small room, in which there was a table,

two chairs, a threadbare settee, and a cooker, with a large bowl of something bubbling on the hob.

Sitting on the settee was a saggingly mournful man. His large eyes were bloodshot. He mumbled, "What do you want?"

"First, the introductions. Mack Tuttle, meet Celia le Dale. Celia le Dale meet Mack Tuttle."

The Doctor rubbed his hands together. "Now, Mack, I thought that it might be helpful if you would tell Miss le Dale what happened to you. I'm hoping that it will be a warning to someone who is working for Mighty McQueen." He looked at Celia, with a trace of a frown, then back at the mournful man.

Mack let out a large sigh and shook his head. Then he said, "I used to be a clerk here in the docks. It wasn't a well-paid job, it wasn't interesting, and there were no prospects of promotion, but I liked it well enough. It was just recording all the fish that were brought in. Then, one day, Mighty McQueen came in to do some business, and she wanted someone reliable to do her clerical work. For some reason, I was chosen, and McQueen arranged for me to go and work for her.

"At the time, I thought that she was just a successful businesswoman. I soon learned that she was a very successful criminal. Drugs, gambling, brothels; all owned by her. It was too late to leave. It always is. When you're in, you have to stay in. But being in just made me more and more miserable. Then I became ill. Then, I lost my job. I suppose I was lucky that she let me leave. She might have just had me shot. She usually does when people become inefficient."

"So you see. . . ." the Doctor began.

Celia explained.

"Ah," the two men said.

Celia smiled. "I'll just take her medicine and play along for a while."

Mack said, "Would you like some soup?"

"No, thanks. I'd better be on my way."

"I wish you great good luck," the Doctor said.

"Are you sure that you won't have some. . . ."

"Sure, thanks." She opened the door.

". . . soup? It's very nice soup. How about you, Doctor? Some soup?"

CHAPTER 6

Celia walked back to the doctor's house and from there she headed back to the casino.

She was about to go in when she saw Mr Hayter approaching.

"In there," he said. "It's all happening."

She followed him in. It looked like a joint convention of gangsters and nervous helpers. The human cards, still dressed for the games, were trying ridiculously to look inconspicuous. All the games had stopped and the tables had been pushed aside.

Mr Hayter leaned against a wall, chewing gum, already looking bored.

Dominating the empty space in size and foaming anger was Mighty McQueen.

A close second was the man who was tied to a chair.

"I trusted you, Jack," roared McQueen. "I promoted you. I made you my brothels manager. Not one, but *all* of them. And what did you do in return?"

"I made a lot of money for you," the prisoner said desperately.

"Yes, but you could have made a lot more, couldn't you, Jack? I mean if you hadn't been selling off my girls to...overseas traders. You stole them, Jack. You stole my tarts."

"They wanted to go. They asked to go. I didn't steal them. I just let them go."

McQueen raised her arms and looked round. "And there we have it. I didn't even have to resort to torture. I find the defendant guilty as charged. What do you say, Mr Hayter?"

"I concur entirely. The evidence is already overwhelming. And now we have a confession."

"What evidence?" cried Celia. "*I* haven't heard any."

"You don't need to hear any. You're not a member of the jury."

"There's a jury?"

"No. And that makes you doubly irrelevant. You're not on the jury which doesn't exist."

"I can't be on a jury which doesn't exist."

"Exactly. And now, while we're doing one execution, it will be no trouble to do another. Guards. Seize her."

"You have no right," Celia shouted.

"Oh? And why not?"

"Well, for one thing, I'm a cop."

"A cop. I see. You don't *look* like a cop."

"Well, I am. I am here to investigate drug-running by Billy Izzard, who, I suspect, is working for you. But now, I have...."

"Yes. What do you have, besides our little discussion group here?"

"I have the dead body of Mr Dormuss in a skip, behind the previous premises of Mr Hayter, who appears to be the prosecuting counsel, although I don't see anyone appearing for the defence."

Mr Hayter was shaking his head. "The skip. So that's where he went. He *had* been depressed. Perhaps he crawled in there to die."

"Perhaps he was put in there after you killed him."

"I? How dare you suggest such a thing?"

"You or your partner, Mr Marcher."

"Slander! Perjury! Contempt of court!"

While Mr Hayter twitched with indignation, Mighty McQueen looked as though about to explode. "I'm hearing you, Mr Hayter," she quivered. "And I agree with everything you say."

She turned and pointed at the prisoner. "You," she bellowed, "have been found guilty and will be executed." She turned and smiled sarcastically at Celia. "Now, before I pass sentence on this one, let's do things the right way. Is there anyone here to speak in her defence?"

"Yes."

That was a surprise. Heads turned this way and that. Mr Hayter gulped, swallowed his gum and began to choke.

Mighty McQueen's head merely rolled round and looked in the direction of the voice.

Celia's head turned to confirm what the voice had already told her.

Captain Lora was standing by the door, looking like someone who was completely in charge of the situation, which she was. The uniform, the determined look, and the Cobalt 42 Beamspray certainly helped, but it was also her emanation of calm, strong superiority.

Even Mighty McQueen wasn't saying anything.

Captain Lora said, "An arrest ship will shortly be landing. Hayter and Marcher will be arrested for the murder of Mr Dormuss. Billy Izzard will be arrested for drug-running. And you, Miss McQueen, will be arrested for various murders, attempted murders and various other offences, including the business which has led to this gathering. Jack Diamond will be arrested for his part in it, and I'm sure that he'll prefer that to what you intended to do to him. All recorded, of course. The voice verifier will confirm the unique wave patterns of your voice."

McQueen tried to sneer convincingly and said, "You'll have to be more specific."

"I shall, later. While you have been distracted by Miss le Dale, we have been recording and gathering evidence."

She turned to Celia. "Thank you, Celia. You have been very helpful."

Celia shook her head. "But only by accident. I didn't follow procedures, and I made a mess of things."

"But valuable experience. Ah, here comes the support team. I'll let them take over."

She directed the uniformed and armed support team, then came over to Celia. "We'll go home now, and review what went on here."

Celia was very pleased. She had been rescued, and she wasn't in trouble, and ahead was the prospect of learning from all that had happened.

They went back in Captain Lora's ship. She explained that going back through a time fabric tear could be very tricky, and if not done just right would leave one with a terrible headache. Celia's ship would be brought back by one of the support team.

Soon, they were rushing up towards the blackness, then, seemingly, floating in the void, and hurtling out into the part of the Galaxy that they knew so well. Even though there was still a long way to go, Celia could feel the nearness of things, and she felt the joy of going home.

———

"Okay," said the elevator. "I'm ready now."

# # #

ABOUT THE AUTHOR

John Guthrie writes speculative fiction for all ages, from children to adults. His books are often set in troubled worlds, whether here on earth or in far-flung planets in other solar systems. At the heart of his books are characters happy with their quiet lives who are ensnared in situations they're desperate to escape from. They don't know whom to trust because trusting the wrong person often leads to the worst possible outcome. You'll find yourself cheering for each of the main characters in John's books as they match wits with the most ruthless of adversaries.

John resides in the UK and, when he's not on the lookout for a stray dog to show up on his doorstep, is continually dreaming up new stories and characters.

If you enjoyed this story, please consider leaving a review at your favorite book site.

Follow John on Facebook at tinyurl.com/5n82ch69.

Find John's books on Amazon:
tinyurl.com/JohnGuthrie-Amazon

www.ingramcontent.com/pod-product-compliance
Lightning Source LLC
Chambersburg PA
CBHW020309200626
46814CB00006BA/2153